War Chief

A Lou Gault Thriller

by Dave McKeon

Dave McKeon

Copyright

Copyright ©2022 War Chief by Dave McKeon

All rights reserved.

No part of this publication may be reproduced, distributed, or transmitted in any form or by any means, including photocopying, recording, or other electronic or mechanical methods, without the prior written permission of the author except in the case of brief quotations embodied in critical articles and reviews. For information, email to contact@ahowardactivity.com

This is a work of fiction. Names, characters, places, and incidents either are the products of the author's imagination or are used fictitiously. Any resemblance to actual persons, living or dead, businesses, companies, events, or locales is entirely coincidental.

Edited by Paula F. Howard, A Howard Activity, LLC

Interior design by Paula F. Howard

Cover design by Bob Hurley, ImpressionsBookDesignServices.com

Published by Aha! Press, an imprint of A Howard Activity, LLC

PRINTED IN THE UNITED STATES OF AMERICA

ISBN: 979-8-9872226-3-8

Available for purchase on Amazon.com and at TheWritersMall.com

Dedication

To Sandy

Thank you for the joy you
brought into my life.

The Territory

Chapter

1

The hunter had been watching the glen since midmorning. The day's sweltering heat didn't bother him as much as the flies that were landing on his bare shoulders and back did.

Should have worn a shirt under my overalls, he chastised himself. Usually, he stayed well to the west but had overhunted that area of the forest. It was also rare that he took a stand this close to a road, even a dirt road like this one, but the game trails that crisscrossed just above the bridge where he was now, looked far too promising to pass up.

Shortly after he had arrived, a doe had walked up the trail, but she spooked when the wooden planks on the bridge below suddenly rumbled under the weight of a passing car. He had brought his rifle up before she bounded off, but only for practice; it wasn't camp meat that he was after today.

Slowly, he shifted his position when he saw the unmistakable profile of a large buck as it approached the edge of the glen. It was the buck's thirst and the smell of cool water just beyond the glen that had drawn him to the spring.

The animal was skittish and had paused before entering the clearing. The only reason the large buck had survived this long was that he was naturally cautious. If he sensed danger, every muscle in his body was ready to take flight. The hide covering his chest and upper front shoulders seemed to shimmer as if in nervous reflex; his ears were constantly moving in all directions, He seemed to dismiss the noise a few kids were making down by the bridge as no threat.

Now, the buck raised his head into the air. The hunter could see the animal's nostrils flare open, then shut, as it searched for the slightest scent of danger. Once satisfied it was safe to enter the glen, the beautiful animal moved forward, his neck stretching forward, almost horizontal with his back. The hunter raised his rifle, carefully aimed, and fired.

--

The young game warden had stopped to talk with two youngsters who were fishing off the bridge.

"How's the fishing?"

"Not so good."

"What are you using?"

"Crawlers."

"Best to keep them out of the sun; they'll stay lively longer." The warden watched the boys fishing for a few minutes, "Do you see that dark pool further down?"

"Yeah."

"Well, leave the bail open the next time you cast; let the current take your bait down into that pool."

"Okay," one said. No sooner had the bait entered the pool than there was a swirl on the water and the line began to race off the young boy's reel.

"Whoa!"

"Set the hook."

The boy pulled back on the rod and set the hook as a nice-sized brook trout surfaced, attempting to throw the barb now caught in its mouth.

"Wow! Thanks, mister!"

"You won't find any trout close to the bridge, it's too shallow. They're waiting behind those rocks just beyond the entrance to that pool. Some wait under the bank that overhangs on the right. I'd put money down there'll be a few more fish in that pool, but remember, you have a daily limit. So, don't let me catch you with more than two trout apiece."

"How'd you know they were there?"

"I used to fish here when I was your age."

Off in the distance, a shot rang out, surprising the warden. "Gotta go boys. Hunting season is still months away, and that was no squirrel gun." He looked back at the boys. "Remember what I told you now, keep that can of worms out of the sun."

"Yes sir!"

--

Just as the hunter was approaching his kill, he saw movement to his left. A wave of panic washed over him when he spied the bright yellow shoulder patch on the warden's uniform and quickly hid behind a tree.

After twenty minutes, when no one showed to claim the deer, the warden figured he had been seen and the shooter was long gone. As he reached the animal, he looked down in disbelief at the enormous hole in the deer's chest.

"What the hell was he using, a cannon?"

Inching out from the tree, the hunter once again raised his rifle and squeezed the trigger. The shot entered the warden's upper back and took out most of his chest.

After reloading, the hunter came forward, knelt next to the deer and took out a small saw. Removing the antlers, he placed them in a plastic bag, stood up, brushed off his knees, and walked away.

The game warden's name was Lloyd Bancroft. He had been a game warden for just under a year; the following Tuesday he would have celebrated his twenty-fourth birthday.

Chapter

2

The sun was setting as Lou Gault stepped out onto the screened porch running across the front of his cottage. Brilliant amber-colored clouds set against a sky rapidly-changing from blue to violet gave the horizon a picture-perfect contrast. Out of habit, his eyes scanned the horizon, searching for anything that didn't seem to belong. As far as the eye could see, the land, wide lake, forest, streams, all of it belonged to him.

There was an enviable independence about Gault, and it was obvious to even the most casual observer that he had found his niche in life and was good at it. The calm, self-confident demeanor he projected masked the warrior's spirit that lay hidden deep within him. His tall, wiry physique belayed the tremendous strength of his limbs. Even though he was no longer a member of Canada's elite Joint Task Force Two commando unit, he still cropped his hair close on the sides. He lived a quiet, simple life now, far away from the carnage that he saw during the Afghan war.

What he didn't know was that his resolve to live a simple life was about to be tested once again.

For the past week, the temperature had been blistering hot in central New Brunswick, Canada, where he operated a sportsman's resort known as *Havre de Poisson*. Even the leaves on the trees had begun to curl under the sweltering dry heat of the day. The only relief came from daily thunderstorms that roared through the valley late each afternoon, pummeling the earth with a force great enough to shred the leaves on the trees.

When a young woman with chestnut brown hair and hazel green eyes joined him on the porch, he turned around. She was dressed in gray tailored slacks and a white fitted blouse, both of which complimented the well-proportioned contours of her body. She handed him a glass of wine and smiled.

"If the breeze coming off the lake keeps up, it should be a lot cooler sleeping tonight."

"I hope so. I'd like to get an early start over to the village tomorrow, Kate."

"Okay." They touched glasses in a silent toast.

"Tell me, what do you see when you look out there?"

"I see the place where I want to be."

"No, really, what exactly do you see?"

"I see the magnificent lake, a beautiful evening sky, a forest beyond with some ancient trees, a few ducks . . . it's a grand view."

"This land is our homeland. It has always belonged to my people."

"It's beautiful."

"I gave my word to Grey Elk that I'd protect this land."

"Protect the land from *what*?"

"From those who would try to take it."

"Does that ever happen?"

"Often enough. Grey Elk has driven squatters off our lands a few times."

"I wish I had known him."

"He would have liked your Irish spunk."

"My Irish *what*?"

"Spunk."

"My spunk?"

"It's a term of endearment," Lou said as he kissed her on the forehead.

"I hope so."

When Lou's grandfather, Grey Elk, had died, stewardship and title for the roughly fifteen square miles of land surrounding the remote glacial lake in central New Brunswick had legally passed to Lou. Other than an Abenaki village some six miles north, the nearest thing that could even be loosely described as a settlement was roughly thirty miles distant, "the way the crow flies."

These days, the only humans with access to the lake were his fishing resort guests who flew in to stay at the resort Lou had named Havre de Poisson.

Operating a business this far from civilization was demanding and only attractive to those who were truly self-reliant. Gault has overcome more than a few challenges in life, by drawing on his natural instincts and the resourcefulness inherent in his mixed French and Abenaki bloodlines.

"I'm glad we've had these past few weeks to ourselves, Lou," she said.

"One of the pleasures of owning your own business, Kate, is taking time off when you want."

It was rare that anyone ever booked the last two weeks in July or the first two weeks in August at Havre de Poisson; the fish were in deeper water then and difficult to catch. Lou referred to those four weeks as "the summer doldrums" and he actually shut the resort down.

In prior years, he might have done a few odd jobs around the resort during the shutdown, but mostly he'd just kick back and enjoy the break. This year, however, he'd been traveling back and forth several times a week to the Village of Grey Elk with Kate, his Irish fiancée.

The following morning, the sky was still gray when Lou and Kate stepped into the 26-foot mahogany runabout that would take them down the lake.

"For years now, I've been wondering if I should be shutting down, or marketing these four weeks as a family vacation opportunity," he said to her.

"That's a different clientele."

"Yeah, tell me . . ."

"How many of the cottages would actually work for a family?"

"One."

"Are you thinking of adding some?"

"Hell no, if I do that, the circus would become too big for the tent."

"The what?"

"I'd lose control. It would be too much for me to handle."

"You can always delegate."

Lou paused while he stowed a few things under the bow, "Nah, I don't believe in that."

"Really?"

"Yeah. Besides, I like the life I live now, and I've got enough on my plate. So, I'm thinking that I'll just leave things the way they are.

"I'm fine with that."

"Actually, the shutdown is a chance for us to spend some time together; maybe do some traveling."

"Well, you'll get no argument from this colleen on that," she laughed.

As he reached down and pressed the button to blow the bilge, he added: "Angelo was saying that Alessandra was talking about going back to Italy next summer to visit her sister. Maybe we should think about going over with them."

"She mentioned that to me."

"Are the lines and bumpers in."

"All clear."

"I think we'd enjoy Italy, Kate."

With that, the powerful inboard came to life, and the throaty rumble that these classics are known for drowned out everything else either of them would want to say as the runabout slowly backed out of the boat house.

Once clear of the dock area, Lou shoved the throttle full forward, and the twin screws lifted the bow out of the water with ease. Lou stayed in the center of the lake as he raced down the glassy surface, to minimize the impact the boat's wake might have on the shoreline.

Kate and Lou had met the previous fall when the Mounties decided to use the sportsmen's resort he ran as the perfect location for a secret operation. Lieutenant Kate O'Grady was sent over as INTERPOL's liaison for Operation Delta-Tango. Her role had been to help the Canadians coordinate with MI6, as the two teams worked to shut down an international smuggling ring. Lou and Kate were sent out on undercover assignments a few times and told to act as a couple. Over time, it had stopped being an act.

There had been no secrets between the two of them; they fought side-by-side, trusted their lives to each other more than once and became best friends.

When Operation Delta-Tango had ended, Kate was aggressively recruited by the Mounties to join them. When they made her an offer that she couldn't refuse, she transferred over from the Irish Directorate of Military Intelligence and now held dual citizenship. While she still owned a residence in Ireland, Havre de Poisson had become her home.

When Lou proposed, the couple decided they would marry in a traditional Abenaki wedding ceremony during the summer break. Then, when the season ended, they planned to travel over to Ireland and renew their vows in front of Kate's Irish Catholic family.

Now, as they approached the small islands sheltering

Moose Cove from the open water, Lou stood up, shifted the engine into neutral, and glided over the shoals that stretched between the islands into the idyllic cove.

"Lou, how old do you think the huge fir trees are on these islands?"

"Some are well over a hundred years old; they don't live much beyond two hundred."

"Every time we come here, I feel like you've brought me to a secret hideaway that's away from everyone and everything. It's so quiet. I think this is my absolute favorite place on the lake."

"Moose Cove has been a favorite swimming hole for ages."

"Do people still come here?"

"Off and on. The raft and dock have been here forever, the picnic tables along the shore are new."

"I can't believe how clear the water is in here."

"The rest of the lake is just as clear. Because it's sheltered. in here, you can see down about fifty feet."

As they set out the bumpers and tied up against the dock, they could feel the warmth of the early morning sun on their backs.

"Kate, let's go for a swim before we head up to the village."

"Aargh, I didn't bring a suit."

"Neither did I."

Laughing at her Catholic school modesty, Kate began taking off her clothes, in between sneaking in more than a few glimpses of Lou's tall muscular frame as he disrobed.

"I think you could have been a stunt double for Clint Eastwood," she said. "You have his build."

"Maybe from the back, but he's nowhere near as handsome as I am from the front . . . besides I'm happy living the obscure and simple life that I have."

As she stepped up onto the dock, she pressed her nakedness against his and placed her hands on his chest. "You're right. You are more fun from the front." With that she hooked her foot behind his ankle and pushed him into the water.

Rising to the surface, he opened his eyes just in time to see Kate's bare bottom coming directly at his face as she cannon balled him.

As soon as she surfaced, Kate yelled to him. "Come on! I'll race you to the raft!"

Lou could have easily overtaken her, but he was enthralled watching her naked backside rock gracefully back and forth as she swam the crawl. He held back to watch. When they reached the raft, he waited.

"Ladies first," he offered. As he watched her climb up the ladder, he thought, *Smart as a whip and just about as fine a figure as I've ever seen.*

"Come on slow poke, aren't you getting out?"

Sitting down beside her, Lou leaned over and began nibbling her neck.

"You do seem to know where all my buttons are, mister."

"Uh huh."

"Lou, what if someone sees us?" she whispered playfully pushing him away.

"Relax, all Abenaki lovers come to the cove to make love on the raft. It's actually a rite of passage."

"I think you just made that whole thing up."

"No, I really didn't."

Laughing, Kate laid back, turned on her side and propped her head up with her left arm while walking her fingers up and down Lou's hairy chest.

"Is that so?" she said, smiling. "I would have made love to

you back on the dock if you hadn't been so clumsy and fallen in."

He looked back at her. "The dock's bad luck, unless you want a little one."

Kate's fingers traveled down toward Lou's manhood as she whispered, "What if we had made love on the beach?"

"Even worse . . . twins. Only the raft is safe."

"I think you're completely full of the Blarney . . .but in a nice way." It wasn't long before they were both fully aroused. Kate gently pushed Lou onto his back, mounted him, and was soon lost to the passion that had built within her until they were both doused in sweat and satisfied. When she leaned down and kissed Lou, he was looking across the lake.

"I think I could spend my entire life making love to you in this private little cove of ours."

"It is peaceful here, but let's swim back; there are two families waiting to swim."

"Where?"

"Just beyond the tree line, they waited for us to finish."

"Finish what?"

"Making love."

"They *saw* us?"

"Yes."

"They saw me on top of you?"

"Yes, that's why they waited. Come on, let's swim back and say hi."

"Lou, I don't have anything on."

"By the time we swim back, they won't either. There's no shame in being naked, Kate, it's how we all came into the world."

Once Lou waved his arms, the two families emerged from the woods, waved back, and began to disrobe and enter the water. As they swam towards shore, Kate reflected on how different her life had become since leaving Ireland.

Chapter

3

Ten miles away from where Lou and Kate were toweling off on the dock in Moose Cove, a game warden was pulling off Highway 17 onto a dirt road that ran parallel along the western border of the Abenaki village lands. It was close to the area where Lloyd Bancroft had been found shot about a week and a half earlier

Bob Connors had retired from the Department of Natural Resources after a forty-year career as a game warden several years ago. When his wife had taken sick and died, Bob let his former supervisor know he was available to work again, if only part-time. Up until this point, Connors had only been brought back to help with administrative work. But this time, he was assigned to the Kedgwick office in an effort to place more game wardens out in the field to bring an end to poaching that had been increasing around Five Fingers, New Brunswick.

Connors was known to be "old school." He always got the job done, but he did things his way. Over his career, he had received a number of written warnings about following departmental procedures in the field. Since retiring the first time, Connors had put on weight, and the new protective vest he had been issued sat on the seat beside him. Not only did he feel the vest was too restrictive, but it was also just too damn hot to put on what he felt was an unnecessary layer of clothing that didn't breathe.

In all the years he'd been out in the field, Connors had never been shot at even though he had gone deep into the woods to confront more than his share of poachers numberous times.

When Connors pulled over to the side of the road, he rolled all the windows down, and parked in the shade. He had just taken off the plastic lid of a large cup of Tim Horton coffee when he heard a gunshot. The noise was loud enough that he instinctively flinched, spilling coffee on his trousers.

Holy shit, that one was close! he thought.

He put the lid back on his coffee, dried his hands on a sweat towel resting on the seat, took the keys out of the ignition, slowly opened the driver's side door, stepped out, and closed it behind him.

Connors knew the shot had come from somewhere on Abenaki lands and thought to himself, *You Abenaki may not need a license to hunt your lands, but that doesn't mean the regulations don't apply to you.*

As soon as Connors entered the woods , he saw the deer lying not more than twenty yards away. *No wonder it sounded so friggin' loud,* he thought, *it was damn close.*

He looked around to see if he could spot the shooter coming toward the kill, but the woods looked empty.

Well, whoever you are, if you thought you were going home with a little camp meat today, you're going to be mighty disappointed. He took a deep breath. *This one's going over to Kedgwick."* A new law required game wardens to bring any fresh kill over to the lab for evaluation before disposing of it, and that's exactly what he intended to do.

Connors partially concealed himself next to a young balsam fir waiting for the shooter to come forward and claim the kill. He listened while ever so slowly, the sounds of the forest began to reappear; however, Connors was only listening for human footsteps.

After a full twenty minutes, he began feeling impatient. *Where, the hell, is this guy?* Tired of waiting, he walked over to where the deer lay. When he reached the carcass, he couldn't believe what he was seeing.

I've never seen a kill like this before, he thought. *This guy must be using a damn cannon to make a hole that big*!

Connors noticed three other bullet holes around the large wound, each looking to be about the size a 30-caliber would make, any one of which could have brought the buck down. The rack was a good-sized one, still covered in velvet.

The shooter had seen Connors as soon as the game warden entered the woods which touched off a wave of panic that immediately washed over him. He knew if he got caught poaching, the beating he'd get from his father would be far worse than any punishment the law could ever hand out.

Connors never heard the shot that ended his life. The fifty-caliber ball that entered the center of the elder man's back shattered his spinal column before blowing his heart, and most of his left lung, out through the front of his chest. The three smaller caliber entry wounds destroyed what was left of his rib cage.

The sheer force of the impact would have knocked Connors' body forward a considerable distance had he not been thrown up against the trunk of an old fir tree. Instead of collapsing to the ground, Connors' body remained upright, held to the trunk of the tree like Velcro by the dead branches that had impaled him.

When the shooter came over to the deer, he knelt beside the animal's head, took out a small pruning saw, cut both antlers off the buck, placed them into a plastic bag, stood up and brushed off his knees, then smirked at the way the warden seemed to be hugging the tree before coldly walking away.

It took the better part of the afternoon before Connors was found. He was the second New Brunswick game warden killed inside of two weeks. Both men were shot in the back and found near a deer whose antlers had been sawed off.

When word reached him that another game warden had been killed, Sargent Major Fletcher Martin decided it was time to bump the investigation up to the Mountie's major crime unit and involve special investigator Kate O'Grady.

Chapter

4

The Abenaki village of Grey Elk was about six miles northeast of Moose Cove. Lou hadn't been back since Grey Elk's funeral several years earlier. But for the past couple of weeks, Lou's cousin had been shuttling Lou and Kate back and forth from the cove until he finally became tired of being "on call" and had given Lou the keys to an extra ATV he owned.

The first time Kate heard Lou addressed as "Raven Claw" it surprised her. "You never told me you had an Abenaki name, Lou."

"It wasn't intentional, it just never dawned on me that you didn't know."

"Will I take an Abenaki name when we marry?"

"Yes."

"Will I be able to choose my own name?"

"No, you will be given a name."

"By whom?"

"The elders . . . they will decide."

"Is that how you became known as Raven Claw?"

"Yes, it goes back to when I was seen by many as masterful

in the game of 'butterfly hide and seek.' It was thought that I must have eyes like the raven to be able to see my quarry so easily."

"Don't you mean like a hawk or an eagle?"

"Those birds can see great distances, but the raven is considered smarter and a more resourceful bird. Ravens will use their claws to carefully uncover what it suspects may be hidden from view. Finding someone who is hiding and doesn't want to be found is what the game of 'butterfly hide and seek' is all about. My uncles said that my name was an easy choice for the elders to make."

"Your cousins were talking about you and this 'butterfly hide and seek' thing yesterday."

"I know. Laughing Gull came and spoke to me. They would like me to mentor their oldest sons in the game, in exchange for sponsoring you at our wedding."

"Will you mentor them?"

"Of course. It is a great honor. . . and you need to be sponsored. It is our tradition, much like a father who gives his daughter away at an Anglo wedding."

"But didn't you say, just a few hours ago, you already had enough on your plate?"

"I'll make room for this." Kate raised her eyebrows, but kept any comments to herself.

"Come, walk with me, Kate. I want to show you the marriage pole I've made for us. Oh, they also said to tell you that they're making your wedding dress." Kate didn't reply.

As they walked across the village, Lou sensed that it seemed a little rundown. He also sensed that more of his people were moving back to their ancestral homeland. *The addition to the schoolhouse should have been finished long ago,* he thought. *The council lodge and guest lodges all need to be re-stained.* Even the paths and walkways weren't being maintained, he noted, and common areas were no longer being cared for regularly. *What is going on?*

When Grey Elk died, responsibility for managing the affairs and upkeep of the village had fallen to the tribal council, along with stewardship of the village lands. However, the decline he was seeing couldn't be for lack of money since the village received ample compensation annually from the logging rights Grey Elk had leased out.

Lou began to wonder. *If the money isn't going toward maintaining the village, what the hell are the elders doing with all the money?* For years, he had avoided accepting an open invitation to take Grey Elk's seat on the village council. Lou believed those who lived in the village should take all responsibility for the care and well-being of their home. But the more Lou walked around the village and spoke to people about village life, the more disturbing the rumors and stories became to him.

A Mohawk, who had married one of his cousins, told him that a professor of archaeology from McGill University had recently visited her father's village.

"He kept asking about the ancient battle between the Abenaki and the Mohawk that happened on the shore of 'the water with many fish.'" She recounted. "My father said this man talked of doing something called 'a dig.'"

"I know of the legend."

"Then, is it true?"

"The round shield and great sword that hang in our council lodge are said to have belonged to the Vikings who fought alongside the Mohawk."

"So, would you say, 'yes,' to this dig?"

"No, the ancient ones should be left to rest; if he comes to me, I will tell him that."

--

Earlier in the day, two young hunters had told Lou of the deer they had come across in the forest. Its antlers had been taken, and the deer had been left to rot where it fell. Another person told

Lou that he had heard Carleton Mountain would soon become a ski resort, and much Abenaki land would be lost.

The more stories Lou heard, the more concerned he became about the amount of unchecked encroachment going on in the Abenaki lands that had once belonged to his grandfather.

"Kate, I think I'd like to stay over and go to the council fire tonight, just to listen to what the village elders have to say."

"If that's what you'd like to do, I'm okay with staying over. Are you thinking of getting more involved in the village?"

"Absolutely not. I have more than enough on my plate . . . and I like my life just as it is. I'm only interested in hearing what the elders have to say about the trespassers. The people who live in the village are the ones who need to care for the village and protect the land around here, not me."

Kate nodded that she understood. "I've never been to a council fire, what's it like?"

"It's like a town meeting. The elders share what's going on, and everyone discusses what should be done."

"And you are going to just *listen*?"

"I'm only going to listen."

He's not pleased with what he's hearing and seeing, Kate thought, *I wonder if he will just sit and listen.* Later, after Kate and Lou had dined with his cousin, Laughing Gull, the three of them walked over to the council ring together. When they reached the natural amphitheater, Laughing Gull took Kate by the elbow.

"Come with me. This is where the women sit."

"What?"

"Come, this way."

"We don't all sit together?"

"No, the men sit alone."

"Are women able to speak at the council fire?"

"No. We speak our thoughts later, when we are in our lodges."

As Kate took a seat, she looked over and saw Lou, laughing and talking among the men. "So much for the equality of the sexes," she said to no one in particular.

John White Owl opened the tribal council meeting with an invocation: "Great Spirit, as we gather at this tribal council, we thank you for this gift of sharing between fathers/mothers and sons/daughters. We thank you for these friends, for all that you have given us, and we ask for your wisdom and guidance."

Throughout the meeting, Lou kept overhearing people behind him talking among themselves about the surveyors they had seen driving stakes into the ground on Abenaki land. Someone in the village had been approached about a "right-of-way." Lou waited for the elders to speak of this subject and about the poaching of deer.

But when the elders began the closing ceremony without saying a word about the land encroachment or the dead deer, Lou could no longer remain silent. The warrior spirit deep within him rose to the surface like an erupting volcano spewing fire and ashes as he jumped to his feet.

"Hear me! This is Abenaki land! The land of our fathers' fathers! I have heard many stories today of those who are trespassing on our lands, killing our deer, driving stakes into our ground; I have heard talk of Abenaki lands being taken, yet our village leaders sit idle and say nothing." Lou looked directly at the elders. "Why is that?"

Not one elder signaled he would speak. So, Lou raised his voice even louder, "Where are your *tongues*?" His powerful voice silenced everyone. Many thought they heard his words echoing among the hills in the valley below.

Lou waited for someone on the Tribal Council to respond, but the only sound anyone heard was the crackling of the fire as the logs shifted.

Astonished that none of the elders were responding, Lou folded his arms across his chest. "Then I claim the council seat that was once held by Grey Elk. I will defend what belongs to our people!"

No one dared challenge Raven Claw. Everyone knew it was his right to take Grey Elk's seat. Most present either nodded their heads in agreement or grunted approval of the words he had spoken.

Kicking Bird, the oldest among the elders on the Tribal Council, at first looked like he was going to get up to say something, but ultimately, just shifted in his seat and narrowed his eyes to stare at Raven Claw.

--

Later, as Kate and Lou were walking back to the guest lodge where they were staying, Kate spoke her thoughts. "Lou, you made some pretty strong statements tonight. Will you have *time* to sit on the council when the second season starts up?"

"Kate, I have no choice," he answered. "When I came back from Afghanistan, I made a promise to Grey Elk that I would protect this land. No one is stepping into the role that he had; no one is managing the affairs of the village. The council isn't doing a damn thing to protect what is ours."

"I noticed two village men sitting in the shadows, off to the side who briefly exchanged glances when you stood up and spoke. I thought it was odd that they said nothing."

"Yes, Kasko and Lone Otter. I will speak with them tomorrow."

"You saw them?"

"Yes."

"How could you have seen them? Lou, you couldn't possibly have seen what I saw, they were sitting *behind* you, way off to your right, back in the shadows."

"Eyes like the raven, Kate."

Chapter

5

The morning after the council fire, Lou awoke with determination. "Kate, I'll be back. I'm off to kiss the toads." Still half-asleep, Kate sat up. "Whoa, Lou, please tell me that kissing toads has absolutely *nothing* to do with this traditional Abenaki wedding you're planning."

"It doesn't," he laughed. "It's one of Grey Elk's expressions. Toads are things in life we'd rather not do but need to take care of. If you tackle them first, the rest of the day goes smoother."

"And what are these toads you're about to kiss?"

"I want to speak with Kasko and Lone Otter. They know something that I don't." He kissed her on the nose. "I shouldn't be long."

Lone Otter was sitting outside his lodge idly whittling a stick when Lou approached.

"Lone Otter, I have come to speak with you and Kasko."

"He is not here."

"When will he return? I wish to speak with you both."

"He didn't say," Lone Otter quietly replied, without taking eyes off his whittling.

Lou smelled a rat. *These two are never apart. Inseparable since childhood, one is always with the other. In a fight, you don't fight just one, you have to fight both.*

When they took wives, they married twin sisters. When they built lodges, they built them next to one another. Kasko had always been the schemer; Lone Otter was the faithful follower.

"Lone Otter, will you tell Kasko that I wish to speak with you both?"

"If I see Kasko again, I will tell him." Lone Otter never raised his eyes.

Lou walked back to his lodge wondering why Kasko had deliberately chosen to dodge him. He found Kate awake and in a good mood.

"Well, that was quick! Where were the toads, all lined up just waiting to be kissed?"

"No, actually, they seem to be avoiding me," Lou answered. "Kate, I think I'd like to meet with my new mentees before we leave the village today. Do you need to go back soon?"

"Nope. I'm on vacation this week . . . and next week, too."

"Really? Then why have you been bringing your laptop and phone with you every time we come over here?"

"Remember when I said my role was similar to being on retainer?"

"Yes."

"Well, that includes vacations. While you were off attempting to kiss a few toads this morning, I received a text from our good friend, Fletcher Martin. It seems the sergeant major wants me to be on a conference call with him at ten this morning, something to do about game wardens. Hopefully, it won't take too long."

"That'll work out fine. While all you Mounties are chatting, I'll meet with my new mentees. Let's go see my cousin Laughing Gull, she wanted to measure you for your dress before we headed home today, anyway."

--

When all four young cousins had learned that Raven Claw would be their mentor, they were more than pleased, backslapping and yipping like the young ones they were. Stories of how Raven Claw had successfully led search parties for lost hunters were still being told around the lodge fires. Now, they would have his attention to themselves. It was exciting.

--

"Did I ever tell you that I used to play hide and seek?" Kate said to Lou as they walked through the village.

"It's not the same game, Kate."

"No?"

"No. Butterfly Hide and Seek is a rite of passage that every young Abenaki male must master on his path toward becoming a warrior. The Pequots originated the game which lasts for days; it's a test of one's self-discipline, endurance . . . and stealth."

"That *is* different."

"The ability to blend into one's surroundings, without being seen by others, is the very essence of the game. Actually, it is said to be good luck if you can remain quiet and stay still long enough that a butterfly lands on you."

"I see," she said, then remained silent for nearly a full minute. "I'm not sure I could do that."

"It all begins when the 'adversary' leaves. They are given a full day to cover their tracks and 'go to ground'."

"Go where?"

"Conceal themselves. The 'seeker' then heads out and uses all their skills to find the 'adversary.' Both players are expected to live off the land, so they carry minimal food and water with them. It is not unusual for the game to last for three, sometimes four days."

Kate laughed. "Our games were over when recess ended; the nuns were *strict* about that." He smiled at her, enjoying her lilting Irish brogue as she spoke.

"You had nuns in school?"

"All the way."

"I don't think I've ever actually seen a nun."

She laughed again. "Oh, at my school, they were *everywhere.*"

When Lou and Kate reached Laughing Gull's lodge, his cousin immediately sent the younger children off to fetch the four youths that Lou would mentor.

For some reason, Lou's instincts told him to turn around. When he did, he caught a glimpse of Kicking Bird, just as he moved off the path.

--

Lou spent some time with the young men to get a sense of who they were. Finally, he felt they were familiar enough with the rules of the game, and wise enough about the forest, that he could send them out on a practice run.

"I have decided that you will begin today," he told them. The youths nodded as their eyes grew wide. "In three days, I will return and listen to your stories, just as Grey Elk did with me. Now, decide among yourselves who will hide and who will seek."

When they had decided, he asked, "Which direction will you travel?"

"I will go in the direction where the sun sets," the tallest one said.

The shorter youth of the four, who would also hide said, "Good, go there, and enjoy the smell of rotting deer and flies. We will go east, where the air is pure."

Lou paused for a moment. "What rotting deer?"

"There are many deer that have been killed in the west and left to rot. Only their antlers have been taken. We have all seen them, Raven Claw," the shorter youth said.

"Raven Claw, why would anyone take only the antlers and leave the meat?"

"I don't know, but we will find who is doing this soon. Now, the two of you who will hide, prepare, and go. Laughing Gull will tell the two seekers when it is time to leave early tomorrow."

As Lou watched his mentees leaving, he noticed a slight movement in the bushes, just to the left of where they had been sitting. When Kicking Bird suspected his presence had become known, he froze, and his hand instinctively went to the hilt of his knife.

Chapter

6

Arthur Turnbridge was the eldest son of Luther and Ruth Turnbridge's fourteen children. The Turnbridge clan had lived in ramshackle buildings along the outskirts of the settlement known as Five Fingers for as far back as anyone could remember.

Nobody knew how many of them there actually were and the only visible means of income they seemed to have was from the moonshine they sold off the back of an old pick-up truck they parked at the edge of town three or four times a year. Except for an occasional trip to the general store, or when they were forced to send their children to school, the Turnbridge clan tended to keep pretty much to themselves.

All the Turnbridge children were special needs students, a result of inbreeding that had gone on within the clan for generations. Arthur was not quite as challenged as most of the younger Turnbridge, but he had also been classified as a special needs student when he was school age.

Now, Arthur stood well over six feet tall and was built solid as an ox. He looked as if he might be clumsy, but he was very agile on his feet. Known to be a brawler when he drank, Arthur and the law had several drunk and disorderly run-ins of record. The one superior ability that Arthur did have was his marksmanship. He could load and fire a muzzleloader faster, and with greater accuracy than most people could load and fire a single shot breech-loading rifle with a high-powered scope. Like every one of his siblings, he knew the ways of the forest extremely well, which is where he spent most of his life.

Arthur's shooting prowess had first attracted the attention of Lee Wong Ying back in late February. Ying had recently entered into a supply chain alliance with Shang Ho Labs. Shang Ho needed antlers and Ying had enough entrepreneurial blood running through his veins that he wanted to become their number one supplier. For that to happen, Ying needed to build his own first line which wasn't going to happen if he stayed in the cities.

For the past week, Ying had been driving around northern New Brunswick in a rental car stopping at pubs and bars, buying drinks, and trying to strike up conversations with the locals, hoping one or two might be interested in becoming one his downline suppliers. But Ying had a few strikes against him: He wasn't a local, he talked with a slight British accent, and he dressed like a city slicker.

Lee Wong Ying was a well-educated man. He was schooled in elite private academies in Malaysia run by the British. He had always tested near the top of his class, however, because he was Malaysian, he was never accepted into what was considered proper British society.

He had spent most of his life living along the fringes of society, drifting from one role to another. At an early age, he mastered Silat, one of the deadliest forms of martial arts. Silat was about only one thing - violence.

As a martial arts crowd favorite when he lived in Malaysia, Ying had competed in numerous tournaments. Not only did he resemble Bruce Lee in appearance, but his prowess and adaptability in the ring, when confronted by a serious challenger, was exciting to watch, and often resulted in heavy betting.

Then one day, when Ying changed his mind and threw a martial arts tournament by faking an injury, forfeiting a match he was heavily favored to win, he had to flee Malaysia.

Ultimately, he settled in eastern Canada where he was introduced to the lucrative world of the Canadian black market. Ying had absolutely no scruples and would sell his services to the highest bidder whomever it was.

Currently, the highest bidder was seeking the velvet that covered a deer's antlers. The velvet contained a raw version of Insulin-like Growth Factor-1. Known as IGF-1, the growth factor was a natural hormone that boosted human endurance and increased muscle strength. It also improved muscle recovery by breaking down carbs faster. The hormone was banned by the World Anti-Doping Agency unless used in a low-dose supplement form.

Ying's client, Shang Ho Labs had recently experimented with IGF-1by using the raw anabolic hormone extracted from the velvet. Their research found that the drug couldn't be detected in human blood because of the inherent DNA differences between the species.

When word of the discovery leaked out, demand for their product went through the roof overnight within the world of sports medicine. The street price had more than quadrupled.

Within hours, Shang Ho Labs' biggest challenge was to establish a reliable supply chain for the velvet.

--

When Ying read an ad promoting a "turkey shoot" in Five Fingers, a few towns over, he decided to stop off and watch.

The 'turkey shoot' was held behind the Grange Hall. When the shoot ended, Ying watched the winner, a slovenly-dressed and foul-smelling young man, walk away from the crowd and find a spot where he could reload his weapon. Ying waited until most everyone left the area, then approached Arthur Turnbridge.

"Sir, I congratulate you on your win. You are a remarkable shootist. Would you care to enjoy a drink with me?"

"I ain't one to turn down no drink, eh? You just leads

the way, mister."

When they sat down Ying raised his glass saying, "I salute you and your fine performance today!"

As Ying sipped his drink, Turnbridge threw back his head, tossed the liquid into his mouth and swallowed the shot in a single gulp.

"Now, that there is some damn fine whiskey, mister. I'll have another if you're still buying."

Ying smiled and nodded, knowing full well where this was going. When the waiter came over, Ying asked him to leave the bottle of Johnny Walker Black on the table.

"Mr. Turnbridge, I believe you and I may have an opportunity to do some business together."

"'*Mr. Turnbridge*,' ha, there ain't nobody that calls me that! Hell, I thought you was talking to my Pa, but he ain't here. I goes by 'Arthur,' that's my given name."

Turnbridge put his huge mitt around the bottle and helped himself to another shot. "What's this business you got in mind?"

Lowering his voice, Ying said, "Arthur, I'd like you to shoot some deer for me. I'll pay you one hundred dollars a deer."

"Hell, I kin git you all the venison you want for *that* price."

"I'm only interested in the antlers."

"All you wants is the *antlers*?"

Ying noticed two men standing at the bar look over at them. "Arthur, please, keep your voice down, but yes, that's correct, all I want are the antlers."

Turnbridge drained his glass and poured himself another drink. "Well, hell, I got *lots* of antlers. Got 'em hung all over the front of the barn, some damn big nice ones, too. How many you want?"

"I don't want any of those."

"You said you wanted antlers."

"I want antlers, but with the *velvet* on them."

"You want the meat?"

"No, I only want antlers with the velvet on them; size doesn't matter. You can do whatever you want with the carcass."

"And you'll give me a hunnert dollars fur each one?"

"That's right . . . one hundred dollars for each set of antlers that you bring me with the velvet on them, carefully wrapped in plastic, so the velvet doesn't dry out."

"Well, I'll be damned! So, how's I get paid?"

"In cash, every other week."

"You want the heads? You gonna mount 'em?"

"No, no heads, Cut the antlers off the head; I just want the antlers."

Arthur thought for a moment. He wasn't stupid. "You know this is poaching. Law don't take kindly 'bout poaching round here. I needs to be careful. My Pa told me if I ever gets caught poaching that he ain't gonna help me out. He says I'm gonna be on my *own*, and when I gets home, he's gonna take the strap to me."

"And I'm willing to pay you *one hundred dollars* to take that risk." Ying said. He saw the conflict in Arthur's eyes between the one hundred dollars and getting caught poaching.

"Tell me Arthur, would you kill a deer if you knew that it's antlers could help someone who was sick get better?" Ying could tell that Arthur was having trouble making the connection between antlers and sick people, so he tried another tactic.

"Arthur, have you ever seen a sick person?"

"My Pa was sick once, he almost died."

"Arthur, the company I represent uses antlers to make a medicine that helps people get well. You'd like to help sick people get well, wouldn't you Arthur?"

"My Pa took medicine once."

"Did it help him get better?"

"Ya."

"Did it make *you* feel happy when the medicine made him better?"

"Ya, and my momma was happy too, 'cuz then me and her didn't have to tend to the hogs alone no more."

"Arthur, don't think of this as *poaching*, think of it as helping sick people get better."

Turnbridge thought about this for a few moments before repeating: "A hunnert dollars?"

"That's right, Arthur, one hundred dollars."

Turnbridge smiled, exposing a mouth full of crooked, yellow teeth that had obviously never seen a toothbrush, let alone a dentist. As he poured himself another glass of whiskey, Arthur said, "Mister, we got us a deal. I'll drink to that!"

"Agreed," Ying said. "So, when should I expect to receive some goods?"

"Say, what?"

"When will you be able to deliver some antlers?"

"How 'bout the first week in March?"

"Splendid, I'll meet you at the far end of the field behind this Grange Hall in two weeks from today . . . at ten o'clock."

When Turnbridge left the grange hall, he mumbled to himself, "Damn if I didn't just meet the dumbest damn fool there ever was! Gonna give me a hunnert dollars for antlers. Shi-i-i-i-it!"

Chapter

7

While Lou met with his four young mentees, Kate linked into the major crime unit's conference meeting. Just fifteen minutes before the call, she had the lead role in the murder investigation of two game wardens recently killed in the line of duty in New Brunswick.

"Good morning, Kate! Thanks for joining us," Fletcher Martin greeted her as he kicked the meeting off. "Everyone, I'm sure you all know by now that a second game warden has fallen in the line of duty. The pressure is pretty intense now to bring into custody whoever is responsible for committing these crimes. Whether these wardens were specifically targeted, we don't know. What we do know is that their deaths were *not* accidental. I've asked Lieutenant Kate O'Grady to take the lead on these investigations. Some of you know Kate, most of you will recall that Kate was instrumental in our ability to bring down the smuggling ring operating down on Grand Manan last year. I'd like you all to give her your full cooperation. Kate, the rest of the meeting is all yours."

"Thank you, Sergeant Major," she said. "Good morning, everyone. I'd like to begin by discussing what we know so far. Let's go around the room virtually; please introduce yourself and share what you already know about the case." She motioned to the first person in the upper left of her computer screen. "Claude, please start us off."

"Claude Benson, Northeast Kedgwick field office here. Pretty much all I know is that both men were shot in the back. Entry wounds were the same, a large hole with three other entry points. In both cases, there was a dead deer in close proximity, each with its antlers sawed off."

"Harland Colton, also from Kedgwick," the next Mountie said. "Both wardens were killed in the area of Five Fingers. If I'm not mistaken, I don't think they're called 'game wardens' anymore, though, I think they're now referred to as 'conservation officers.'"

"Thank you," Kate nodded, "for the correction."

"Hi Kate, it's Arnold Cunningham, Fredericton headquarters. I believe one warden was actually found on Abenaki land."

"Hi, Arnold, nice to be working with you, again."

Harland spoke up. "That's true, he was found just off the dirt road that comes off route 17 about three miles south of Five Fingers center. The road runs along the boundary line separating the Abenaki lands from Five Fingers. They found him not even thirty yards into the woods, pinned up against a tree."

"Do we know if these wardens, or officers, had any history of working together?" Kate asked. "Did they work together on any arrests?"

"Jim Harvey, here, from the Southeast region. Ma'am, to my knowledge, they never worked together. Bob Connors started out working at the Kedgwick field office, but he spent the last thirty years down here in Moncton before retiring. Lloyd Bancroft was much younger and didn't even become a warden until after Connors retired."

Kate took a deep breath when she heard the word "ma'am," but let it slide. "Bob Connor's was retired?"

"Arnold Cunningham here, again, Kate. Yeah, Bob retired a couple of years back. He came back in from time to time, usually to help out with administrative work. But this was the first time he was assigned to any field work, that I know of."

"Okay, so it's fairly safe to say that these two weren't being *targeted* for something that they had both been involved in," Kate said. "What else do we know?"

"Jim Harvey here. That may not be entirely true, Kate, the Lloyd Bancroft that was just killed was a junior. His dad, Lloyd Bancroft, Senior, was *also* a warden. He and Connors may have done some work together up in the central region before he transferred down to the southeast years back."

"I understand," she said. "Jim, I'd like you to go through all three wardens' arrest logs and see if there's anything they may have done that overlapped or connected them in any way."

"Yes ma'am."

"Bruce Kendall here, Northwest Grand Falls office. We've known someone's been jacking deer in the greater Five Fingers area for a while; we started getting reports going back to March, maybe even earlier. Whoever is doing the shooting doesn't seem to be interested in the meat or the hide; all they're taking are the antlers."

"Do we know what the market price is for a rack of antlers?"

"Kate, Claude, again. That's another thing that's odd about this, they're not taking the *whole* rack, they're just sawing each antler off at the base."

Kate raised her eyebrows. "Claude, I'd like you to check with the taxidermists in the area. See if anyone is currently doing any work with antlers."

"Yes ma'am."

"What else do we know?"

"Steve Andrews, Central Region, New Castle. As far as we can see, both wardens were acting alone, and for some reason, neither one was wearing their protective vest."

"Arnold here, Kate. This comes under a different heading, but I think we should advise all wardens working in that area to start patrolling in teams of two until we capture this shooter."

Kate smiled that someone was thinking proactively. "Arnold, have a conversation with the natural resource folks covering that region and let them know we're strongly suggesting their wardens go out in teams of two for the time being. And reinforce the fact that *everyone* wears their protective gear."

"Will do."

"Okay, is there anything else we know?" No one spoke up. After a brief pause, Kate continued. "Let's talk for a moment about what we *don't* know. Does anyone have any thoughts on a motive?" No one responded.

"What else *don't we* know?"

"Harland here. We don't know whether the wardens were bushwhacked, or if they were held at gunpoint and executed."

"Good point, Harland. Take a look at the crime scene photos and see if there's any indication of a struggle."

"Yes, ma'am."

Kate paused. She'd had enough. "Folks, I need to say this: I go by the name of 'Kate.' Please don't call me *ma'am*. Now, do we know if the ballistics are a match for both shootings? Do we know what *time of day* the wardens may have been shot?"

"We should have the coroner's report on the second shooting back by tomorrow, Kate."

"Harland was that you?"

"Yes, ma'am . . . ah, *sorry*, I meant to say, 'Kate.'"

"Harland, take a look at both coroner reports; we need to know what may be similar . . . anything that could help us get a handle on how this shooter operates."

"Okay, will do."

"Arnold, when you talk to the natural resource folks, see if they can give you an idea of how large of an area this poacher has been operating in."

"I'll ask."

"Okay, here's a wild question, and I know it's a longshot, but it's one that needs to be asked so we can rule it out: I'd like someone to do a background check on both of these wardens just so we know there wasn't something in their *personal* lives that might have been a factor in any of this."

"This is Arnold . . . I'll take that, Kate. Headquarters will end up being involved in this one anyway."

"Okay, great. Thanks, Arnold. Now, is there anything else we should have talked about, but didn't? Anything that we should have at least put out on the table as an unknown?"

"Nothing that I'm aware of, Kate," someone said. "I think this was a good start."

She didn't catch who spoke but thought it might have been Harland. "Okay. Anyone got anything else?"

Silence.

"Right, well, let's get together again in two days. I'll arrange for a conference line. In the meantime, I'll do a little research on what the market for antlers is this time of year. If anyone has any breakthrough news to share, don't wait until our next call, share it."

--

By the time Lou returned to the guest lodge, Kate had finished her call.

"How'd the call go, Kate?"

"Not bad for a kickoff, but we're just at the beginning of these investigations."

"So, you're still on vacation?"

"Absolutely," she laughed. "I only took on what I felt I needed to do and delegated everything else. That's how I ran the INTERPOL team when I led it."

"You delegate a lot?"

"As much as I can; makes my job much easier. You should try it."

"Nah, the devil is in the details. Besides, getting my hands dirty gives me a sense of actually doing something."

"You are so old school."

"Hey, it works, and I'm successful."

"You *are* successful," she said. "How'd the meeting go with the mentees?"

"It went well, they were anxious, so I sent them out to the woods . . . just to see how they'd do."

Chapter

8

The two gentlemen sat in plush high-backed, overstuffed leather chairs, facing one another in the lounge of Ottawa's prestigious Rideau Club. Neither one had seen the other since they were fraternity brothers at McGill University nearly two decades ago.

Buxton Thomas was Elwood Pritchard's senior brother during rush week. They had never been close friends during school, and the following spring, when Buxton Thomas graduated, they'd lost touch.

Buxton's family had deep ties to the Rideau Club, five generations earlier, his namesake was one of the club's original incorporators. Now Buxton was a private investor and came from a family that many would describe as "old money." His exquisite attire, pencil-thin mustache, gold-rimmed glasses, and slicked-back hair, all combined to give him the look of a wealthy aristocrat complete with an air of aloofness. He was quite proud of his pedigree and often invited people of "lessor means" to lunch at the club.

Today, his guest was Elwood Pritchard. A mutual acquaintance had reconnected the two of them several months ago, however schedules being what they were, this was the first opportunity that both men were free to meet.

Elwood Pritchard's sole interest in reconnecting with Buxton Thomas was to talk him into becoming an investor in his Carleton Mountain Development project. The overwhelming majority of Pritchard's past business ventures had ended as financial failures; as a result, he was "persona non grata" within the banking industry. However, the one thing Pritchard always did have going for him was the ability to dress as if he was prosperous. He also had an uncanny ability to con people into investing in his visions of grandeur. Lastly, he was able to bounce back time after time from one failure after another with no one seeming to be the wiser.

"Buxton, I am delighted to finally be able to reconnect with you. It's been a number of years, old fellow."

"Yes, it has, Elwood. How have you *been*?"

"Well, thank you, yes . . . yes, very well, and you?"

"Apparently, I am well also, Elwood, only last week my physician advised me that I have the constitution of a man half my age."

"That's splendid, but please, call me 'Woody.' Now, Buxton, you are a busy man, so rather than beat around the bush with pleasantries, I am going to come straight to the point. I'm here to offer you an opportunity to get in on the ground floor of the Carleton Mountain Development project."

While Pritchard shared the key objectives of his project, Buxton sat back in his chair, unconsciously pulling on his pencil thin mustache, as he listened with interest.

"I don't believe I'm familiar with this project, Woody, exactly *where* in Ontario is this Carleton Mountain?"

"Actually, Carleton Mountain is in New Brunswick, not Ontario. We're still very much in the early rounds of acquiring capital, which is probably why you haven't heard of it. Buxton, this project will open up the entire central part of New Brunswick to further economic development and is a marvelous opportunity."

"How so?"

"The first phase of the project will establish the entire area as a destination point for winter sports. Once that happens, phase two will kick in and we'll begin transforming the surrounding area into high-end vacation homes; this will obviously attract a variety of retail businesses. I'm sure you can see where this is going. The projected return for every investor fortunate enough to get in on the ground floor on this project will be tremendous."

Pritchard noticed Buxton purse his lips and nod his head as if he could visualize in his mind what he was hearing.

"We've already started surveying portions of the land, and we're meeting with representatives of the railroad to discuss infrastructure strategies. Our research has shown that many eastern Canadians, as well as Americans, are already traveling to the western provinces to ski because there's nothing comparable in the east. Developing Carleton Mountain will change all that. We plan to create an experience that will be equally as challenging, equally as *desirable* as in the west. Carleton Mountain will be right in the easterners own back yard," he paused a beat.

"Phase two is the icing on the cake, so to speak. Phase two includes several ice-skating arenas, a bobsled run, a ski jump, major restaurants, more hotels, and an airport. Quite frankly we see the Carleton Mountain area as having a legitimate potential to someday host the winter Olympics."

"You don't say . . . just where in New Brunswick *is* this Carleton Mountain?"

"That's the beauty of the whole thing, it's in the middle of absolutely *nowhere*! The cost of acquiring the land will be dirt cheap . . . pardon the pun. We've already identified the tracks of land that we'll need, secretly, of course. Everything will be purchased in bits and pieces using multiple shell companies, just the way Disney did down in Florida back in the mid-sixties."

"So, what are the obstacles?"

"Well, funding, of course, that's number one. Some of

the land is Crown land, but we have a way around that. Lastly, of course, will be getting the infrastructure in place to reach the mountain."

"I assume you are coming to me for funding. Who currently has title to the land?"

"As I've said, there's some Crown land involved. However, we believe we'll be able to make a land swap in exchange for a ninety-nine-year, non-forestry development lease. We've quietly acquired the rights to purchase an equal amount of land that abuts a very popular, but landlocked provincial park in southern New Brunswick, which we suspect the parks and recreation people will be very happy to annex in a trade deal." Buxton was still listening, so Elwood continued.

"Another reason for the provincial leaders to say 'yes' to the land swap is that this whole project will be a huge shot in the arm for New Brunswick's economy. This project will create jobs for New Brunswick like nothing else on the horizon; no politician is going to stand against it. Think about it, the rail corridor alone will immediately open up the area for further growth. The tipping point for them will occur when they realize what social and institutional capital will be created by this project. Of course, a few campaign contributions in the coffers of the right people won't hurt either."

"Money does seem to talk."

"Yes, it does; and we've done our homework, we know who the key players are."

"What about the rest of the land?"

"A logging company controls a good portion of the land that we'll need, as does another landowner. We figure that once we have the lease on the Crown land, the courts will allow us to acquire whatever else we need by expropriation. We'll acquire a couple of tracts of land in the area at a low-cost point, just to establish the current value for the land. The Abenaki also have a village in the vicinity, but that land only comes into play from an infrastructure perspective. We're working on obtaining a right-of-way across their land."

"Well, I must say, Woody, I'm quite impressed with the thumbnail sketch you've just provided. I believe this might be just the type of investment that the people I represent could be interested in. Precisely what are you looking for from me?"

"To be frank, Buxton, seventy-five percent of Phase One capital, and your political influence to help us navigate through all the twists and turns this project will encounter as it goes forward."

Once again, Buxton Thomas sat back in his chair subconsciously pulling on his pencil-thin mustache. Those who knew Buxton Thomas well seemed to understand that when he began fiddling with his mustache, he was deep in thought, or about to make a decision. Pritchard had observed this behavior often during their college days. Now he waited for Buxton to respond.

"Well, I'm not certain how much *political* capital I personally have in New Brunswick, Woody, but I suppose that's what networks are for. I believe the next step is for your people to meet with my man, Solicitor Aaron Blake. He'll need to see all of your financials, including your burn rate, and of course, the complete development plan for both Phase One and Phase Two. I'll rely upon him to advise me on how much capital we might want to put up. He's with Lafleur, Blake, and Rogers, over on Exchange Street."

Elwood Pritchard was delighted.

"Thank you, Buxton, this has been a very enjoyable lunch. I'll have my people follow up directly."

"I'm sure you will. Now, unfortunately, I need to excuse myself. Meetings you know."

As soon as Buxton Thomas returned to his office, he put in a call to Aaron Blake, his long-time family solicitor.

"Aaron . . . Buxton here, listen, I've just met with a fellow named Elwood Pritchard. I'd like you to do a little research on him. Find out what he's been up to professionally. Also, see what you can find out about a Carleton Mountain Development Group. Yes, Carleton Mountain . . . no, I've never heard of them, either; they're somewhere in New Brunswick. Sure, a couple of days will be fine, and if you go over the retainer, just bill me. Right, thanks, speak with you soon."

Chapter

9

Kasko left his lodge in the predawn hours of the morning after the council fire. When he reached the edge of the village, he chose the trail that led to the western boundary of the Abenaki lands. The trail Kasko followed had been used for centuries by his people.

It wasn't long before he entered a long, flat valley. The area had been an important resource for his people for generations. Not only was the area rich with game, but in the fall, when the river that ran through it was little more than a stream, Abenaki fathers, and their sons, had always walked along the dry riverbed searching for pieces of flint.

In the summer, the valley was where the men harvested new shoots from ash trees which they used to make shafts for their arrows. Often, the men would camp along the riverbed for several days, some would sand and shape the shafts so they were perfectly straight, while others hunted the ruffed grouse and prepared its feathers for the fletching. Arrow-making was another skill that had to be mastered before one could become a warrior.

Creating the arrow tips was the only part of the process that wasn't seasonal. Forming arrow tips from raw flint required special skill and patience There were always craftsmen within the village with whom one could trade for arrow tips.

Very little flint ever went unused since every fragment had a purpose. The smaller pieces of flint were used to make tips to hunt birds, the larger tips were used when hunting larger game or when defending the land against adversaries.

Kasko had traveled the trail many times, yet he still looked for trail markers that had been carved into the ancient trees which measured the distance to and from the village.

Kasko had traveled the equivalent of three miles before the sun finally began to reach the valley. He knew what he was looking for but wasn't exactly sure how much further he needed to travel. When he finally saw the brightly colored markers that had been driven into the earth and were tied around the trunks of trees, he sat down on a hill and waited.

It wasn't long before Kasko heard the sounds of an all-terrain vehicle off in the distance. When the surveyors arrived, Kasko stood up and made himself visible.

"Bud, look yonder, we got company again," one of the men said.

"Yeah, don't unload any gear until we hear what he has to say," the other answered.

As the surveyor walked up the hill, he raised his hand in a peace sign. "Hey, good morning, Chief, how you doing today?"

"I am not a chief," Kasko replied.

"Well . . . okay. What can I do you for?"

"My people are not happy that you have come to drive stakes into our land."

"Well, we're not doing anything beyond marking a trail here. No harm in doing that, is there?

"This is Abenaki land. You have no right to be here."

"Relax! Nobody's going to build houses on your land and try to move in; they just wanna put a road in to go *across* your land."

Kasko just stared at the two surveyors, feet spread apart, arms defiantly folded across his chest.

"Look, we don't want any trouble. We're just here to do a job. All we're doing is marking a trail, nothing more than that."

"This is Abenaki land," Kasko repeated. "You have no right to be here."

"Okay, I'll tell ya' what, how about I tell *our* chief to come talk with *your* chief, how's that?"

"That would be good. Now go, there are enough trails to follow."

"Whoa, listen! We've been hired to do a job here. We're not going to just pack up and go home."

"This is not your land. This is *our* land. You have no right to be here."

"Now wait just a darn minute . . ."

"No! You must go, *now*."

"Bud, I think we should let Pritchard straighten this out, we've got a couple more jobs that we can go do."

"No, we're here now, let's finish the job we've started."

Kasko repeated himself: "This is not your land. This is *our* land you have no right to be here."

"Bud, I think we should just go."

Kasko stood his ground in front of the two men. "This is not your land, you must go."

The lead surveyor whispered to his colleague, "Yeah, maybe you're right." Turning to Kasko, he said, "Okay, Chief, tell ya' what . . . you win, we're gonna leave."

As they drove away Bud's assistant asked, "Was that the same one you talked with before?"

"I don't think it was, but who the hell knows."

"Did Pritchard talk to them."

"Apparently not."

"The other jobs will keep us busy for a while. Do you want me to call Pritchard and let him know that his job is on hold?"

"No, I'm the one he's been dealing with; I'll call him when we get back."

Kasko remained where he stood until the surveyors had left, then he proceeded to pick up every stake, every marker, every ribbon and every flag that had been placed on Abenaki soil.

--

Elwood Pritchard was totally immersed in the preliminary railroad proposals that he had spread out across his desk when his assistant buzzed.

"Mr. Pritchard, you have a call on line two."

Pritchard sat back in his chair momentarily, just to clear his head before picking up the phone. "Hello, Pritchard here."

"Mr. Pritchard, Bud Gleason of Gleason and Barry Surveying. How are you this morning, sir?"

"Yes, Bud, just fine. How's the survey going on that right-of-way?

"That's what I'm calling you about sir, it's not."

"What's the problem?"

"We were told that we had no right to be on Abenaki land today, and not to come back until you've spoken with them, giving us their permission to be there."

"I thought you said you'd done that?"

"No, sir, what I *said* was that I had spoken to *an* Abenaki who happened by and I explained what we were hired to do. I assumed that *you* had spoken with them and that we had permission to be in there on their lands."

"No, I hadn't spoken with anyone. I had planned on talking with them once you'd finished the survey work and I knew what the plan was. But we can pull that up. How do I get to this village of theirs?"

"There's an access road off of Route 17 that leads to their village over near Five Fingers. It's not marked, but I can show you where it is."

"Good, I'd like you to come with me anyway. What kind of gifts should I bring?"

"What?"

"What kind of gifts should I bring?"

"These folks are all pretty well educated. You're not going to persuade them with gifts."

"All right, let me take a look at my calendar." After a brief pause, Pritchard came back to the call. "I could do Tuesday of next week, or I could do Wednesday. What's best for you? I'll have my assistant set it up."

"Either day works for me, sir, but I doubt that your assistant would be able to set anything up. I'll take a run over there and find out when we could come and speak with their tribal council."

"I thought all these tribes had a chief! Are you saying we need to go before a *committee*?"

"Their system of government is probably more democratic than ours. I'll go see when their tribal council is meeting next and get back to you."

"All right, just set it up, this right-of-way is essential."

As Pritchard hung up, he yelled out to his assistant:

"Marsha, try to keep my calendar open for next week, and find out what airport is near a place called Five Fingers, New Brunswick, where I can fly into."

"Yes sir."

"And see if you can get Canadian Northern on the line, I'd like to give them the go ahead."

"Yes sir."

Chapter

10

Kate had sent an email out earlier with the bridge line information for her next conference call, and was waiting for a few more members of the major crime unit to dial in. Within a short time, everyone had clicked on to the call.

"Okay, it looks like everyone's here, so let's start. We had a number of action items from our last call, so let's go over those first," she said.

"Jim Harvey here, Kate, I'll go first. I went through all their arrest logs; there's no record of the two deceased game wardens ever having worked together, nor is there anything in the files that indicates that Lloyd Bancroft, senior, and Connors, had ever done anything together when they were both in the central region."

"So, we can rule that out. Okay, who's next?"

"Claude Benson here, Kate, I've checked with all the taxidermist; no one has done anything with antlers since last hunting season, and they only do full head mounts."

"Good, next?"

"Harland here, Kate. I had the crime scene photos blown up and asked a couple of people to look at them, in case I missed something. There really isn't anything noticeable that would suggest there might have been any type of struggle."

"Harland, weren't you also going to compare the coroner's reports?"

"Yes, and I've done that. Both men were shot in the upper back and sustained significant damage to their upper torso. The massive entry wounds sustained by both men were similar enough that the coroner made a footnote that the wounds were most likely made by the same weapon. Based on the bleeding around the entry wounds, it appeared that only one shot each time was fired. Both men would have died instantly from their wounds. There was no powder residue found on either body, so each kill shot was fired from a distance of at least five feet away. Both projectiles completely passed through each body, however microscopic metal fragments found in both wounds were determined to be a match. Time of death was estimated to be anywhere between nine in the morning to one in the afternoon for both bodies. The only difference between the coroner's two reports were the additional wounds Connors received as a result of being impaled against the trunk of a tree."

"Okay, so we can assume that the same weapon was used, and perhaps we're only dealing with one shooter. Good report."

"Yes ma'am, ah, Kate. My guess is that the shooter used a 'buck and ball load'.

Kate was unfamiliar with the term. "Harland, so that everyone is familiar with that term, would you please explain what a 'buck and ball load' is?"

"Sure, a buck and ball load can only be used with a black powder muzzle loader. Two or three thirty-caliper shots are loaded, then a fifty-caliper ball is shoved in. It'll knock down a damn elephant. It was a common gun load in grizzly territory."

"Thank you Harland."

"Oh, uh, one more thing Kate, both wardens had their side arms, wallets, and watches still on 'em, so we can rule out robbery as a motive."

"So, we've determined that the weapon this shooter used is a muzzleloader, and we can rule out a crime of opportunity, or robbery, as a possible motive. Claude and Harland, check with everyone in your region that sells ammo to find out who's been purchasing black powder and caps and might be using a muzzleloader."

"Will do," Harland answered.

"Arnold, you had a couple of actions."

"Yes, I did. First off, I spoke with the regional conservation director and told him that we were advising they send their people out in *pairs* until we bring this shooter into custody. He said they'd follow your advice.

"I, also, had legal do an audit on both Connor's and Benson's personnel jackets. Neither man had any record of a criminal, civil, or domestic disturbance charge in their personal life that would have even remotely played a role in their deaths. As far as the geography that this shooter may be operating in, the conservation folks believe that he's pretty much staying within a ten miles radius around Five Fingers. Of course, they have no real way to verify that at this time."

"Okay," Kate said. "so what we know is that both men were shot from behind, from a distance of at least five feet, most likely with the same weapon. They may or may not have known that the shooter was behind them. In both instances, a poacher had shot a buck and removed its antlers. Neither warden had anything in their past that would have made them a target, so we can rule out revenge as a motive. Neither warden had their wallet, watch, or side arm taken, so robbery was not the motive."

"Kate, Benson here. I'm wondering if these killings may just be a case of being in the wrong place at the wrong time combined with a poacher who'll do anything to avoid being caught."

"Let's hope not," she said. "That's a wild card that we don't need to deal with. I suspect that if we can determine the motive, then we'll be able to bring this shooter in quickly."

"Kate, Jim Harvey here. It's interesting that this shooter isn't taking either the meat or the hide."

"Yeah, Claude, I was thinking the same thing. This time of year, poachers are out for camp meat. This guy, and I'm just *assuming* it's a guy, is only taking the antlers," she said, "and it does seem to come back to the antlers, doesn't it? I did some research on antlers since our last call. The primary market for antlers is basically set by what the rustic home décor industry is willing to pay, which is only a few dollars a pound," she said. "Some eastern herbal medicines contain *ground* antler, but that's a limited market. There's a few knife companies, offering knives with handles made from deer antlers, and then, there's the do-it-yourself hobby kits for antlers, but you supply your own antlers. There's just isn't enough money in antlers for that to be a motive."

"Jim Harvey, here, Kate. You mentioned eastern herbal medicines. I wonder if there might be some connection to that Asian aphrodisiac we keep hearing about?"

"Is this in reference to rhino horns being ground down and sold as an aphrodisiac?"

"Yes."

"That's been proven to be an urban myth, Jim. That being said, the Chinese do use rhino horns in a few traditional medicines, but that's the only thing that seems to be creating a market for rhino horns. I know the Chinese do have a traditional medicine that calls for ground-up tiger bones. There are still a few cultures out there who believe if you ingest certain parts of an animal, you'll gain the strength of that animal."

"Yup, just a thought," Jim said. "True Crime and Justice magazine ran a story on it a while back."

"I wouldn't put a lot of faith in anything that I read in that tabloid, Jim."

"Harland here. Arnold, when you talked to the conservation folks, did they mention if the wardens were wearing any kind of radio or body mic when they're in the field?"

"That never came up in the conversation, Harland."

"Well, I'm thinking that the only way we're gonna get this shooter is by catching him in the act. The wardens are our eyes and ears on this, not the constables driving around on patrol. Now, if these wardens were equipped with radios like our guys have, and we maintained a good number of Mounties in the area of Five Fingers, say between the hours of nine and two, why we just might have a better chance of catching this guy. What do you think Kate?"

"I like that idea. Arnold, do we have a dozen or so body mic's sitting around in headquarters we can lend out?"

"I'll find out."

"Arnold, have a conversation with the conservation director and let him know what we're thinking about doing," Kate said. "Okay, next question: How many additional constables do we have patrolling that area now?"

"Benson here, Kate. We have four additional assigned to the area, which makes a total of nine."

"When are the four additional constables out on patrol?"

"I'll have to check on that."

"Make sure they're out on patrol during that nine to one window mentioned in the coroner's report. It won't add much value if we're flooding the area with extra patrols after dark."

"Will do."

"All right, does anybody have anything else?" She was met with silence. "Okay let's meet again in two days."

--

Later, as Kate was making a pot of tea, thoughts ran through her head. *This is the middle of August; why is someone killing deer and taking antlers now?*

While leaning against the kitchen counter waiting for her tea to steep, she continued her thoughts. *What's so unique about deer antlers this time of year that someone would want to kill for them?*

Returning to her computer, she keyed in a search: *What is unique about deer antlers in the summer?*

The first response popped up: *"In summer, the entire cartilaginous antler of a deer is in a pre-calcified growth stage, covered in a living velvet that contains a growth hormone called insulin-like growth factor 1, or IGF-1."*

Unfamiliar with the term "IGF-1," Kate did a query and found out that "the hormone is proven to reduce the recovery time after an injury and also improve human endurance. However, use of the hormone, in its purest form, was currently banned in the sports world."

Hmmm, maybe Jim Harvey's question about the rhino horn wasn't as far out in left field as I thought.

As she drilled down further, she discovered a number of links to technology efforts aimed at increasing the body's natural production of the hormone. There was also a link to a laboratory in China that has been experimenting with the use of IGF-1 extracted from deer velvet. When she clicked on the link, the text was in Mandarin.

She copied the text and began searching for an English translator service for Mandarin; she was becoming highly interested in the fact that there was a trail to be followed.

Chapter

11

Lou hiked up to the village to meet with his four young mentees who had just returned from their adventure. Now sitting in a circle, he addressed the two who had acted as seekers.

"What have you learned?"

"It is not easy to find an adversary who doesn't want to be found, Raven Claw."

"I walked past my adversary many times, but it wasn't until he moved that I saw him."

Lou nodded, then spoke again. "The two of you who were hidden, what did you learn?"

"That it is impossible to remain still when bugs are crawling all over you, especially on your face, in your ears, and on your nose."

"I left a trail that was far too easy to follow."

After asking several more questions and listening to what had been learned by each of his mentees, Lou stood up. "I will return in a few days and begin teaching you the ways of the forest, how to read signs, and how to hide your trail."

"Raven Claw, before you go," one young man said. "I heard

gun shots every day when I was in the forest. Someone is hunting on our lands to the west."

"We will find who it is that hunts our lands," Lou said.

The young boys picked up on the seriousness in their mentor's voice.

When Lou returned home to his cottage, he sent a text to his cousin, Jake: *"Bring hiking shoes when u fly in on Friday."*

Within minutes, Jake acknowledged with a "thumbs up" reply text.

--

It was late on Friday afternoon when Jake dipped the wings of his Twin Otter and entered the far end of the valley. He glanced over at the well-used hiking shoes on the seat next to him and wondered what his cousin had in mind for the weekend.

The big lake had been as calm as a mill pond all day, but now that the sun had set, the wind was picking up. However, a little chop wasn't going to prevent Jake from landing; he'd earned his wings as a bush pilot long before he took over the mail route, and he was quite familiar with the lake that was listed on the maps as "Number 980."

When Lou and Jake had been orphaned at a young age, the tribal council had decided that both boys would be raised by their maternal grandfather. Grey Elk had welcomed his grandsons into the hunting and fishing lodge that he operated.

It was at Havre de Poisson that he patiently taught them how to hunt and fish along with the ways of the forest, and the values they would need to live an honorable life. He raised them as he had raised his own sons, the two boys had grown up as inseparable as twin brothers, rather than cousins.

Lou ended up taking after his grandfather, Grey Elk, and was the more stoic and pragmatic of the two. Jake was always the family comic, playing for a laugh. He had always been a free spirit . . . and an opportunist.

Over time, both boys had come to know every sector of Grey Elk's land like the back of their hands. When they weren't in school, they would serve as a guide for many of the guests who came to hunt at Havre de Poisson. Their tracking abilities eventually caught the attention of the Canadian Mounties, and their services were regularly called upon to help find lost hikers and hunters throughout the entire province. In recognition of their years of service, they were designated as honorary auxiliary members of the Royal Canadian Mounted Police.

When they came of age, both joined Canada's elite Joint Task Force Two, a special forces unit. Lou was deployed to Afghanistan and spent close to two years on the front lines. Jake became the martial arts instructor for new recruits, and never left Canada.

For the past four years, Jake has flown the mail plane out of Kedgwick, delivering mail five days a week within a radius of 150 miles. Jake was also the *sensei* at the local dojo, which he ran for youngsters, and their parents, in the area. He was pretty happy with his way of life.

--

Hearing the faint sound of the float plane approaching, Lou instinctively turned his head and looked toward the far end of the valley, then called to Kate who was nearby.

"Kate, that old Twin Otter Jake flies is coming up the valley. Let's take a walk over to the dock and jockey a few boats around so he has room to tie up."

"How can you tell that's Jake?"

"If you listen to the motors, you'll hear one sputter and miss on the fifth stroke."

"Is that dangerous?"

"Nah, he can fly with only one engine, if he has to. It's just a signature of that particular plane. He said they're planning to rebuild the engine once the budgets are settled."

--

When there weren't any guests at Havre de Poisson, everyone at the resort dined together family-style. It was a rare treat to have Jake there in the summertime, even though he was a frequent visitor during the offseason.

As soon as they sat down, the banter at the table erupted as if Jake had never been gone.

"Kate, if you pass me the eggplant caponata, I'll pass you the lyonnaise potatoes."

"Not until you pass the butter."

"Lou, pass this down to your wife."

"Alessandra, can you pass me the rolls, please. Angelo, I brought you some hand-rolled Cuban cigars."

"Good, I'm out."

"So, Lou, we're going hiking, are we?"

"We'll talk about it after dinner."

"All right, but Angelo and I are going to enjoy a cigar and brandy after dinner while we watch *'Skyfall'.*"

"How many times do you two need to watch that movie?"

"Lou, it's about the comradery. Besides, we keep getting the dialogue mixed up when Bond's fighting on top of the train and they're heading toward the tunnel."

Angelo slapped his right hand on the table. *"Mi scusi un minuto!"* Pointing his index finger in the air, he growled: "It is not WE *who gets confused,* it is YOU!. It is *you* who does not know the lines," Angelo yelled.

"The words are this: *'Can you get into position . . . There's no time, mum . . .Take the shot . . . I said, take the shot . . . I can't, mum, I might hit Bond . . .Take the bloody shot . . . Agent down, mum.'* It is YOU who keeps wanting to mention the tunnel again. Now, no more does she-talk about the tunnel!"

Kate looked over at Alessandra, Angelo's wife, and the two of them just rolled their eyes that anything so frivolous could be taken so seriously by two grown men.

Angelo and his wife were the only other year-round residents living at Havre de Poisson. A middle-aged couple who came over from Italy years ago, they had never left. Chef Angelo was a favorite with all the guests, not only because of his personality, but because he transformed anything a guest happened to catch, or shoot, into the most delicious mouthwatering epicurean delight anyone ever tasted.

Alessandra was the resort's housekeeper, and her husband's *sous* chef in the kitchen. They both considered Lou to be the son they had always wanted, but never had. And that was the way they treat him.

Since meeting, Kate and Alessandra had developed a relationship that fell somewhere between best friends and sisters.

Sometime after dinner, Lou and Jake walked down to the dock. "Jake we've got a poacher that we need to deal with."

"A little camp meat never bothered you, Lou, what's up with this one?"

"This one's a little more complicated than someone going after a little camp meat. A number of bucks have been shot and their antlers sawed off, but the deer have just been left to rot."

"They're leaving the meat *and* the hide?"

"Yeah, that's the strange part; it's just the antlers they're taking, I'm told. It seems to be concentrated over to the west. Now, here's what I'd like to do: We'll fly down the lake early tomorrow morning, moor the plane in Osprey Cove, and go ashore. It may take us a while before we pick up any tracks, but maybe we'll get lucky and hear someone hunting."

"Okay, how early?"

"Daybreak."

"That's fine."

"We'll stay down there overnight. I'll take care of the weapons; we'll travel light, and we'll go in cammo."

"Whoa, why the hell aren't we wearing underwear?"

Lou closed his eyes for a second, shook his head, and took a deep breath, "I said *cammo*', as in camouflage, not commando' you knucklehead.'"

When he turned his head and looked at his cousin, Jake was smiling from ear to ear, "I gotcha again, cuz!."

Chapter

12

The next morning, the ground was covered with a heavy dew as Lou and Kate walked down to the dock to join Jake who had gone there earlier. Both engines on the Twin Otter were already running. Alessandra was also on the dock, passing a prepared 'grab and go' breakfast inside the plane to Jake, along with a bag of supplies for an overnight.

"Lou, once you secure those kayaks to the struts, untie the ropes and get in, I'm ready to go," Jake called from inside the plane.

Lou turned to Kate. "We'll be back Sunday afternoon."

"I'll be waiting."

It took no time at all before Jake taxied away from the dock, skimmed along the surface of the lake, and was airborne.

As Lou looked out the window, he realized it had been years since he had gone as far west as Osprey Cove. The flight was short, and as Jake circled the cove, Lou pointed to an unobstructed stretch of shoreline where they could beach the kayaks. Far off in the distance Lou saw thin lines of smoke rising from the lodges in the village of Grey Elk. The imaginary boundary line that separated the Village of Grey Elk and Havre de Poisson was only about a half dozen miles north of the cove.

As Jake started his decent, he turned on the intercom system. "Flight attendants, prepare the cabin for landing," he announced.

Lou smiled. "Jake, have you ever thought about flying commercial?"

"What, and give up all *this*?"

"No, I'm serious."

"Nah, there's too many needy, whinny passengers nowadays. Hey, when we land, mount the pontoon and throw the hook!"

"Where is it."

"Under your seat, and hold on to your end of the rope, that's the only anchor on board."

The cove was perhaps two hundred yards wide, open to the lake and extended four hundred yards inward. Once they landed inside the cove, Jake taxied close to shore so the plane would be protected from winds traveling up and down the lake.

"I doubt anyone will bother the Otter Lou, but I'll disconnect a few wires in the ignition and fuel line, anyway."

When they reached shore, they dragged the kayaks up onto the sandy bank and secured them to the trunk of an old spruce tree.

"No sense in trying to hide the kayaks Jake, a float plane sitting in the middle of the cove is a pretty good indication that someone has come ashore." Within moments, the two cousins were silently moving through the forest.

"These woods are pretty dense, Lou."

"I know."

"You might want to consider having someone come in and do a little selective logging."

"I've thought about it; the only thing is that they'd have to cut a logging road in here to do it, which would encourage more people to trespass on our lands."

"You're going to lose a lot of good lumber out here, if you don't. The loggers could always come down from the village." Before Lou could respond, they heard a gunshot.

"Sounds like we've got a shooter in here, Lou. How far away do you think he is?"

"A couple of miles at most. Let's spread out, but not too far."

As they ran through the forest, both men smelled the putrid carcasses of rotting deer before seeing them. Antlers had been cut off the heads of each one.

It took only a little over fifteen minutes for them to find the fresh kill. Like the others, the antlers had been sawn off, and the rest of the body had been left where it fell. There was no sign of any attempt to harvest the meat.

"Now that's an interesting shot pattern Lou. What the hell was he using, a friggin' cannon?" Jake said.

"A huge hole with separate holes around it and only one shot?" Lou said, "think about it. The shooter has to be using a 'buck and ball load' to make a pattern like that."

"You think?"

"Yeah."

Jake looked a little closer at the wound. "I think you're right."

"Well, this guy certainly isn't concerned about covering his trail, look at the friggin' tracks he left."

"Must figure no one's around."

From the size of the footprints and long stride, they could tell it was a large man. They followed the tracks for several miles, finally coming to a dirt road. "We're beyond Abenaki lands now, Jake. We crossed the only road on our lands, awhile back."

"I'm not exactly sure where the hell we are, but I'd say we're pretty close to Five Fingers, if I had to guess."

"Let's see where this road takes us," Lou said. A little over a mile down the road, they came to a two-lane paved road.

"This has to be Route 17, Lou; it's the only paved road in the area."

Several logging trucks barreled past them before a farmer came along sitting atop an old tractor which was pulling an empty hay trailer. "You fella's wanna save some shoe leather? Hop on . . . I'll take ya' up as far as the center of Five Fingers."

As they approached Five Fingers, Lou whispered, "Still not much of a town center, is it?"

"Hey, at least it's got a diner."

The outside of the diner had certainly seen better days, but the inside was clean though it looked a little worn.

"Howdy fella's, what'll you have?"

"Cheeseburger, I guess."

"That it?"

"And a fresh coffee."

"Make that two coffees, and another cheeseburger."

"Coming right up."

The proprietor turned his back on Lou and Jake and began preparing the grill as they made themselves comfortable sitting at the counter.

"Ain't seen the likes of you two in here a 'fore . . . are you new 'round here?"

"We're down from Kedgwick," Jake offered. "Just doing some varmint hunting, that's all."

"Figured that when I saw them rifles; ain't nothing else in season now. Town folk been complaining about coyotes, lately.

Nobody's gonna say nothing, if you shoot a few of them, actually that'd be doing us a favor."

"Do people around here hunt with muzzle loaders much? We heard one go off in the woods earlier today."

"Darned if I knows. That's a question for Mathew over there at the general store. He knows just about everybody in these parts, and what they hunt with. Where 'bouts did you boys say you was from?"

"Kedgwick."

"Funny, I ain't never seen you in here before, Kedgwick being so close by and all."

"Yup, first time we've been in here."

"You said cheese on them burgers, right?"

"Yes, please."

"American or cheddar? I got both."

Jake looked at Lou, shrugged his shoulders. "American, I guess."

"Okay, American, it is."

Jake didn't see any condiments on the counter. "Do you have any Grey Poupon?"

"Any grey, *what*?"

"What kind of mustard do you have?"

"Nothing but the best! French's."

"Really?"

"Yessir! I'll bring a squeeze bottle over and some ketchup in a moment. Just shake it up before you squeeze it, otherwise that first squeeze will be watery."

"Right."

Finishing lunch, the two men headed over to the general

store. As they left the diner, the owner dropped a dime, and made a phone call.

--

As they neared the general store, Lou cautioned his cousin. "Jake let me do the talking this time. I wanna see what I can learn from this shopkeeper."

"No problem, if you need me, I'll be over in ladies lingerie."

Like every small country store, there was a little bell that rang as soon as Lou pushed open the door. In less than half a minute, the owner came out from the back room.

"Howdy, fellas, how can I help?"

"I'm wondering if you have any percussion caps?"

"Don't get much call for caps these days. I'll have to check out back. Might still have a few boxes."

"Don't bother, I've got a percussion pistol and was just checking, that's all. Funny though, I was sure I heard what sounded like the boom of a muzzle loader go off earlier today."

"Well, if you did, it was most likely one of the Turnbridge clan that done it. They're the only ones I know of in these parts that still shoot muzzle loaders. They come in once a year and order a few bags of Prime-All. That's about all the business I do with them."

"Do they have a large collection of antique firearms?"

"Nah, the Turnbridges ain't collectors. They're just a bunch of hillbillies. They pretty much live off the land. They've been in these parts for generations; most folks say they're all illiterate inbreds."

"Sounds like the kind of people we'd wanna give a wide berth to," Lou said. "Can you give us a clue as to where abouts they are, so we can stay clear?"

"They're just a few miles south on Route 17 . . . just beyond a dirt road, off to the left."

"Thanks." As they left the store, Jake said, "Sounds like you've identified a possible perp, Sherlock."

"Perhaps, but whoever it is, we'll have to actually *catch* them in the act."

As they walked back down the highway, a dark green SUV slowly pulled up directly behind them. Turning, they both noticed the round game warden emblem on the vehicle's door as a very young warden got out.

"Howdy, fellas. Saw you walking along the road and thought I'd just check your licenses."

"We're Abenaki . . . not required to have a license to hunt our lands."

"I'm aware of that. Only thing is, you're not on Abenaki soil. So, I need to see your varmint licenses."

"I just told you; we don't carry licenses."

"If that's the case, I'll have to confiscate those rifles."

In a very nonchalant voice, Lou said, "Well, I really don't think that's going to happen, son."

The warden backed up, pulled out his handgun. "Drop the weapons, turnaround, get down on your knees, and put your hands on top of your head." He was dead serious. Neither Jake nor Lou made a move.

"I said, *drop* the weapons, turnaround, get *down* on your knees, and put your hands on top of your *head*!"

"Well, Lou, you wanna take him, or you want me to?"

The young warden backed up a few steps, after realizing how dangerously close he was standing to the two men he had drawn upon.

Just then, a second warden's car came to a screeching halt directly behind the first SUV. He saw what was happening, and jumped out of his vehicle, shotgun in hand. Almost simultaneously, a third vehicle came blasting to a stop from the opposite direction and a Mountie jumped out.

"Jake? Lou? What the hell are you two doing way over here in Five Fingers?!"

"You *know* these two men, Constable?"

"Yeah, they're both auxiliary Mounties. What's the problem, Warden?"

"We got a call about two strangers carrying rifles. We're following every possible lead and they refused to lay down their arms."

"Well, these two are okay. I can vouch for them. Incidentally, you're damn lucky you didn't try to disarm them." Turning toward Lou and Jake, he said, "You're a long way from Havre de Poisson, guys, what brings you way over here?"

"Someone's been poaching on Abenaki lands. Quite a few of our deer have been killed and just left to rot. We found a fresh kill, today, and the poacher's trail led us to a dirt road just down this road a piece."

Both wardens had relaxed a bit. Now, the second warden asked, "Can you describe the bullet hole on the fresh kill you saw today?"

"The chest was blown out, antlers were gone, and the carcass was left to rot."

"Were there multiple entry wounds on the deer?"

"Yeah. But we only heard one shot. The shooter must be using a 'buck and ball' load to leave a pattern like the one we saw."

"Sounds like the guy we're after. You're lucky he didn't know you were trailing him. He's 'back shot' two of our wardens already, killed 'em both."

"We'll keep that in mind."

After the two wardens returned to their vehicles, their Mountie friend turned to Lou and Jake. "Be careful, guys, this dude's dangerous."

"Can you give us a lift back to that dirt road a few miles back?" Lou asked.

"I'm not supposed to, you know that . . . but sure, hop in."

Once their friend had dropped them off, Jake turned to Lou. "Okay Kemosabe, me been to town, now what?"

Chapter

13

It took all of three minutes for Lou to pick up the poacher's trail on the opposite side of the dirt road. "Jake, there's a fresh trail over here."

"There's more than a couple of old trails over here Lou," his cousin replied. "Looks like whoever it is, just does a friggin' beeline."

"Let's see where this one goes."

"Wanna choose up? See who goes first?"

"Just keep your eyes open for traps."

The two Abenakis moved cautiously through the woods and undergrowth that was primarily a carpet of knee-high ferns.

"Looks like somebody's been selectively harvesting these trees."

"Have you noticed there's no deadwood laying around either?"

"I did. This place has been picked clean."

The further into the wooded area the two men traveled, the more open it became. It appeared as though they were on a plateau of some type. A couple of miles further along, Lou caught a faint smell of burning wood.

"Smell that?"

"Sure do."

"We're coming up to something, so stay alert."

Jake yawned before saying, "Aye, aye, Cuz."

Always joking, Lou thought. "Jake, seriously, there's most likely buildings up ahead. We won't be under cover much longer. As we get closer, we'll need to drop down and low crawl."

For the next mile, they traveled through field upon field of ferns; trees so widely spaced out, it almost felt like being in a park. Upon Lou's signal, both men dropped to the ground and began low crawling as they approached what appeared to be a ridge. When they reached the top of the highest point, Jake worked his way over to Lou.

In a hollow below them, was a cluster of buildings. They weren't much more than rust covered metal roofed shacks that seemed to be built directly into the sides of the ravine. Both men pulled out binoculars to get a better look at the scene below.

"It looks like a bunch of women sitting around, Lou, see 'em?" Jake whispered. "Over to the left . . . on the porch . . . all ages. They seem to be watching a horde of barefoot kids."

"Any men among them?"

"Not that I can see. The kids are chasing each other around; they're playing some kind of game."

"The men must be somewhere in the hills, working the stills the storekeeper told us about."

"Yeah. Oops, here comes an old gent out of one of the houses. Looks like he's only got one leg."

"That's the reason he's there and not at the still. Most likely lost it to gangrene. Doesn't look like they pay much attention to hygiene down there."

"Yeah but, look at the laundry hangin' . . . must wash clothes a lot; every shack has a line or two running to the next one over. Lots of laundry hanging," Jake shifted his binoculars. "Get a load of the old pickup truck over on the right, next to the barn. That one's seen better days."

"Could be the truck they use to take moonshine into town." Lou said.

"Any guesses on when the last time that barn saw a coat of paint?" Jake said. "Looks like the chickens are all free range. I see goats roaming, too."

"Yeah, I see that."

"Take a look at the number of hogs in that pigsty to the right of the barn. Now, that's one huge pen . . . how many hogs you think are in there."

"Don't know . . . looks like it continues around behind the barn . . . I can see about fifty, maybe more," Lou said. An odor wafted on the air toward them. "Smell that? Kinda takes your breath away, doesn't it?"

"Yeah. I don't see any fields. They must not have any cows or horses."

"If they're running stills, they have to have corn fields somewhere."

"You're right. There's probably a crude mill somewhere, too."

"If all they've got is that pickup truck, there's got to be draft horses somewhere."

"You think?"

"They need something to plow the fields with."

"I can see the beginning of a garden just beyond the barn; must be fields below. It's hard to tell; looks like the land begins to drop off."

"Other than a couple of mangy looking dogs lying in the

shade over by that pile of firewood, I don't see anything else."

"So, you think that old pickup is the only vehicle they have?"

"Yeah, a farm this size would need an underground tank for gas, if they were running a lot of vehicles."

"Yeah, but where'd they get money to pay for gas?"

As Lou put his binoculars down, he looked over at Jake. "The store owner said the Turnbridge clan pretty much lives off the land. They probably don't need any more vehicles, or anything else."

"At least there's no huge trash heap adding to the squalor."

"I would think what little trash they generate, would be biodegradable. Probably gets tossed into a compost heap somewhere."

"Lou, with all those damn hogs, smart money says chitlins and jowls is a regular on the menu for these folks,".

"Well, at least now we know who's been killing our deer."

"Yeah, but why? They're not taking any meat, only antlers."

"Well, maybe they've become vegetarians," Lou smiled over at him, ". . . or they don't eat venison."

"Yeah? Well, take a look at the front of that barn, there's quite a few racks on it, that sure as hell tells me they eat venison."

"Those racks are pretty grey; they've been there for more than a few seasons. Maybe the ones that ate venison all died off Jake." Jake looked at his cousin, and just shook his head.

"It could happen."

"The question is, why the hell are they killing so *many* deer if they're not taking the meat?"

"And only the bucks."

"Exactly. Find out why they want the antlers, and we'll

know why it's bucks only."

"Whoever is doing the shooting either has a lot of time on his hands or is a damn good hunter."

"There doesn't seem to be a lot going on down there to keep a fella down on the farm," Lou said, "maybe it's a combination of both." He shifted his position. "Sun's starting to go down, I'm not sure how much more we're going to find out from up here."

"Just when I started getting comfortable . . . "

"Jake, I think we found what we needed to find out. At least, now we know who's killing the deer."

"What now?"

"Let's head back, make camp, and figure out how we want to deploy tomorrow. Could be we might even catch this shooter on *our* land."

"I'm ready."

"Me too; let's go."

Just as they were backing up, preparing to leave, a stick suddenly snapped directly behind them. Lou closed his eyes, thinking, *Damn it, one of us should have been paying attention to the back door*

Chapter

14

Earlier in the day, at just about the time that Lou and Jake were having lunch over in Five Fingers, Jarl Ohlson was turning onto the access road that led to the Village of Grey Elk. Ohlson was a fully tenured professor of archaeology at McGill University. His colleagues tended to shy away from him for no particular reason other than he made them feel . . . uncomfortable . . . sometimes. He, also, rarely accepted invitations to faculty social gatherings.

He usually came across as surly, and somewhat pompous. Due to his short stature, many believed he suffered from a Napoleon complex. Not long after Ohlson had arrived at McGill, one of his students had nicknamed him "the weasel," largely because of his dark beady eyes and his shifty mannerisms. The name stuck and had been passed down each year to incoming freshmen eagerly seeking acceptance.

When Ohlson reached the village, he parked his car in front of the largest building he saw and waited. When two men finally came out of the building, Ohlson jumped out of his car.

"Excuse me! Hello, excuse me, over here! Yes, I was wondering if you gentlemen could help me. I'd like to speak with whoever's in charge."

The men looked at each other; one shrugged his shoulders. "What do you mean, when you say, 'who's in charge?'"

"You know, the *chief*! The guy who runs this place. I wanna speak to *your chief*."

"We have no chief."

"No chief? Why, that's great! Okay, then, so let me put it this way: Who runs things around here?"

"We have a tribal council."

"Then that's who I want to speak to. Where is their office?"

"They have no office."

"That's odd...well, then, where can I find them?

"Two of our tribal leaders are inside this building now."

"Great, then thank you." As Ohlson began walking up the stairs, he suddenly stopped and turned around, calling back to the men: "Hey, am I okay parked there?" He pointed to his car parked in front of the building. The two Abenaki paused, turned to look at him, then continued to walk away. They had no idea what he was asking.

Entering the building, Ohlson went over to the only occupied table where two men were engaged in conversation. When they failed to immediately acknowledge his presence, Ohlson cleared his throat several times . . .loudly . . . which caused them to look up.

"Good afternoon, my name is Jarl Ohlson, do you have a minute?"

Without waiting for a reply, Ohlson pulled up a chair, turned the chairback toward them and sat down. "I'd like to talk to you about a tremendous educational opportunity that I'm prepared to offer the Abenaki people."

The two elders were completely taken aback by his rudeness and continued to stare at him in silence.

"Gentlemen, are you both part of this 'tribal council' thing?"

They understood the words, "tribal council," and the elders nodded.

"Okay, great. So listen, here's the deal: In exchange for your cooperation, I am able to offer a full four-year scholarship to McGill University to any Abenaki student who qualifies and wants to attend McGill. We're talking room, board, books, tuition, the whole nine yards. That's right, I'm talking about a 'full boat.' How's that grab ya?" His expression looked nearly as patronizing as a lap dog with its tongue hanging out.

The two elders only had a vague idea of what Ohlson was trying to say. They simply stared at him with blank faces.

"Gentlemen, in return, I'd like your permission to run an archaeological dig at the site of an ancient battle that occurred centuries ago between the Abenaki, the Mohawk, and some Vikings here on this land. Are you familiar with that legend?"

Before either of the elders could respond, Ohlson looked up and saw the ancient Viking sword and shield that hung from the rafters. He pointed excitedly to it. "*There*, up there! That's what I'm talking about! I want to dig around where the battle was . . . where those artifacts came from."

Finally, one of the men spoke up. "The legend that you speak of has been told many times, but the battle was not fought on the lands of our village."

But Ohlson would not be put off. "The Mohawk told me that it *was*, that it was fought near some lake that had a lot of fish in it. Isn't that lake near your village?"

"The lake of which you speak is in the land of Grey Elk."

"Okay, so how far of a drive is that from here?"

"The only way an outsider can go there is by float plane. You must first make arrangements to visit Havre de Poisson."

"Float plane! You're kidding me, right? I can't drive there?" Ohlson pulled out his cell phone, "Okay, let me google this. What's the name of this place again, Harvey. . . what is it?"

"Havre de Poisson."

"Oh, *Havre*, okay now I've got it. Okay, thanks, guys."

With that Ohlson, the weasel, got up and left. As he sat in his car, he impatiently punched in the phone number listed for Havre de Poisson.

"Come on, come on, pick up the phone," he muttered. After a number of rings, the phone bounced over to an answering service.

Ohlson recorded his name and phone number along with the message that he'd like a call back as soon as possible.

Chapter

15

When the stick snapped behind them, Lou whispered "Jake, on three you roll left, I'll go right, let's get him."

In seconds, the men rolled in opposite directions, expecting to hear the boom of a muzzle loader, hoping one of them could return fire. Then, sitting up, rifles ready, they were surprised to see the eyes of a scrawny waif of a girl, not even six years old, standing before them.

The first thing Lou noticed about the child was that her eyes seemed far too large for her small head. She couldn't have weighed more than thirty pounds. The simple, tattered dress she wore was badly soiled. For a moment, the three of them simply stared at one another. Then, without a word, as if a voice had spoken to her, the young girl turned and disappeared, seeming to dance across the tops of the ferns and over the ridge without looking back.

"Jake, I think we just met a member of the Turnbridge clan,"Lou said.

"That little one's not 'right in the head,' but she damn sure knew how to come up on us without making a sound," Jake said.

"Yeah, I'm beginning to think the shooter may be just as adept in the woods. Let's head back, make camp, have something to eat and talk about tomorrow."

"Good idea . . . I brought the Grey Poupon."

By late afternoon, Lou and Jake had returned to the lands of the Abenaki and quickly constructed a lean-to. Even though they were deep in the forest and the sky was clear, their structure's opening faced away from prevailing winds as it always did.

"Lou," Jake hesitated, "I just heard something out there. I'll be right back."

"Take your rifle. I'm going to try and text Kate, just to let her know what's happening."

"Tell Kate I said, 'Hi.'"

Within a matter of ten minutes, Jake returned with two rabbits, "Lou, how do you like your rabbit: regular, creamy, or *al dente*?"

Lou was reading emails on his smart phone. Without really listening, he responded, "Regular, I guess. Kate said 'hi' back."

"Have you thought about tomorrow?"

"A little. If this guy is as adapt in the woods as I think he might be, I'm thinking the smarter move for us would be to take a stand and see what shows up. If we hear a muzzle loader go off, we can head in that direction, if it's close enough."

"Sounds like a plan. What time do you wanna head back?"

"I'd like to be back for dinner, this is the week Kate and I are getting married. I'm sure there are things we have to do."

While the rabbits were slowly roasting over a bed of coals, Lou mentioned to Jake, "The other day, Laughing Gull asked me to mentor her son and three others in 'butterfly hide and seek.'"

"That's a great honor.

"I know."

"You got the time for that, Cuz?"

"Did Grey Elk have the time for us? No, but he made the time."

"Point taken. Have you met with them yet?"

"A couple of times; they're as eager to learn as we were. I sent them out once; they did okay, now I'll begin teaching them. They were the ones who told me about the dead dear out here in the west."

"They travel out this far?"

"Well, remember, Jake, we traveled all over Grey Elk's land, and the village lands. Come on, they're *young,* just like we were."

"Yeah, I guess we did. Hey, you wanna baste those rabbits? Here's more Grey Poupon."

"Throw me that squeeze bottle."

Except for the endless whistling between a couple of saw-whet owls calling to one another, the night was uneventful. In the morning, they dismantled the shelter, leaving no evidence that anyone had spent the night there.

Later that morning, they positioned themselves in various stands, hoping for a glimpse of the shooter, but the woods were silent.

Around two in the afternoon, Lou decided to pack it in. They hiked back to Osprey Cove. Then, minutes after Jake reconnected everything, the Twin Otter lifted off and was heading up the lake to Havre de Poisson.

Chapter

16

Elwood Pritchard knew it was time to make the phone call that could change his fortunes forever. With only a slight hesitation, he picked up the phone and punched in the numbes.

"Good afternoon, RE/MAX, how may I direct your call?"

"This is Elwood Pritchard, is Robert Fulton in?"

"I'll check sir."

After a pause, the receptionist came back on the line. "Mr. Pritchard, Mr. Fulton said that he will call you right back. Is this the best number to reach you?"

"Yes, thank you."

Moments later, Fulton was punching Pritchard's number into his cell phone.

"Woody, sorry, but I didn't want to take your call on the company phones, they record everything, supposedly for *training* purposes, but who knows. Anyway, I've just closed on thirty-seven acres in the boonies a little over thirty miles north of Nictau, right off Route 385 on behalf of Eastern Timber Associates. Nictau is the closest town to the south of Carleton Mountain, so this transaction will definitely show up on any future land evaluation in that area.

"I was also able to get the seller down close to the price you wanted. Initially, he wanted one hundred an acre, which was way overpriced and I think he knew. I was able get him down to four-fifty by telling him another woodlot in the vicinity with better access was about to come on the market at that price. So, he bit. Title should transfer to Eastern Timber Associates in about five business days."

"Excellent. Thank you Robert."

As soon as Pritchard hung up, he intercommed his secretary. "Marsha, see if you can get Barry Colvin on the line over at Colvin Realty for me."

Within minutes Barry was on the line. "Hello Woody, I was just about to call you. It looks like we have a deal on that sixty-acre wood lot we talked about that's a few miles east of Five Fingers, close to the Abenaki lands. We should be able to sign papers in the next few days. We were able to get the land for fifty an acre. Title should transfer to Eagle Enterprises in thirty days."

"Perfect. Thanks, Barry, I appreciate your follow through on this."

"My pleasure; I'll send the deed over as soon as it's recorded."

Satisfied that he now had been able to establish the value of undeveloped land in the greater Carleton Mountain area at a low price, Pritchard wrote, "Done," next to the action item on his white board. Next on his list was contacting Tiverton Realty to give them the go ahead to pick up the option he had on eighty-nine acres of land abutting Grand Lake Provincial Park.

As he dialed the number he thought: *I know I'll pay more than a grand an acre, but that land is exactly what will tip the scales my way when I get into negotiations with New Brunswick's Natural Resource people.*

The number at Tiverton Realty was busy. He left a voice mail for a call back.

He had one more important call to make. Since New Brunswick's provincial elections were only a few months away, Pritchard was very much aware that certain politicians seemed to have more influence than others when it came to leasing crown lands.

"Marsha, see if you can get my attorney on the line for me."

Pritchard had done his research and knew exactly which politicians were up for reelection and which of them rewarded their contributors.

"Mr. Pritchard, I have Solicitor Israelian on line one."

"Thanks." Pritchard pressed the button for line one. "Izzy I'm just calling to give you a heads up. I'm going to fund the PAC that we set up with fifteen grand. I'd like you to disburse it equally to three legislative assembly members on behalf of The Carleton Mountain Development Corporation. Yes, Monday will be fine. I'll fax over the names of the assembly members who I'd like the money to go to. Let me know when the money has gone out, okay? Fine. Gotta run, talk with you later."

--

Since March, Lee Wong Ying had been landing a small ultralight helicopter at the far end of the field behind the Grange Hall, every other week. Within a matter of minutes, Arthur Turnbridge would emerge from the line of trees, with a cloth sack containing antlers covered with velvet, all carefully wrapped in plastic.

Arthur Turnbridge wasn't the only hunter that Ying had recruited, but he was proving to be the most prolific of the lot.

The quantity of antlers Turnbridge delivered was never the same; sometimes he had a dozen antlers, other times more. To date, Turnbridge had delivered about ninety sets of antlers to Ying, the most of any of them. Ying carefully inspected each antler before accepting it. Only once, did he reject a set of antlers that Turnbridge had brought to him for being too dry.

The other hunters Ying had recruited into his downline, never had more than a half dozen antlers. And they weren't nearly as careful about keeping the velvet moist as Arthur Turnbridge was. Yes, he was special.

The first time Ying took out his wad of one-hundred-dollar bills and casually peeled off what he owed, Turnbridge was wide-eyed and speechless.

But he had other worries. As discreet as Ying tried to be, it was difficult to land an ultralight every other week in a small community like Five Fingers without attracting attention. There wasn't a lot going on in Five Fingers, and after a while, the same group of locals who would park their cars at the dump at night (hoping to see some bears rummaging around in the trash) began sitting behind the Grange Hall waiting to see his ultralight fly in. He had attracted unwanted attention. Word soon reached the Mounties that something odd was happening twice a month in back of the Grange Hall at the far end of the field.

Corporal Harold Burkett was dispatched to observe whatever the citizens were concerned about and, if needed, to take whatever appropriate action he felt was necessary.

A little after noon on the day the ultralight was next expected, Burkett pulled onto the grassy area next to the Grange Hall and waited in his vehicle.

It was a beautiful day, and Burkett could think of any number things he'd rather be doing but, at least, he was parked in the shade underneath the huge tree next to the Grange Hall.

It was just about two in the afternoon when the ultralight passed directly overhead at tree top level, circled the field once, and set down in the far end. Almost as if on cue, someone emerged from the tree line carrying a bag and approached the ultralight.

Burkett smelled a drug deal.

He shifted his SUV into four-wheel drive and began racing across the field toward the ultralight. About halfway across the field, the man who had emerged from the tree line began frantically pointing at the oncoming vehicle. The operator of the ultralight quickly initiated a vertical takeoff and disappeared above the trees. The man who had come out of tree line immediately blended back into the forest.

Burkett exited his vehicle and checked if anything had been left on the ground but found nothing.

When Burkett submitted his report, he added a footnote that the next time the ultralight was expected, he'd be waiting in the woods at the far end of the field behind the grange hall.

Chapter

17

Long before dawn, Lou had walked over to the rocky point that jutted out into the lake. Rocky Point was where Lou always went when he wanted to be alone with his thoughts.

As he sat down, a gust of wind came off the water, filling his senses with the fragrance of balsams that lined the distant shore. At this time of morning, the lake was still quiet; in another hour, the eerie, wavering call of loons would signal the start of a new day. Once the loons where awake, Lou would return to his cottage, as the loons had become Kate's morning wake up call.

Lou and Kate had decided that their wedding would be a blend of traditional and contemporary rituals. The village elders had assured him that there were no right or wrong ceremonies, that he should just do what his heart told him to do, that all his relations and ancestors would understand and accept whatever was chosen to do.

For weeks, Lou and Kate had traveled alone to the village of Grey Elk. Today, Angelo, the long-time resident chef at Havre de Poisson, his wife Alessandra, and Jake, would accompanying them to celebrate their marriage.

Lou was pleased that so many villagers had come to their "gathering" the previous week to hear their intent to be joined. He interpreted the large turnout as recognition that he was now seen as a leader in the village.

When the elders were satisfied that no one objected to their marriage, a blanket was placed at the base of their marriage pole where gifts for the couple could be left.

Finally, today was their wedding day.

When Lou's entourage was ready, they all walked down to the boat house. Once the huge Chrysler engine came to life, Jake untied the lines and stepped into the 26-foot mahogany Chris-Craft. They traveled down the lake at close to top speed, reaching their destination in under fifteen minutes.

As they approached Moose Cove, Lou backed off the throttle, and glided over the shoals that stretched between the islands. Two of Lou's relations were waiting at the dock with Jeeps that would transport them up to the village, once the bumpers were in place and a canvas tarp covered the boat.

As soon as Kate and Lou entered the village, Kate was whisked away by Laughing Gull to be changed into the traditional white deerskin dress that had been made for her. The dress had been carefully tailored to Kate's figure. Rows and rows of long thin tapered thongs hung from the underside of both sleeves. Images of the sun, the earth and the moon, had been painstakingly made from beads and quills creating a border around the neckline. Her sponsors had also made a pair of moccasins, with matching beadwork. She looked radiant.

Once Lou had changed into his traditional formal Abenaki deerskin attire, their purification ceremony began.

Lou had decided upon the traditional purification ceremony which emphasized prayer and contemplation. Once Lou and Kate entered the temporary structure he had created, they sat motionless as an elder scattered the sacred herbs in all four directions. First sage, to purify the area of negative energies, then sweet grass to encourage the spirits from the other side to join them, then cedar to create an atmosphere for the spirits to work within, and finally tobacco to bless the earth.

"Let us honor our relations so that they may bless this joining," the elder said.

The elder was the first to offer his prayers, by saying, "Spirits, remove the darkness that dwells within us and carry our prayers to the sky father and the earth mother so that we may rejoice in this joining."

When he had finished, each person took a turn. Once everyone had spoken, the elder working with spiritual energies blended all of the prayers together into a mystical tapestry, that would dwell in the nonphysical world and forever bless this joining.

When the ceremony was complete, a blue blanket was placed over Lou's shoulders and another was placed over Kate's shoulders, signifying their individuality.

A pipe ceremony and prayers followed, then traditional songs were sung while their entire circle of sponsors underwent a purification ceremony with sweet grass. Finally, the elder, who was also a licensed officiant in New Brunswick, stood up and asked those in the circle, "Are you willing to give these two to one another?"

Jake led the response. "Yes, we are."

"Families and friends, we are gathered together in the sight of the creator to witness and bless the joining together of Raven Claw and the woman that is known by her people as Kathryn O'Grady in marriage to one another." The elder then stepped forward, removed the two separate blue blankets and placed a single white blanket over both of their shoulders, signifying that they had now become joined as one.

"Kathryn O'Grady, in the presence of the Creator, and all of your relations, do you declare your intention to enter into this sacred union?" He looked at Kate.

"I do. I will have Raven Claw to be my husband, to live together with in sacred marriage."

"Will you love him, comfort him, honor and keep him,

in sickness and in health, and be faithful to him as long as you both shall live?"

"I will."

"Raven Claw, will you have this woman who will be known to all as, Wyanetta Wikimak, to be your wife, to live together in sacred marriage? Will you love her, comfort her, honor and keep her, in sickness and in health, and be faithful to her as long as you both shall live?"

"I will."

"We are pleased by your marriage and pray for the Creator's blessing upon you. The words of your vows have now been forever woven into the blanket that is upon you." The elder then spoke to all who were in attendance.

"Will all of you present uphold and care for these two people in their marriage?"

This time Alessandra led the response by saying, "We will."

A great feast followed the wedding ceremony. There was contemporary music and dancing that continued well into the night. Somewhere during the festivities Kate was escorted by her sponsors to a lodge that had been prepared for the newlyweds. When the women returned to the celebration, the men who stood up for Lou lifted him upon their shoulders and carried him to the lodge where Kate awaited.

When Lou entered the lodge, Kate had already changed into a very provocative black lace negligee and was lying in the middle of the bed.

"Well now, that negligee doesn't leave a lot to the imagination, my love."

Kate smiled and slowly wet her lips with her tongue. "Welcome home, dear," she said in a sultry voice. "The negligee is only the wrapping."

"And all this time, you had me thinking that you were really demure."

"Let me slip out of this negligee first, it belongs to my cousin. She said it was really good luck because every time she wore it, the sex was so great, she didn't give a damn whether or not she ended up getting pregnant."

As Lou slipped into bed beside her, he asked, "Then, why'd she give it away?"

Wrapping her soft arms and long legs around her new husband, she whispered, "Because she figured that eight kids in six and a half years was lucky enough."

After some time, when they had made love and were completely satisfied, Lou rolled over on his back and looked at his lovely, new wife. "Kate, do me a favor."

And what might that be?"

"Don't be in any hurry to return that negligee."

She smiled and looked at him with a warm smile. "I won't. Now tell me, what does my Abenaki name translate to?"

"Wyanetta Wikimak?"

"Yes . . . what does it mean?"

"It comes from the Algonquin . . . it means 'Beautiful Wife.'"

The following morning, the newlyweds enjoyed the breakfast that had been prepared for them.

"Lou, I had no idea how closely a traditional Abenaki wedding would parallel a Christian wedding ceremony," Kate said. "It was absolutely beautiful."

"Weddings are fun, aren't they? They give everyone a chance to come together and rejoice."

"They do, and there's one thing that I'm especially rejoicing about."

"What's that?"

"That I didn't have to kiss any toads or take your Abenaki last name."

"I'm not sure I know what you're talking about."

As she tousled Lou's hair, she said, "Raven Claw. The Irish colleen you just married would never have been pleased if she ended up with the last name of Claw."

"Hmmm, so being called 'ma'am' is out, and now being called 'Mrs. Claw' is also out. You once said that you're not one to be trifled with. Is there anything *else* that your new husband should be aware of?"

Kissing him lightly, she said, "Actually yes. Right now, this new wife of yours is really in the mood for a morning delight. You do know what that is, don't you?"

"Oh, I *do*," he said, reaching for her, again.

Chapter
18

As soon as Corporal Burkett woke up, he could tell it was going to be another one of those sweltering hot August "dog days of summer." He was thankful the Mounties' summer uniform had an open collar and that ties were only required during a court appearance.

When he arrived at the Grange Hall, he parked beneath the huge sugar maple that stood next to the building hoping the shade would help keep his SUV cool. Since he was early, he waited in his vehicle for over an hour before deciding to get out. Then, he radioed his position, letting dispatch know that he was going to reconnoiter the wooded area at the far end of the landing field, then stake it out.

He unclipped his twelve-gauge shot gun that hung along the front edge of the bench seat by his knees before taking a few shells from the console. Satisfied that he had everything needed, he secured his vehicle and headed directly across the field. As soon as he entered the woods at the far end of the field, he looked for a comfortable log to sit on, one that offered a good view of the field.

Burkett had grown up in Toronto and wasn't a hunter; he had very little knowledge about the ways of the forest. Most importantly, he was totally unaware that he had been observed from the very moment he had stepped out of his SUV and began crossing the field.

A short distance from Burkett, young Turnbridge was hiding among the trees. When he saw that it was a uniform coming at him, he became confused and began to fidget. He knew Ying would expect him to come out of the woods as soon as Ying arrived, yet Turnbridge was terrified of what his father would do to him, if he was ever caught poaching.

Corporal Burkett hadn't been in position more than ten minutes when the audio on his radio came to life. The voice was directing another patrol car to a domestic disturbance somewhere in Kedgwick. Burkett turned the volume control knob off and tried to make himself comfortable on the log he was sitting on. He hadn't had much for breakfast but remembered a granola bar in his shirt pocket and reached for it. As he looked down to take a second bite of the breakfast bar, he wondered where the warm sticky red liquid was coming from that was flowing down the front of his shirt. Then everything went black.

Burkett never heard his assailant come up from behind, nor did he feel the cut from the razor-sharp blade that ended his life. The wound severed both carotid arteries in one swift motion and Burkett bled out in a matter of seconds, without uttering a sound.

Turnbridge wiped the blood off his knife onto Burkett's trousers before placing it back in its sheath. *That weren't much different than cutting a hog's throat*, he thought, *except there weren't no squeal.*

Then Turnbridge looked at the Mountie's shot gun, for a moment, but decided he didn't want it and walked a few yards over to where he normally sat every time he waited for Ying to arrive.

Today will be an extra-big payday, Turnbridge thought, *'cuz two weeks ago, Ying took off in a hurry before he could pay me last time.* The dead body lying several yards away, gave him no thought at all.

It was close to two-thirty in the afternoon when the Mountie, who had been dispatched earlier to Kedgwick, pulled up on the lawn in front of Grange Hall and parked next to Burkett's SUV. As he walked across the field, he noticed turkey vultures soaring in the thermals at the opposite end of the field. *Hmm, something must have died,* he thought.

It had been well over five decades since a Mountie had died in the line of duty in such a gruesome manner in New Brunswick. Emotions among Burkett's detachment ran high after they found him. Flags at every RCMP detachment across the province were ordered to half-mast and would remain there until sunset on the day of Burkett's funeral.

Mounties representing every provincial and territorial division in Canada flew in to attend Corporal Burkett's funeral. The contingent from New Brunswick's J Division was well over two hundred strong. The honor guard that carried Burkett's casket from the church to the cemetery were all members of his own detachment in Kedgwick. He would have been honored that they cared for him.

Headquarters announced that New Brunswick's major crime unit would run the investigation into Corporal Burkett's murder, along with assistance from multiple RCMP detachments and other supporting agencies. They intended to catch the bastard that killed one of their own.

--

Once Elwood Pritchard had clear title to the eighty-nine acres of land that abutted Grand Lake Provincial Park, he was eager to meet with Albert Weeks, New Brunswick's Minister of Forest, Lands, Natural Resource Operations, and Rural Development.

Pritchard was amused at the length of the minister's title. "I can't wait to see this guy's business card," he chuckled to himself.

Minister Weeks was up for re-election and had been severely criticized in the press for his lackluster performance. Weeks was also burning through the meager campaign money that he had accumulated, spending it on advertisements and personal appearances a whole lot faster than he had raised it.

Even though, Week's wanted to be seen, Pritchard's assistant was unable to get her boss on Weeks' schedule, but she was able to arrange a meeting with Weeks' campaign manager.

When Pritchard met with the campaign manager, he explained that he would like to make a land swap in exchange for the ability to lease a parcel of Crown land which was doing absolutely nothing to further New Brunswick's economy. But his idea would.

The campaign manager gave Pritchard the impression that he'd rather be somewhere else at the moment or doing anything other than listening to all of his drivel.

However, when Pritchard mentioned that he was prepared to make a significant financial contribution to Weeks' campaign, the manager suddenly became all ears. The moment the campaign contribution was put on the table, the deal Pritchard was looking for was literally etched in stone. All that remained before a lease could be signed, was approval by the minister's legislative oversight committee, three of whom had already received the maximum allowed campaign contributions from the PAC that Pritchard had set up.

When the proposed lease of Crown lands encompassing parts of Carleton Mountain and surrounding acreage was presented to the oversight committee, two of the five members voted against leasing the land, primarily on the basis of Pritchard's horrendous track record as a developer. However, the measure passed three votes to two.

One of the legislators who voted in favor of the lease did have rather serious concerns, since she had accepted a sizable campaign contribution from the Carleton Mountain Development Group. But she decided to vote in favor of the lease since it would allow her to bring the action back to committee at a later date.

When word reached Pritchard that the lease was

approved, he smiled knowing that his shenanigans were beginning to pay off.

Pritchard's next move was to ask one of the legislators, he had in his back pocket, file an "expropriation legislation" in Parliament that would identify the Carleton Mountain Development project as an essential economic initiative within the province. This would enable him to acquire by eminent domain any additional lands that his project needed.

Canada had no constitutional protection of private property rights, Canadian law however, did specify that property owners were entitled to receive full and fair indemnity for any property taken by eminent domain. The cost of such land was usually established by recent transactions of like property in the surrounding area. The law also stated, however, that owners of any property involved in any expropriation legislation had to be notified by certified mail no less than thirty days prior to any legislation being advanced in Parliament for a vote.

Pritchard smiled, knowing that the two recent land acquisitions he had just made would establish the current market value of undeveloped property in the greater Carleton Mountain area, and it was very *reasonable*, indeed.

Coincidently, The Canadian National Railway filed a notice of intent with Transport Canada that they planned to put a spur track down over to Carleton Mountain off an existing line which ran through New Brunswick from Edmundston to Moncton.

Knowing that Transport Canada would view the expansion request as a mere formality, Canadian National moved forward and arranged for a survey crew to be dispatched to the area.

Chapter

19

Lou had decided to only stay at the village the night of the wedding. The following day, just before noon, the entire contingent from Havre de Poisson traveled down to Moose Cove, stowed their gear in the runabout and took a seat. As soon as Lou cleared the shoals, he opened up the Chrysler engine to full throttle and raced up the lake.

After docking inside the boathouse, Angelo and Alessandra headed over to the lodge to prepare lunch. Jake went over to check on his Twin Otter while the newlyweds carried all the gifts they had received, over to their cottage.

"Kate, I know I've got a full camp starting on Saturday and promised to spend some time with you first, but I need to return to the village tomorrow. The tribal council is meeting in the afternoon for an important issue that has come up. Kasko surprised me last night by saying that he wanted to speak with me soon, so I don't want to put that off. I also promised my mentees that I'd be back right after our wedding. I might as well get everything out of the way tomorrow, so that I have at least a couple of days to relax with you before people start flying in."

"You're a big boy, Lou, if you want to go off to kiss more toads tomorrow, it's okay with me. Just don't burn the candle at both ends. I'll be on conference calls, myself, with two different Mountie investigations and a couple of 1-on-1 calls most of tomorrow anyway. Are you planning on staying over?"

"No, I'll be home for dinner, but I'd like to get an early start in the morning."

"Did you see the blinking red light on the desk phone?"

"Yeah, I saw that when we came in. I might as well take the messages now. Angelo will have lunch ready so why don't you go ahead over. I'll join you shortly."

It wasn't long before Lou joined everyone at lunch. It was a bit of a sad farewell as they wouldn't see Jake again until he flew in the following week with the mail. Even then, his stay would be brief.

"Kate, you had a couple of messages from your cousins calling to congratulate us on our wedding."

"Was one my cousin, Tim?"

"Yes."

"I knew he'd call."

"Did anyone leave a message that tomorrow's been declared a provincial holiday, and there's no mail delivery?" Jake asked.

"No, but some professor from McGill left a message that he wants to speak with me about an archeological dig."

"A what?"

"A dig."

"What the hell is a 'dig?'"

"Jake, that's when they burrow down into the earth with little spoons and brushes looking for old things from ancient times," Angelo piped in. "Half of Rome was roped off the last time we were there. Traffic was all screwed up. Whenever there's any construction in Rome, they end up doing a dig. And, If no one gets paid off, it could take *years* before they finish. In the end, anything they find ends up in the basement of some museum collecting dust anyway."

"Oh, Angelo, you make it sound so awful," Alessandra said, letting out a sigh. "It wasn't that bad."

"Not bad, huh? My nephew, Matteo, my own sister's boy, said he waited two years before he could build his restaurant, because he stood up to them and refused to pay! For two years, they dug with those tiny little spoons and toothbrushes while they held everything up. In the end, they found nothing. *Nothing!*"

"Well, I'll listen to what this fella has to say, but my mind is already made up."

"Any cancellations, Lou?"

"None that I'm aware of, Kate. The booking agency left a message that they've had a couple of new inquiries. It looks like we'll be operating close to, if not at full occupancy, throughout the last nine weeks of the season. So, let's all enjoy the remainder of this calm before the storm when we'll really be busy," he said. "By the way, I gave Laughing Gull a call before I came over here, Kate. I asked her to have my mentees waiting for me at Moose Cove when I arrive tomorrow. It'll save time if I meet with them as we walk up to the village."

"Lou, how did Laughing Gull get *her* name?" Kate was intrigued with the Abenaki tradition of naming people, including herself.

"An old woman gave it to her. She was always flitting around the village telling funny stories and making others laugh. One day, this old woman said that she was reminded of a laughing gull flying all around squawking; the name 'Laughing Gull' just stuck, I guess."

"Does she have a husband?"

"Tall Tree is her husband. He's the big man who she was dancing with all night. He looks intimidating, but he's very easy going. There was never any question about who'd wear the leggings in *that* lodge."

"Really? Who does?" Kate asked.

"Laughing Gull is very strong-willed," Lou said.

After finishing lunch, Jake stood up and placed a hand on Lou's shoulder. "I gotta go, but if you're smart, Lou, you'll give Kate one of your leggings *now,* and be happy that you get to keep the other one."

Kate tousled Lou's hair as she got up to help Alessandra clear the table. "Jake has a point, darlin', happy wife, happy life!"

Chapter
20

The minister of Indigenous Services was surprised when he received notice from his legislative assistant that lands belonging to the Abenaki in New Brunswick had appeared on a list of properties connected to an expropriation legislation working its way through Parliament.

He no sooner read that notice when his assistant placed a letter on his desk filed by the Canadian National Railway stating an intent to lay track through lands that belong to the Abenaki. The minister made a note to contact the tribal council in the Village of Grey Elk immediately to see if there were any questions they might have.

I'm sure they will, he thought.

After several attempts to reach the Village of Grey Elk by phone, the minister of Indigenous Services finally asked his administrative assistant to send a fax alerting the village elders about the pending expropriation legislation, and of Canadian National's intent to lay track on their land.

--

Meanwhile, on the other side of Ottawa, Elwood Pritchard sat in Buxton Thomas' outer office. With the land swap now agreed to, and the expropriation legislation working its way through the system, Pritchard felt confident that things were moving forward.

Still, investment money was a problem, so he had decided to circle back and, once again, gauge Buxton Thomas' interest in his project. Pritchard had arrived a few minutes early, but it was now twenty minutes past the time they should have met.

Suddenly, the door to Thomas' private office flew open.

"Woody! Come in, come in. I apologize for the delay," Buxton gestured him into the inner office. "Meetings run over now more than ever. My son tells me that's the new norm these days."

"I've noticed it too, Buxton. I've come to share some news with you, then I'd like to hear where your current level of interest lies in the Carleton Mountain Development project."

"Yes, yes, of course, of course! I anticipated that was the reason why you were here."

"Buxton, the land swap for the Crown land has now been completed, and legislation is working its way through Parliament that will allow us to acquire by eminent domain the additional land needed.

"Why that's excellent."

"We were fortunate to have been able to acquire two sizable wood lots in the area. Those purchases will ensure a very reasonable price point when we acquire the additional land by eminent domain. Canada National is now moving forward with plans to lay down a spur line. We're moving forward by leaps and bounds."

"Well, I'm sure there's been a lot of hard work that's gone on behind the scenes, Woody," Thomas was all smiles. "I must say, that is astonishing progress, since we last spoke."

"Very true, Buxton, it has been. Now, if I may be so bold as to ask, what exactly is your level of interest in this project?"

Buxton immediately started fiddling with his mustache.
"Well, after conferring with Aaron Blake, our solicitor, we are willing to invest seventy percent of the phase one

funding, in exchange for a sixty-five percent ownership, and two seats on the board."

Pritchard's jaw nearly dropped. He was astonished to hear what Buxton wanted in return, but recovered quickly. He cleared his throat before speaking again. "I'm very pleased that you have that level of confidence in the project, Buxton, but, naturally, I'll have to run this by the present Board to get their approval. You must realize that sixty-five percent ownership is not what anyone anticipated."

"Of course, of course, entirely expected," Buxton Thomas wanted this meeting over as quickly as possible. "Well, I do need to run, meetings, you know."

Pritchard left somewhat dejected. This was not anywhere near the deal he had wanted, and he had no intention of allowing an investor to become the majority stockholder after all his hard work. Now that he had the Crown land, the project should be attractive to a number of banks; perhaps, he could even save some cash by acquiring additional land with non-voting shares in the project.

What Pritchard did not know, was that Buxton Thomas was heavily invested in several ski resorts in western Canada. He saw Pritchard's project as an opportunity to further expand his own level of influence within Canada's ski industry.

As soon as Pritchard left, Buxton Thomas called his solicitor. "Aaron, Buxton here. I just met with Pritchard. I know we surprised him with the cost of our money; undoubtedly, he'll now try to make another pitch to the banks. I must tell you, though, he's made considerable progress, and his project just might be seen as an attractive investment to some lenders . . . we can't let that happen."

"I agree," Aaron said.

"Let's put the brakes on that legislation he's so sure is going through Parliament in his favor. Once the banks find out that the bill is stuck in committee, it'll sour any deal that Pritchard has in the works."

"Any special way you want me to handle it?"

"No, I don't care how you do it, just stall it in a committee somewhere. When he comes back looking for our political influence to move the thing forward, the cost of money will have gone up . . . considerably."

"It won't be a problem, I'll make a couple of phone calls today."

"Thanks, Aaron."

Chapter

21

Kate sat in front of her computer screen with a cup of Irish breakfast tea, getting ready for the next major crime unit phone call that was about to start.

"Good morning everyone."

There was a chorus of good mornings from the participants.

"Alright, I have some news to share, but first, let's go over the action items people took away from the last call."

"Claude Benson here. This wasn't an action, but it appears the Abenaki have joined us in the hunt for this shooter. Last week, a couple of Abenaki were stopped over here in Five Fingers. It appears they're all riled up about the amount of poaching that's being done on their lands. Seems like the poaching on their land fits the same mode of operandum that we're seeing everywhere else."

Kate knew that Lou and Jake had been stopped but kept that info to herself. "That'll certainly help, Claude, more feet on the ground. Thanks for sharing that. Arnold, what were you able to find out regarding the body mics?"

"Kate, we have enough body mics to loan to all wardens," Arnold said. "I've spoken with the division head; he's onboard with the idea."

"Great, will you oversee the implementation?"

"Yes. I've already set up a hands-on training session for the wardens, we'll do it up in Kedgwick."

"Thanks Arnold."

"Claude, back to you. What's the situation on how we're deploying the additional Mounties?"

"I'm glad I looked into this, Kate. The four additional Mounties are now working an eight to three shift. They had them coming in on all three shifts, giving the local guys a break from pulling the dog shift."

"So, how many patrols do we have during the prime window now?"

"Six - two original patrols, and four additional vehicles."

"How does everyone feel about that? Is that enough coverage?"

"Harland here, Kate. That's a lot of patrols for our area. As long as these wardens use the radio and wait for one of us before going into the woods, it should be sufficient."

"Is everyone in agreement that six patrols will be sufficient?"

"This is Jim Harvey, Kate. Six is more than enough."

"Bruce Kendall here. As long as the wardens use their body mics, six should be enough."

"Alright, let's move on. I did some research on what the market for antlers with velvet is. It appears there's a lab over in China that has found a way to extract IGF-1 out of the velvet, and they're actively seeking suppliers."

"What's IGF-1?"

"It's a growth hormone. IGF-1 is an acronym for insulin-like growth factor 1. This appears to be the 'X-factor' drug for a lot of professional athletes. It promotes faster healing and fosters higher performance. The sports world has banned it for obvious reasons. When word got out that this Chinese product was undetectable in human blood, their product started flying off the shelves. They can't keep up with the huge demand. Right now, I can't think of any other possible motive for someone harvesting a large number of antlers as we're seeing at this time of year."

"Kate, Jim Harvey here. China is a long way from here. They'd have to have one hell of a supply chain in place if these antlers are going all the way over to China."

"Right now, my guess is that this has all happened so fast, there's a lot of freelancing going on. That being said, when we find our shooter, we'll find out what he's doing with the antlers," Kate said. "All right, new business. I'm sure you've all heard that Corporal Burkett was murdered over in Five Fingers. We're being asked to take that one on, too."

"Kate, are they thinking Burkett's murder is connected to the poaching?"

"I haven't heard anyone say that. Burkett's report indicated that he thought it was a drug deal. Apparently every other week, an ultralight lands in a field, and someone comes out of the woods. Then there's an exchange of something and the ultralight takes off. That's all we have to go on presently."

"Claude here. I'd be surprised if anyone in our region has enough cash to spend on drugs."

"It does take a lot of cash to sustain even a recreational drug habit," Kate said. "Claude, take a look at the bookings in your area; let's see who's been brought in on drug charges, or on repeat robbery charges. Also, talk to the banks in your area. See if anyone is suddenly falling behind on their mortgage or car payments. Talk to the 'ma and pa' stores that allow people to run tabs. Find out if anyone has suddenly developed a pattern of falling behind."

"Will do."

"Bruce Kendall, are you still on the line?"

"I am, Kate."

"Bruce, let's see if we can find that ultralight. I'd like you to contact every airport within a radius of two hundred miles of Five Fingers whether it's private, public, or commercial. Find out if anyone has an ultralight landing there on a regular, or even irregular, basis."

"Okay. Nothing outside of two hundred miles?"

"No. Ultralights only have a range of about a hundred and eighty miles."

"Two hundred miles will stretch into Quebec and the States; are you okay with me going there?"

"Let's stay within New Brunswick for now."

"Got it."

"Claude, Harland, Corporal Burkett's last report indicated that there was a known pattern of when the ultralight was flying into the field behind the grange hall in Five Fingers. Have a detail standing by the next time that ultralight is supposed to fly in. I don't want the detail to *do* anything beyond alerting us that the ultralight is approaching. We need to find out where his base is. Once we get word that he's approaching, we'll scramble one of our aircraft to follow it."

"Will do."

"Anyone have anything else?"

"Bruce, Arnold here. When you visit these airports, find out if anyone is pumping avgas into gas cans and taking it off property."

"You think this guy may be keeping it offsite?"

"Might be. There are a lot of old barns around. He could be using one as a hanger."

"Gotcha."

"Good call, Arnold," Kate said. "All right, does anyone have anything else?" Kate waited five seconds before saying, "We'll regroup in a couple of days."

Chapter
22

The following morning, Bud Gleason arrived at the Village of Grey Elk shortly after eight-thirty. He parked in front of the council lodge, stepped out of his car, and walked over to read all the notices posted on the message board near the front door.

As soon as he finished reading one notice stating that a tribal council meeting was scheduled for that very afternoon, he looked inside the building to see if anyone was there. As he turned to leave, someone asked, "Can I help you?"

"Hello . . . yes. Who would I speak to about getting on the agenda for today's tribal council meeting?"

"You're talking to him right now."

"Great. I'm Bud Gleason." Gleason stuck out his hand which the other man shook. "Elwood Pritchard and I would like to come and speak with the council about constructing a road that would cross through Abenaki lands."

"We have heard rumors of this. We would like to listen to what you have to say."

"Any chance of getting on the agenda today?"

"If you can be here by two o'clock, yes."

"Great . . . and your name is . . .?"

"I am John White Owl."

"Thanks, John."

When Gleason returned to his vehicle, he immediately phoned Elwood Pritchard. "Mr. Pritchard, Bud Gleason here. Listen, there's a tribal council meeting this afternoon. If you're available, they're willing to listen to us."

"Hold on just a minute," Pritchard said. Gleason heard him speak to someone in the background.

"Marsha, did you find out if there is an airport near Five Fingers that I could fly into?"

"The closest one is in Kedgwick, Mr. Pritchard."

Then Pritchard returned to their conversation. "Bud, can you pick me up at the Kedgwick airport?"

"Sure. The tribal council meeting starts at two. If you fly in by noon we'll have plenty of time to get there."

"Fine, let me see if I can get a flight. I'll call you back." After hanging up, Pritchard stood by his office door. " Marsha, see if you can get me into this Kedgwick airport by noon."

"Yes sir."

--

The right-of-way was the final piece of the infrastructure puzzle for Pritchard. The rail line was going in, he had the Crown land that he needed, legislation was going through Parliament that would allow him to purchase the additional land he needed at a low cost per acre. The only thing he hadn't nailed down was the capital to manage it all.

While Marsha checked on flights into Kedgwick, Pritchard began pulling together the information he believed would help him obtain approval for a right-of-way from the Abenaki.

"Mr. Pritchard, the only way I can get you into Kedgwick for noon is on a charter. I can bring you back on a regular carrier."

"That's fine, I'll take it Marsha. Oh, and let Bud Gleason know what flight I'll be coming in on."

"Yes sir."

--

Later, when Pritchard arrived at the airport, he was somewhat surprised to find that another passenger had also booked a seat on the charter to Kedgwick, an Asian.

"It looks like we'll be traveling together. Name's Pritchard, Woody Pritchard, and you are?"

"Ying. Lee Wong Ying." The Asian bowed ever so slightly in Pritchard's direction.

Always on the lookout for investors, Pritchard asked, "If you don't mind me asking, what brings you to Kedgwick, Mr. Ying?"

"I have a farm in the area."

"You do? Potatoes or dairy?"

"Actually, it is experimental, we're . . ." Before Ying could finish, his cell phone rang. "Excuse me, I must take this."

Ying was the last to board the plane and sat in the rear seat. Pritchard and Ying never finished their conversation.

Chapter

23

As Lou walked with his mentees toward the village, he pointed out various signs along the pathway to his young charges..

"Who can tell me what animal crossed here?"

"A fox."

"It wasn't a fox; that wasn't even a close guess. Look at the tracks. What do you see? What's the story that these tracks tell?"

"Was it . . . a skunk?"

"No, the back feet are too large for a skunk."

"A weasel?"

"Come on! A weasel doesn't walk, they hop like the rabbit."

"A porcupine!"

"Do you see any quill marks? If it was a porcupine, you would see quill marks in the dirt. Look at the tracks closely. What's the story that's being told?"

"Raven Claw, it was a raccoon."

"Are you guessing, or do you know that?"

"I know that."

"How?"

"The hind feet are much larger than the front feet, and the front paw prints have five distinct fingers. The tracks are deeper on the far side of the puddle, so, he must have found something to eat, cleaned it in the water, and sat up while he ate. You can see where his front paws came down at the edge of the puddle. His prints aren't as deep on the other side of the puddle as he walked away, but here, you can see where his wet tail brushed the earth when he came out of the puddle."

"Good. Now you kept referring to it as a 'he,' how do you know it wasn't a female raccoon?"

"Can you tell the difference?"

"This time of year, yes. The sow raccoon is still teaching it's young, so you would see small tracks in the mud near the sow. Look closely. Do you see any small tracks?"

"No."

"Then *that* tells you it was a boar."

As the small group continued walking up the path, Lou began demonstrating different techniques they could practice to hide their own trail and create a false one.

A couple of times, Lou had a feeling that someone was watching them, but then, he dismissed it, and focused on his mentees.

He could sense that the young boys were anxious about being sent out into the woods, again, so, he said: "Divide yourselves into different teams this time and decide who will seek and who will be the adversary."

When they reached the village, Lou stopped and gave instructions. "Those of you who will be the adversaries, go now, and travel to our lands in the east. Those who will be seekers will be told by Laughing Gull when it is time to leave tomorrow. I will be back in three days."

After watching his mentees scurry off, he headed over to find Kasko, someone he truly respected. When he approached the lodges of Kasko and Lone Otter, he found Lone Otter sitting outside his lodge whittling, again.

"Kasko saw you coming. He will return," Lone Otter said. With that, Kasko came from around the back of his lodge carrying a sack.

"Raven Claw, it is good to see you."

"It is good to see you, too, Kasko. it has been many years since we have hunted together."

"Too many years have passed. Lone Otter and I are glad that you have returned to take the seat of Grey Elk. The council has been without a leader for too long. Kicking Bird tried to lead, but he is selfish, and no one will follow him. White Owl tries, but he is not a very good leader. But many will follow you, Raven Claw."

Lou knew that whatever was in the sack, was something that Kasko wanted to show him, but he had to wait until Kasko was ready to talk about it.

"I am glad to hear your words. I will do my best to protect our lands. Are you interested in joining the council?"

"No, that is for others, but we will sit and listen to what is said."

"There is a council meeting today, will you come?"

"We will be there. Our council seems to have no eyes and no ears. I have brought you something that will tell the truth." With that Kasko opened the sack and dumped the contents onto the ground. "These are the markers left by those that seek to make a new trail in our land from the west. I told them to go away, until they come and talk to us."

"These are surveyor's flags. You found all this in the west?"

"Yes. Their trail goes beyond our lands, but I did not take those flags."

Hardly believing what he was seeing, Lou said, "You

picked all of these up?"

"Yes. Some I had to dig out of the trees with my knife. I told them that our people do not need any more trails."

"Who did you tell that to?"

"The men who came to drive in the stakes. I, too, have heard stories of the many flags, and I went to see for myself. All that is left there now are the tracks from their ATV, but the forest will soon hide those."

"Kasko, no one will be able to deny that there are people trespassing on our lands now. I will take this to the council today."

"Be careful. Kicking Bird watched as I gathered all of these. He did not offer to help, and he walked away, thinking I did not know he was there."

"Kicking Bird . . . that's interesting."

"He will not bother me as he knows he would have to fight two of us," Kasko said.

With that they clasped forearms, and Lou walked over to Laughing Gull's lodge.

"Laughing Gull, can you feed a hungry wanderer?"

"Hah! I thought you would never come.," his cousin said. "My son, and another, have already left for the east. I will tell the seekers when to leave tomorrow. Unlike my husband, they are young and still listen to me."

Chapter
24

When Lee Wong Ying circled the field behind the grange hall in the ultralight, he saw two RCMP vehicles parked at the edge of the tree line along the road, and his defensive instincts immediately kicked in. Unaware that Turnbridge had killed a Mountie two weeks earlier, he didn't know why the area was now under heavy surveillance.

Below him, Arthur Turnbridge sat waiting at his usual spot for Ying to appear. Two young Mounties assigned to monitor the field had worked their way up through the woods earlier and were now, unwittingly, positioned about fifty yards to the left of Turnbridge.

Ying knew exactly where Turnbridge would come out of the tree line and began to set the ultralight down parallel to the line of trees where Turnbridge normally waited.

The major crime unit's objective was to trail the ultralight once it left the field with a pursuit chopper. The two young Mounties assigned to the surveillance detail had been specifically instructed to take no action, beyond calling in that an ultralight was approaching.

Unfortunately, both men were anxious to make corporal and when they saw the ultralight descending, thought that an arrest would be an excellent collar to have on their records.

Just as Turnbridge was about to walk over to Ying, the two Mounties emerged from the woods, side arms drawn, running toward the ultralight. When Turnbridge saw the Mounties, he panicked, and froze in his tracks.

Ying was taken completely by surprise when the Mounties flanked both sides of his cockpit, weapons drawn. He hadn't seen them approach since the ultralight had no rearview mirrors.

The Mounties' first mistake was not calling in that the ultralight was approaching. Their second mistake was to stand as close as they did to the cockpit. In a heartbeat, the Mountie on Ying's left was taken out with a vicious kick to the neck that crushed his windpipe. Upon seeing his fellow officer go down, the second Mountie subconsciously stepped back a foot, stood straight, and yelled, "Hands in the air, *now!*"

Ying immediately raised his hands causing the second Mountie to relax for a nanosecond thinking he had control of the situation.

"All right, out of the cockpit, now!"

With lighting speed, Ying's left knee knocked the cyclic stick far to the right, tilting the swashplate assembly, altering the pitch of the rotating blade to almost a forty-five-degree angle. The Mountie's severed head bounced a good twenty feet before coming to a rolling stop. His torso collapsed to the ground directly underneath the outer edge of the rotating blades.

Turnbridge remained frozen in place, shocked by what he had just seen happen.

Then, Ying returned the blades to full horizonal position and waited for Turnbridge to show. When nothing happened, Ying finally cupped his hands and called out, "Arthur are you there?"

Turnbridge immediately emerged from the woods, bag in hand. Ying took the usual amount of time to inspect each antler, then counted out the hundred-dollar bills like nothing had happened.

Before Ying lifted off again, he said to Turnbridge, "From now on, meet me at the tree line in the field behind the general store in Five Fingers."

The crushed windpipe had not killed the first Mountie, but he stayed prone on the ground while he pressed his lapel mic. However, his injury was so severe that his speech was unintelligible.

Receiving the call, and understanding there was trouble, the sergeant on duty immediately dispatched a backup ground patrol that he had waiting in the area to the GPS coordinates being transmitted from the Mountie's phone.

Again, Flags at every RCMP detachment across the province of New Brunswick were ordered to half-mast.

Mounties representing every provincial and territorial division in Canada flew in to attend the constable's funeral. The contingent from New Brunswick's J Division was, again, well over two hundred. The honor guard that carried the casket of the fallen Mountie, were all members of the RCMP detachment based in Kedgwick.

New Brunswick's Major Crime Unit, was told to add another Mountie killed in the line of duty, to their case load.

Chapter
25

At a quarter before two, Lou entered the council lodge carrying his large sack. A number of village residents were already seated. Two tables had been arranged at the front of the room and the rest of the room had been set up theatre style.

Kicking Bird and another member of the tribal council were already seated at the head table going over the agenda and checking the handouts. Lou acknowledged them and took a seat at the opposite end of the table.

By two o'clock, the gallery was nearly full and all seven members of the tribal council were present and seated.

Just as John White Owl was about to call the meeting to order, he paused as two non-villagers walked into the room and quickly took seats.

White Owl signaled for everyone to stand and led them through a traditional invocation: "Great Spirit, as we gather at this tribal council, we thank you for this gift of sharing between fathers/mothers and sons/daughters. We thank you for all you provide and ask for your wisdom and guidance."

As everyone was seated, White Owl began the meeting. "First, let us welcome Raven Claw to the council. His wisdom will add much to our discussions." Lou raised his hand in acknowledgement as grunts of approval came from the audience.

"We have visitors among us today; they have come to speak to us. We will listen to them now. Mr. Pritchard, Mr. Gleason, please come forward."

Pritchard and Gleason immediately rose and walked to the front of the room. "Gentlemen, thank you for giving us this opportunity to come and speak with you. My name is Woody Pritchard and this is Bud Gleason. Now, you may not be aware of it yet, but there's a project underway that will bring much wealth to this area of New Brunswick. That's what I'm here to talk to you about today. The project doesn't involve any of your lands *directly*, however, what we are looking for is a right-of-way to travel *across* your land, a trail, if you will, to allow people from the west to travel to Carleton Mountain."

Kicking Bird spoke first, "Who has asked for this trail?"

"Good question! The trail is needed so people from the west can go to Carleton Mountain." He knew he had ignored answering his question. "You can rest assured that there will be no provisions made for anyone to be able leave the trail as it passes across Abenaki lands."

Another spoke up. "There are already trails that go to Carleton Mountain."

"That is true," Pritchard said. "There are trails from the north that go to Carleton Mountain. However, far more people that live in the west over by Grand Falls will soon want to travel to the mountain."

Tall Tree stood up. "There is nothing to see there. Why would more people choose to go there?"

"People will want to travel there to enjoy winter sports, like skiing."

Kasko spoke up. "But there are no trails there to ski. Why would they go there?"

Seeing the direction that the conversation was heading toward, and not wanting to discuss the development of the mountain, Pritchard decided to shift gears. "The trail that we are talking about will only be a two-lane road; that's all it will be. We'll bank the road so that it drains well; we'll use culverts whenever we encounter a stream or wetlands. We don't intend to build damns like the beaver does." Pritchard thought he'd get a laugh out of that, but his audience remained quiet. "We'll also enclose the trail with fencing to further ensure that no one is able to leave the trail or enter Abenaki land."

Lone Otter stood up, surprising everyone. "No fence, the game has always run free on our land." There were more than a few grunts of approval at Lone Otter's comment.

"Okay, we don't need to put up a fence. If a fence is an issue, there won't be one," Pritchard nodded. "Problem solved. We're flexible, and we're willing to work with you to make this happen."

"Where will this trail be?"

Pritchard was happy that he had been able to shift the conversation away from talking about the development on and around Carleton Mountain.

"We haven't figured that out yet. Everything's still on the drawing board, so to speak. We're just here now to talk to you about it, answer any questions you may have, and get your permission."

Raven Claw spoke up. "Then you haven't started any survey work, yet? We can still influence where any trail might be developed?"

Pritchard briefly glanced at Gleason before answering. "Why, yes, that is correct."

At that, Raven Claw stood up, lifted the bag off the floor that Kasko had given him, and dumped its contents onto the table. "Then whose survey markers and flags are these that have already been driven into our land?"

Pritchard felt the flush of blood to his face. He hadn't seen the trap that he had just stepped into until it was sprung. He had underestimated these people.

"That was just an . . . ah, an *exploratory* effort. The . . . ah . . . the trail can be *actually* placed *anywhere* as long as it goes from west to east, isn't that right, Mr. Gleason?"   Pritchard hoped to take the heat off himself by introducing Gleason to speak.

Gleason recognized Kicking Bird as the man he had first spoken to. "Yes, that's right, it can be located anywhere. I spoke to the gentleman sitting at the end of the table over two weeks ago when we first started doing the initial survey. I told him that we were looking to build a trail. As a matter of fact, he was very helpful. He let me know exactly where the village was located; that way we were able to stay well south of it."

Raven Claw turned to Kicking Bird. "How is it, Kicking Bird, that you have known of these trespassers that seek to take our land, for weeks now, and you have said nothing to the council?"

Kicking Bird remained calmly seated. "The council has not met since I spoke with him."

"The council met at a council fire just over a week ago, I was there," Lou, as Raven Claw, said. "I even heard people talking about rumors that surveyors were on our lands, yet you did not speak."   Raven Claw said nothing further, as Kicking Bird was an elder and had been shamed enough in front of the village.

White Owl stood up. "Is there anything else that you wish to tell us, Mr. Pritchard?"

"Not really, we've told you what we came to say. Can you take a vote on this? It looks like you have enough people here for a quorum? We'd like to know before we leave that we have your permission to proceed."

"Now that you have spoken, we will talk among ourselves, then we will make a decision as to whether this is a good thing or a bad thing for our people."

"Okay, we'll hang around, just in case you have any

further questions."

"There is much to discuss; this will not be decided upon today."

Pritchard was taken aback. "Oh, well, how long will this take? I mean, look, if this is about compensation, we're prepared to compensate you for the right-of-way. If you don't want a fence, that's fine by us, too."

"Our people must talk before we can answer that."

"Well, I guess I was misinformed about your process. Okay, here's my card, get back to me when you've made your decision." He handed a card to the nearest one at the table. "Thanks, again, for the opportunity to come and speak with all of you. Call me if you have any questions." With that, Pritchard and Gleason left the council lodge.

By the time they reached Gleason's SUV, Pritchard was livid. "Those bastards! I went out of my way to come all the way up here, explained what we were trying to do, and they move it into a *committee*? Well, screw them! I'll get the rights by eminent domain."

"You'll be able to do that?"

"Yes, the only thing that's changed, Bud, is that *you're* on hold until I get this straightened out."

Once Pritchard and Gleason left the meeting, a call for the next agenda item was made. It was a discussion on the poaching that had been going on in the west.

As Raven Claw spoke of the freshly killed deer that he and Jake had found, and of the many other deer they had seen rotting in the forest, every Abenaki present voiced their anger.

When Tall Tree stood up, the whole room turned to listen.

"Raven Claw, it is good that you sit on our council. We must stop those that are killing our deer and defend our lands from those that wish to take it away from us. I will follow *you*. You will be our *war chief*."

Kasko and Little Otter also stood up, also pledging their support to follow Raven Claw, as did others.

"I will need to think upon this," Raven Claw said. "We have found where the killer lives. However, the one who is killing our deer is wise in the ways of the forest. He has already killed two people who would stop him."

Next on White Owl's agenda was the upkeep of the village.

"Kicking Bird, do you have an update for us on the maintenance of the school and the new addition?"

"No work can be done until we receive more money," Kicking Bird said. "There is no money."

Raven Claw couldn't believe what he had just heard.

"Kicking Bird, how is it that there is no money? Where has all the money gone?"

"We have bought many things; there is no money left. Once we have more money, then work can begin again."

"White Owl, I know how much money comes in from the logging rights. There should be more than enough money to maintain the village. Have there been any large expenses?"

"We have had no large expenses. Kicking Bird, tell Raven Claw where the money has gone this year."

"I did not bring the books. He will have to wait until next time."

Raven Claw was incensed that Kicking Bird was being evasive and had not come to the council meeting prepared to answer. "No! We will have a special council meeting, and you, Kicking Bird, will help us understand where the money has gone."

Kicking Bird looked to White Owl with a look that asked him to intervene. Instead, White Owl said, "Raven Claw is right to ask for this. We will meet, again, next week. Does anyone have anything else they wish to discuss?"

Kasko stood up. "What about the one who seeks permission to dig on our lands?"

"He was told that what he seeks is not in the lands of the village."

"White Owl, is this the man from McGill University of whom you and I spoke?"

"Yes, Raven Claw, it is the same."

"He wishes to speak with me," Raven Claw said. "When he does, I will tell him no!"

Before closing the council meeting, White Owl spoke again. "I have one more thing. A fax arrived today from the minister of Indigenous Services. He is telling us that Parliament will pass a law that will take land away from us. That the railroad will build a track across our land."

The room was silent. It took less than a moment for the message to register with everyone present before an uproar occurred. Someone from the back shouted: "This is *our* land! They cannot *take* it!" Another yelled out: "Raven Claw! You are our war chief! We must council for *war*!"

Raven Claw stood up and everyone quieted.

"White Owl, ask the minister to send someone to our next council to talk with us, so that we may hear the truth, and can ask questions, This is the path we must follow."

White Owl nodded assent, then having no further agenda items, he prepared to end the meeting.

"Let us stand and form the Tribal Circle of Unity to close our meeting. Let us join hands as a symbol of our unity, and the bond that holds us together."

Once the circle was formed, they all recited a traditional closing prayer:

"Great Sprit, who's loving hand cares for all things,
from the highest of majestic mountains,
to the smallest of flowing streams,
look with favor on these humble ones that stand before you.
Grant that we may see the sunset of another day.
We ask of Grandfather Sky,
the wisdom to live in peace with all peoples,
and we ask of Grandmother Earth,
the wisdom to live in harmony with all things in nature.
For all these things we are truly thankful,
as you guide us along the great trail of life."

When the meeting ended, Kasko pulled Raven Claw aside. "Be careful, Kicking Bird is vengeful and you have shamed him. He knows enough not to fight me, as he would have to fight two, but you are only one."

"I will be watchful."

By the time Raven Claw reached Moose Cove, the mental transformation back to Lou Gault had occurred as it always did after he left the village.

When his runabout reached open water, Lou shoved the throttle full forward glad to have a fresh breeze in his face. He backed off only slightly once the boat came up to plane. then he relaxed as he headed due east toward home.

Chapter
26

Officials at McGill University were completely unaware that their fully-tenured and revered professor of archaeology, Jarl Ohlson, had failed to disclose on his teaching application that he had been convicted several times for stealing objects of antiquity, nor that he had sold them on the black market. So, unsuspecting his deceit, they had hired him.

When Ohlson first began hearing stories of an ancient battle involving the Vikings in North America, it had piqued his interest, since authentic Viking artifacts were always in demand. As he researched the legend, he became less interested in the *battle* site and more interested in the *burial* site of the Viking chief who had been killed.

Ohlson had grown up outside Philadelphia and saw himself as a man of action, but in reality, he was a poor excuse for an *"Indiana Jones"* wannabe. He lacked friends and, apparently, a moral compass. Overseeing a half dozen graduate students for five to six weeks at an archaeological dig site was definitely something he could endure if it helped him gain access to the possible burial site of this historic figure.

But when he had visited the Abenaki Village of Grey Elk, he didn't feel he had been taken seriously enough, so he decided to leverage the full weight of McGill University when he spoke with Lou Gault. To do that, he had arranged for a letter to be sent from the office of the Dean of Social Sciences to add weight to his words.

--

Once beyond Moose Cove and in the open water, Lou buried the throttle and raced up the lake. As he approached the boathouse he shifted the runabout's powerful inboard into neutral. When he had glided halfway into the slip, he shoved the engine briefly into reverse which brought the boat to a stop just before the bow would have struck the dock.

As soon as he killed the powerful inboard, he heard the mail plane circling overhead as it prepared to land. Securing the runabout to the cleats in the boathouse, he walked over to the dock and waited for the plane to taxi in.

"Hey Jake, didn't expect to see you again until Saturday."

"Yeah, me neither; you've got some certified letters, and those require 'same day' delivery."

"I don't get many of those."

"Yeah, well if one of them is from Publisher's Clearing House, and you've won, don't forget us little people."

Lou laughed at the inference. Shaking his head, he thought, *is there even a single serious bone in Jake's body.* "Wanna stay for dinner? Angelo's just about ready to serve a fancy new dish tonight, one he's planning to add to the menu."

"I can't, Lou, this old Otter's going in for an engine rebuild tomorrow. I've got one last stop to make over at Five Fingers, then I gotta get this baby back to Kedgwick and swap my radios over to the loaner."

"Okay. Things were interesting over at the tribal council meeting today. I'm now being referred to as the 'war chief.'"

"Cowabunga! Are we going on the war path?"

"No, we're not going on any war path. The village just

needs some leadership."

"Be careful how much you take on, cuz. You've already got a full-time job."

"I know, I know. Kate keeps hinting at that."

"All right, I gotta skedaddle."

Lou pocketed the letters and headed over to the main lodge. As he walked in the door, Kate looked up.

"Was that Jake who just flew in?"

"Yeah, he had some certified letters for me. I'll take a look at them when we get back to the cottage. How'd your day go?"

"Not good; a Mountie was killed over in Five Fingers today, and another was transported to the hospital with severe injuries."

"I'm glad I only run a hunting and fishing lodge."

"Sure, and that would be nice if it was all you had on your plate," she said.

--

When Lou and Kate returned to their cottage, Lou was surprised to see not one but four certified letters among the stack of mail Jake had delivered.

The first one Lou opened was from McGill University. After reading it, he said, "Kate, listen to this one: McGill University is requesting permission to conduct a six-week archeological dig beginning the second week of August. A professor and six graduate students would be onsite looking for the burial site of some *Viking*. It says, 'they'll provide their own accommodations and meals, however, they'll need access to water, toilet facilities, and refrigeration. In exchange, the university will provide a full four-year scholarship to a qualifying Abenaki student including room, board, and books.' It's signed by some dean."

"That's a great deal."

"Kate, I'm totally not interested in this. The ancient ones

need to be left alone."

"So, it's a 'no?'"

"A *definite* 'no.' Like you said, I have enough on my plate."

"I won't argue with that."

Lou inhaled deeply, as he reread the letter.

"Lou, I've heard you, and others, mention this Viking legend. What's it about?" He tilted his head, suddenly realizing Kate hadn't grown up listening to all the legends told around lodge fires as he had.

"Actually, there are two versions of the legend. There's the Abenaki version, then there's the Mohawk version."

"They're not the same?"

"No, the Mohawk legend begins earlier than ours."

Kate came over to the table with two glasses of wine, sat down, raised her glass to him and said, "Tell me the legend."

"Okay, I'll begin with the Mohawk legend. The lands of the Mohawk lie just beyond our northern border and stretch east all the way to the mouth of the Saint Lawrence River. The Mohawks were known within the Iroquois Confederacy as, 'The Keepers of the Eastern Door.'"

"Are the Abenaki part of the Iroquois Confederacy?"

"No, the Abenaki were aligned with the Algonquian Confederacy. Neither of the two tribes were exceptionally warlike, but they were enemies and would frequently raid one another. The Mohawk were known to trade with the 'warriors with hair the color of the sun' many times for metal knives."

"Those were the Vikings?"

"Precisely. The Vikings would enter the mouth of the Saint Lawrence and travel upriver. In the beginning, they only came to explore and trade with the Mohawk, but at some point, they traded for land and stayed."

"So, the Vikings had a settlement in Quebec?"

"According to *Mohawk* legend, yes. Over time, they learned enough of the other's language that they were able to communicate with each other. Both cultures were friendly, but very different. The Vikings were fish eaters even though they had little success fishing in the strong current of the big river."

"The Saint Lawrence?"

"Yes. But legend says the two groups would gather and listen to each other's stories. The Vikings were always intrigued with tales of 'the water with many fish' that lay to the south."

"Meaning *this* lake?"

"Exactly. That's what it was known as back in the day. Well, the Viking chief offered the Mohawk many gifts just so they would bring them here. Finally, one early fall, the Mohawk chief agreed. Ten warriors set out, five Mohawk and five Vikings, which was a large enough party to discourage any roving Abenaki who they might encounter. It also ensured that neither group outnumbered the other."

"Sounds like a war party."

"It *was* a war party. They traveled south through the boreal forest, but once they entered the land of the Abenaki, they stayed clear of the trails and at night, made a cold camp, and slept hidden under the balsams. Now, I'll switch over to the Abenaki version of the legend."

Kate nodded and took a sip of wine.

"When the Mohawk arrived at the lake, they came upon a small band of Abenaki who had been camped along the shore for over a week, spearing and drying fish. My people did this every year to carry their lodges through the long winter."

"When the Abenaki saw that they were outnumbered, the leader held up his hand in the sign of peace. Using sign language, he asked why the Mohawk had come to the land of the Abenaki? The Mohawk chief signed back that these 'others' had come to fish. The Abenaki signed that they were welcome to fish, but that there were few fish left on this side. He said they should go to the *other* side of the lake where the fish would still be plentiful. But when the Viking chief saw the racks of fish they had already caught and were drying over the coals, he also saw the baskets that were overflowing with more fish the Abenaki women had prepared. At that point, he just wanted to trade for the fish. But the Abenaki refused.

"Gutsy call, given that they were outnumbered."

"Yeah. Well, on their way to the opposite side of the lake, the Mohawk and the Vikings planned how they would kill the Abenaki and take what they wanted."

"How many Abenaki were there?"

"It was a small band, maybe only four or five warriors. Well, at sunset, a large band of Passamaquoddy joined the Abenaki and learned of the Mohawk. They pointed out that these strangers who *said* they had come to fish, had brought no baskets, nor women to do the work. That's when they realized it was a Mohawk war party and they prepared for the attack they knew would come," Lou said.

"In the hours just before dawn, the sentry furthest from the camp saw the Mohawk approaching through the woods and mimicked the call of the whip-poor-will. When the war party entered the outskirts of the camp, the trap was sprung. The Abenaki and Passamaquoddy warriors, who had concealed themselves, sprang out from every direction wielding battle axes. The enemy was taken by surprise and forced to retreat, leaving their dead where they lay."

"Sounds like the arrival of the Passamaquoddy really turned the tables."

"Three Mohawk and two Vikings were killed outright in the skirmish but not one of our people were hurt. The Mohawk say the Viking chief escaped, but that he later succumbed to his wounds. He was buried at the eastern end of the lake."

"Even more evidence that Christopher Columbus wasn't the first to arrive."

"Yeah, this all happened a few hundred years before Columbus even set sail. There's a Viking shield and a broad sword captured during the raid that hangs from the rafters in our council lodge."

"Absolutely fascinating," Kate smiled, sitting quietly a few moments, then took a sip of wine. "You said you had four certified letters. Who's the next one from?"

Picking up another letter, Lou looked at the return address. "This one is from the office of the Minister of Indigenous Services." Lou opened the envelope and read the first couple of paragraphs to himself before putting the letter down. "I can't friggin' believe this."

"What?"

"I'm being notified that there's a piece of legislation going through Parliament that will give something called the 'Carleton Mountain Development Group,' the right to take whatever sections of my land . . . Abenaki land . . . that they choose, by eminent domain."

"Can they do that?"

"Only over my dead body will *anyone* take our land. I'll fight this tooth and nail."

"How?"

Lou thought for a moment. "First, I'll get ahold of the solicitor that Grey Elk had do all his legal work."

"Do you know his name?"

"Barnard, something or other. I've got the information in the safe."

"Who are the other two certified letters from?"

He quickly picked up another envelope and read the return address. "This one's from the Minister of Forest, Lands, Natural

Resource Operations and Rural Development." Ripping open the envelope, Lou read the letter aloud: "Gentlemen, this letter serves as legal notice that portions of your property northeast of and abutting route 385 will be subject to acquisition by eminent domain by the Carleton Mountain Development Group. For further information please contact this office."

Lou read the letter once more, to himself. "What the hell *is* this? My land doesn't even go as far south as 385. They're talking about the land that's leased to the logging company."

"May I read the letter?"

"Here."

Lou looked at the return address of the last certified letter. "Now this one is from the Canadian National Railway. What the hell do *they* want?" Ripping open the last envelope Lou, again, read the letter aloud: "Dear property owner. Under provisions granted by the Canadian Federal Transportation Board of Regulators, Canadian Transport, and the legislature, you are herewith notified that Canadian National Railway is exercising its right to establish a right-of-way across your property. You will be compensated for any lands taken at the current market value for comparable land in your immediate vicinity. Should you care to dispute this action, or require more information, please contact Canadian National Railway, 12 Union Street, Ottawa, ON."

Lou rubbed his hand across the back of his neck, letting out a loud sigh.

"Kate this is *un-friggin' believable*! I'm being attacked from all sides! I don't even know *how* I'm going to do it, but I'm fighting this. This newly-minted war chief is going on the war path!"

--

Later, rummaging through his safe, Lou found the legal documents that a solicitor had drawn up for Grey Elk decades ago when he had divided the land into three segments. He spoke aloud. "Here it is: Barnard, Sumter, and Lewis, and signed by Felix T. Barnard. Well, Mr. Barnard, you and I are

Chapter

27

The following morning, when Jarl Ohlson called Lou Gault, he couldn't have chosen a more inappropriate time. "Hello, is there a Lou Gault there?" he asked.

"Speaking."

"Mr. Gault, my name is Ohlson, Jarl Ohlson, and I would like to talk to you about a tremendous educational opportunity that McGill University is prepared to offer the Abenaki people."

"Is this about the dig?" Lou asked dryly.

"Why, yes it is. Have you read the letter from Dean Roberge?"

"I have . . . and the answer is 'no.' I'm not interested. We're too busy that time of year, and it's just not happening."

"Look, Mr. Gault . . . may I call you, 'Lou?'. . . This is a tremendous opportunity. We're talking about a full ride here. We really need to have this conversation."

"No, Mr. Ohlson, you may *not* call me 'Lou,' and the answer is still 'no.' We already receive funding for students to attend college. For anything that isn't covered, we make up the difference. I'm not interested. I don't want our lands dug up, and that's my final answer."

"All right, it sounds like I may have caught you at a bad

time. I'm going to give you a couple days to think about this, and call you back, Mr. Gault. How does that sound?" Jarl Ohlson failed to realize that no one else was on the other end of the line, until he stopped speaking. "Hello? . . . Hello? . . ."

"Who was that Lou?"

"Someone from McGill. He called to try and talk me into that dig. I told him 'no.' He kept talking, so I hung up. It's funny, some people just don't understand that the word 'no,' can be a complete sentence."

Kate smiled and looked at him. "So, what are you up to today? You've only got a couple of days before your guests start arriving."

"I'm not sure, except that the first thing I'm doing is giving Grey Elk's lawyer a call."

"Do you have the number?"

"Yeah, it's on the letterhead." Lou punched the number into his phone. The receptionist on the other end answered, "Provincial Law Partners. How may I direct your call?"

"Ah . . . yes, I'm trying to reach the law firm of Barnard, Sumter, and Lewis. Is this the right number?"

"Yes, it is. The name of the firm was changed several years ago. How may I direct your call?"

"I'd like to speak with a Felix T. Barnard."

"Felix Barnard is no longer with us, sir."

"Which firm is he with now?"

"I'm sorry sir, I wasn't clear, Felix Barnard *passed away* a few years ago; could someone else help you?"

"Who took over his practice?"

"His son *Milton* Barnard took over his practice, however *that* Mister Barnard retired this past June. I can connect you with *Josh* Barnard, one of our associates, if that would help?"

"Yes, please do."

"Let me place you on a brief hold." After several minutes, the receptionist came back on the line. "I'm sorry, sir, no one is answering that line, he must be out of the office. May I take a message?"

"Yes, tell him I'd like to speak with him about some legal work done by a Felix T. Barnard."

"I'll relay that message sir. Is this the best number for him to call?"

"I haven't given you my number, yet."

"The number you're calling from is showing up on my screen, sir, is it the correct number?"

"Yes, thank you." As soon as Lou hung up, he looked over at Kate who looked up from her laptop.

"No luck?"

"It's the right law firm. They just changed their name and the guy Grey Elk used is dead. His son, who took over the practice, just retired. I'm waiting for a call back from the grandson, I guess."

"How long ago was it that Grey Elk used that solicitor?"

"I don't know . . . let me see." Lou took a closer look at the documents. "These papers are dated June 5, 1921."

"Lou, even if the solicitor was fresh out of law school at that time, he'd be well over a hundred years old by now."

"Okay, it was a chance I took. I'm gonna go over to Rocky Point now. I've got some things I need to noodle through."

"Fine. I'm on a conference call shortly, anyway, Ottawa will be dialing into this one."

--

Lou had a favorite rock over at the point where he always sat whenever he needed to be alone with his thoughts.

Weighing heavy on his mind was the thought that he might potentially lose Havre de Poisson to developers. The place where he lived, loved, and which his grandfather had literally carved out of the wilderness, and entrusted to him.

His thoughts turned to the stories which Grey Elk had shared with him, about the early days, and about how he had desperately tried to get publicity to market the resort. Once, Grey Elk had even invited some well-heeled bankers who had lent him money for his resort, up for a complimentary week of fishing. After that, word spread among the rich and famous. Over time, Havre de Poisson had become a frequent topic of conversation in the well-to-do circles. The resort had literally become a "rite of passage" for the more adventurous, well-heeled sportsmen in eastern cities.

From April through October, the wealthy had traveled in groups as they journeyed north to the remote resort. The first leg was always by train, stopping at a siding by a logging camp near Grand Falls. Next, was a full day on horseback, through the wilderness, crossing rivers and navigating heavily wooded terrain, before finally reaching the camp.

It was on the very shores of this obscure glacial lake where Lou Gault and his cousin, Jake, had been raised in the ways of the Abenaki, by their maternal grandfather.

When Grey Elk had died, responsibility for protecting the land had passed to Lou Gault, along with the sportsmen's retreat known as Havre de Poisson and the roughly 15 square miles of wilderness surrounding the lake.

Under Lou's stewardship, the resort had remained one of the more desirable fly-in fishing resorts in eastern North America. Like many lakes in the sparsely populated areas of Canada, it was identified on maps merely with a number. Lou Gault's lake was simply known as Lake 980.

Lou returned to the cottage by mid-afternoon. Kate was sitting in front of her laptop, headphones on, fully engaged, leading the call and scribbling notes. Lou decided to head back out and left her a yellow sticky on the door: *"Gone to village. Back B 4 dinner."*

Before he fired up the runabout, Lou turned the key to "accessory," just to see how much gas was in the boat. The gauge showed less than a quarter tank left, hardly sufficient for a run down to Moose Cove and back.

As he filled the runabout's tank, he watched the needle on the gauge of the huge red gravity flow fuel tank that sat outside the boat house. It dropped below half full. Usually, a single delivery of gasoline was enough to carry Lou through an entire season. This year, he had used a lot of gas going back and forth to the village during the doldrum weeks. Now, with bookings at or near full occupancy for the next nine weeks, the last thing he needed, was to run out of gasoline. To be safe, he sent a text to his supplier, requesting they top off the tank and bring over twenty cases of two-stroke oil before Saturday. It would be simpler to have his supplier premix the gas and oil, but then he'd need a separate tank of gasoline for the jeep, the four-stroke generator, and the backhoe. Always something.

Still, satisfied there wasn't anything else needing to be done at the moment, Lou blew out the bilge, fired up the runabout, and once again, headed down to Moose Cove.

Chapter

28

Lou had the peddle to the floor driving his ATV up the trail to the village, slowing down only briefly to pass two young families heading down to the cove for a morning swim.

When he reached the village, a large group of men had already gathered at the front steps of the council lodge. Turning off the ignition key, he heard Tall Tree say, "Raven Claw comes, he will tell us what must be done."

Lou's thoughts were still on the certified letters he had received yesterday; he only half heard what else Tall Tree said: "Raven Claw, these letters say that outsiders will take our land away!"

"What did you just say?" The words jolted him back to reality

White Owl waved a couple of envelopes he held in his hand. "The mail from Five Fingers came early today. These letters are telling us that someone is going to take away our land."

"I received similar letters, White Owl," Lou said, "and we will fight this. I will speak with the law firm that Grey Elk used. This will not happen. No one will take our lands."

His words had a calming effect on the crowd. Through the corner of his eye, Lou saw the four Abenaki youths he had sent on the "butterfly hide and seek" journey, now walking back into the village, shoulders slumped and heads down. As soon as they saw Raven Claw, their spirits lifted.

When Lou, as Raven Claw, turned and saw them, he spoke. "Were those who went to hide, so careless, that their brothers found them in one day?"

"No, Raven Claw, some men told us to leave the woods."

"Did you travel beyond our lands?"

"No, we stayed within our own boundaries."

"Then who told you to leave?"

"The men who are driving stakes into the ground told us to leave. When Little Fox said he would not go, and started picking up the stakes, they knocked him to the ground. We made the call of the whip-poor-will and those who were hidden came to join us."

By this time, Lou had made the full mental transition into his persona of Raven Claw. He was beside himself with anger. "We have frigging *surveyors* here again? I will put a stop to this!" He turned to the group of men who had gathered in front of the lodge. "Those who choose to follow me, gather your bows. We will go see these people who trespass on our lands and drive them off."

Within minutes, fifteen Abenaki were moving through the forest as swift as deer toward the direction where the youths said they had encountered the survey team. In no time, the Abenaki found the four-man survey team who were sitting down, taking a break.

Raven Claw motioned his followers to stay in the trees but to encircle the surveyors so they had no escape. Once they were in position, Raven Claw shot an arrow into the trunk of a tree closest to where the lead surveyor was resting. It landed inches above his head. Tall Tree immediately let loose another arrow which landed mere inches in front of the crotch of a second surveyor.

When the first arrow struck, the startled surveyor shouted, "Whoa! What the hell? What is this?" When the second arrow landed, the second surveyor yelled, "Holy shit!" Immediately, the group of them jumped up and tried scrambling over to their ATVs.

"Stay where you are!" a menacing voice cried out.

As Raven Claw emerged alone from the woods, he spoke again in a deep growl. "Who trespasses on Abenaki land and drives wooden stakes into the earth?"

The lead surveyor turned and looked at the lone Abenaki coming toward them. "We're doing work for Canadian National Railway," he called out defiantly. "I have a work order authorizing us to be here."

This man knew whose land he was on. He had grown up hating the Abenaki. Ever since he was a child, he had listened to stories of how the Abenaki had driven his own grandfather off his family farm and had burned the house and barn to the ground. Unfortunately, the part he had never heard was that his own grandfather had been a squatter with no right to be on Abenaki lands to begin with, nor that he had been warned many times to leave.

"Does that work order give you the right to knock down to the ground one of our sons, or to tell our sons they must leave their own land?"

"He was pulling up stakes we'd just put in."

"The Abenaki have not given you *permission* to come onto our land. Leave now and take what you have placed on our land with you."

"I've got a work order that says I have the right to be here! The railroad has the right to take whatever land they need to put in a track line. That's the law!"

Lou grew angry that someone thought they had a right to take Abenaki land. However, he controlled himself, and said in a quiet, but menacing tone: "I said *leave*. I say you have *no* right to be on Abenaki land. I say that you are *trespassing*. I say that you will pick up what you have done, and leave, *now*."

"Yeah, you, and what army?" the surveyor responded defiantly.

Raven Claw raised his hand and fourteen more Abenaki emerged from the woods with bows and arrows already notched in hand.

"Holy shit, Bruce, there's a bunch of 'em!"

"Screw them," Bruce said. "They won't do anything, that'd be assault and battery."

"This is Abenaki land. Only Abenaki law applies here," Raven Claw said. "You are trespassing."

"We have the *right* to be here, I have a work order!"

"Show me this work order."

The surveyor foolishly handed the work order to Raven Claw who immediately gave it to Tall Tree who tore it into pieces and smiled.

"It appears you have no work order now."

"You *bastard*! There's over a dozen of you and only four of us."

"Bruce, let's go," another surveyor finally spoke out. "Let the railroad figure this out. Let's not make the situation any worse than it is."

"Go, and as you leave, pick up every stake, every marker, and anything else that you have left on Abenaki soil."

"And if we refuse?"

Lou turned and winked at Tall Tree before turning back to face the lead surveyor.

"Then I may not be able to control *this* man. It was *his* son who you threw to the ground. You have insulted him and disgraced his son."

Tall Tree put down his bow and unstrapped his quiver as if he was getting ready to enter a boxing ring.

"Oh, what's he gonna do, fight me?" the man said. "This is *bull*shit, I'm bringing the law down on your ass, buddy, you can't threaten me."

"This is Abenaki land. Only Abenaki law applies here. It is Tall Tree's right to avenge what was done to his young son."

"Bruce, listen, let's just leave, okay," the second surveyor was clearly concerned about the team's safety. "This just isn't worth it, man."

"They're bluffing!" the first surveyor said. "They ain't gonna do nothing."

Tall Tree had laid his hunting knife beside his bow, taken his leather vest off, neatly folded it before laying it down, and was now crouched over. He began swaying back and forth, the muscles in his powerful build now tense. He looked like a raging bull ready to charge.

When the lead surveyor realized what was about to happen, he backed off. "All right, we'll leave. But we'll be back, even if we need a police escort."

"Go! And pick up every stake and ribbon that you have placed on Abenaki soil as you leave," Raven Claw repeated.

"Screw you!"

"Tall Tree, this one apparently likes to negotiate. Let us see how well he can wrestle."

For a large man, Tall Tree moved with unbelievable swiftness. In an instant, he had his arms wrapped around the lead surveyor, squeezing him like a python does to its prey. Lou waited a moment before saying, "Many have said that something inside of Tall Tree snaps when he fights, that he becomes a wild animal. He has chewed off two ears; no one will wrestle with him now."

The surveyor was wincing in pain and having difficulty

breathing. "Get him off me!"

"Will you leave?"

"Yes."

"And will you take all these stakes and ribbons?"

When the surveyor named Bruce, hesitated, Tall Tree suddenly increased the pressure he was applying.

"Yes! Yes, just let me go." Tall Tree smiled before releasing his hold.

"Ben, Charlie, bring up our ATV's," Bruce said. "Let's pack up and get outta here."

"No, you will pick up your stakes first."

"Screw you. We're taking our equipment and leaving."

Lou nodded, and Tall Tree began circling the man once more as if he was going to charge again.

"No! First you will walk out and pick up your stakes and flags."

"Come on, Bruce, let's just do it," the second surveyor said.

The Abenaki followed the four surveyors as far as the northern boundary of their lands, watching carefully as the men picked up every stake, flag, and marker that they had laid down. When they reached the far edge of Abenaki land, Raven Claw spoke again. "Now go! If you return, we will not be as forgiving."

"What about our equipment?"

"You must not have wanted it. Why else would you have abandoned it."

"You *bastard!* You'll pay for this!"

"Tell the railroad men they must first come and council with us *before* they send any people to our lands," Raven Claw warned. Once the surveyors had gone, Raven Claw turned to his followers. "When we get back to the village, file the serial numbers off their ATV's, repaint them, and give them to lodges which have none."

As they rode back to the village, Raven Claw explained what his strategy would be to stop the poaching in the west. "You must all be ready when I return early tomorrow morning."

As Lou's boat sped back down the lake to Havre de Poisson, he was deep in thought. *What the hell else can go wrong? This was certainly a wasted day.* Then his cell phone went off. The display read "Josh Barnard." Lou took the call and tried yelling over the noise of the powerful inboard.

"I'm out on the lake. I'll call you back in twenty minutes."

Chapter
29

When Lou reached Havre de Poisson, he immediately went over to his cottage to return Josh Barnard's call. Kate had just signed off her last conference call for the day, and was cleaning off her work area when Lou came in.

"Oh, hi, Lou!" she greeted him.

Lou let out a loud sigh.

"Well, we're in a marvelous mood."

Lou stopped and briefly returned his wife's smile. "Hi, Kate, I'm just feeling completely overwhelmed. The village received a couple of certified letters this morning about the railroad taking over Abenaki land, and now the village is involved in whatever the hell is going on. They're all looking at me, their new war chief, to solve everything. I didn't get a single thing done today that I wanted to accomplish over there."

"What happened?"

"When I arrived, my mentees were walking back into the village. Some surveyors had chased them off our land. Then we spent the day running the surveyors off. Now, I've got one less day to get this damn poacher off our western lands before my guests start arriving. On top of that, I need to find a way to stop Parliament, and the railroad, from taking portions of my land. I don't know whether to let my warrior spirit completely loose, and literally go on the warpath, or just accept that maybe I can't do it all."

"Well, if we were in Ireland, I'd take you down to the pub. After a few pints, we'd have put all our troubles behind us."

"Sounds enticing. But yeah, well . . . let me call this Josh Barnard back. He called when I was coming up the lake."

Lou collapsed into the chair at his desk, and with a heavy sigh, dialed Barnard's number. After the second ring Josh Barnard picked up the phone, "Josh Barnard."

"Hello, Josh, this is Lou Gault calling you back. Listen, I need some legal help."

"Okay, so what's the problem?"

"I guess it was your grandfather that may have done legal work for *my* grandfather some time ago. Anyway, I received a couple of certified letters that Parliament is going to pass legislation allowing some development group to take over my land. The railroad sent me a letter too, informing me that they'll be taking land for a new track. I don't believe they have the right to do any of this. My grandfather hired your grandfather decades ago to legally transfer the land to him."

"Well, I can certainly look into this for you, Lou. Can you fax over the letters you received along with a copy of the property deeds you have?"

"Sure, I'll do that as soon as we hang up."

"Fine. After I take a look at them, I'll call you with whatever options we might have. It might take a couple of days before I get back to you, though, but I will tell you that the courts seem to rule in favor of the railroad, most of the time. If your lands are being specifically mentioned in a piece of expropriation legislation, that may require an amendment to the original legislation. Let me take a look into it and get back to you."

"Thanks, I'll fax these documents over to you right away." Lou ended the call feeling even more disheartened than he had felt before he made the call.

Yep, one hell of a wasted day, he thought.

Chapter

30

Jarl Ohlson had been pampered for years by the university administration and had become accustomed to getting his way. He had expected that by offering the McGill scholarship to the Abenaki, it would have given him access to the area where legend said a Viking chief had been buried centuries ago. The scholarship would be on the university's dime, so it wouldn't cost him a thing. Therefore, thinking he was very clever, it shocked him when the scholarship offer was turned down.

Viking artifacts were rarely found on the North American continent, and thus, commanded an unusually high price in the marketplace. Ohlson then decided to reread his handwritten notes about the legend he made earlier in the year when he had first met with the Mohawk.

- Mohawk traded land with Vikings for metal knives / hatchets.

- Vikings wanted to see 'water with many fish' (in land of Abenaki)

- Eagle Spirit (Mohawk chief) bribed w/ gifts to take Vikings

- Small band of Abenaki

- Viking wanted to trade for fish Abenaki had but

Abenaki would not trade.

- Raided Abenaki

- Mohawk beaten back - forced to retreat

- Mohawk war party too small

- Viking chief died in battle

For years Ohlson had studied ritual Viking burials and knew that any chief would have been buried not only with his weapons, but also his amulets, the traditional jeweled belt, his shield, and whatever valuables his men had that might help their chief make the journey to Valhalla to serve the god Odin.

Although the grave was said to have been skillfully concealed, the location of the burial site, along with the story of the battle, had passed down from generation to generation among the Mohawk. Ohlson's last note read:

- Buried at east end of lake, near outlet, near mountain

Having every reason to believe the grave was on the property of what was now known as Havre de Poisson, Ohlson was now willing to spend a little of his own money to find it. Authentic Viking era artifacts would command a price quadruple to his annual salary with the university at the very least.

Pulling up the fishing resort's website, Ohlson dialed the number on the home page. "Hello, I'd like to speak with someone at Harvey Dee Po-something . . . I may be mispronouncing it."

"You've reached Havre de Poisson, how may I help you?"

"Yeah, well, I'm thinking of going there. Do you have any rooms available?"

"Just a moment, sir, and I'll check. Did you have a specific week in mind?"

"No, just tell me what you have available."

Within a few moments, the booking agent returned to the line. "Sir, I have one cottage available the last week of August, and I show two cottages available the first and second weeks of October . . . ahh, no, I'm sorry, there's actually only *one* cottage available the second week of October. How large is your party, sir?"

Ohlson knew that it would be impossible to take time off once the fall semester started. "It's just me. Do you have anything earlier?"

"No, sir, we're completely booked."

"Okay, what's the end of summer deal you're running for that last week in August?"

"There is no deal, sir."

"Okay, let me ask it this way: What's the discount that McGill University gets?"

"I'm not aware there is any discount for the university, sir."

"Now that is surprising, *everybody* gives the university a discount. Okay, okay, never mind, can I get a room facing the water?"

"Sir, every cottage faces the water."

"October doesn't work for me. How much are we talking about for August?"

"That cottage is fifty-four hundred for the week . . .before taxes."

"Whoa! You gotta be *kidding* me! Sweetheart, I'm not trying to *buy* the place. I just want a room."

"That's the only cottage available that week, sir, it sleeps four."

"I don't *care* that it sleeps four, I'm only *one* and I promise to use only *one* bed and *one* set of towels."

"Sir, that's the weekly rate for that cottage. The rates go by size of the cottage, and that's one of our largest. However, the resort is all inclusive once you arrive."

"I've heard there aren't any roads to this place. So, how am I supposed to get there, fly?"

"That is correct sir, you will need to fly in. Where would you be coming from?"

"Montreal."

"There are float planes that fly in from a number of local airports, sir. Kedgwick is the closest, Grand Falls is another. Guests do fly up from Fredericton, as well. We have a travel agent that I can recommend should you need someone to help make your connecting flight arrangements."

Ohlson let out a long sigh. "You're certainly pricey. How much do you need for a deposit?"

"Payment in full is required to confirm your reservation, sir. I can take your card over the phone now, if you'd like."

Ohlson knew he'd never get the university to cover the cost of what basically amounted to a personal vacation.

"Yeah, listen, put that cottage on hold for me, will you. I'll get back to you."

"I'm sorry, sir, the only way I would be able to hold the cottage for you is if you book it."

"Is there a penalty if I cancel?"

"Unfortunately, this reservation is being made within two weeks of your arrival date, if you were to cancel, you'd forfeit the entire amount."

"Whoa."

"However, you would be entitled to receive a twenty percent discount the following year."

"I'll get back to you." With that Ohlson hung up. Before shelling out fifty-four hundred dollars, Ohlson decided to replay the recording he had made when the Mohawk had told him about the legend. After listening to it again, he was convinced that he had a good chance of hitting paydirt. So, he called the booking agent back.

"Yeah, hi . . . we spoke a little while ago. I'll take that last week of August."

"Fine, sir, may I have your credit card number?"

Ohlson hated having to use his own credit card, but he had no choice, and gave her the information.

"Thank you, sir."

"Yeah, I'll need the name of that travel agent, too."

"Yes sir, Adrianna Bowles."

When Ohlson heard the travel agent's name, his kneejerk reaction was to ask what her handicap was, but he just smiled at his own sense of humor.

"You're all set, sir. Where may I send your confirmation and receipt?"

"Ahh . . . send it to my attention at McGill University."

"I'll get this right out to you, sir, along with Adrianna's contact information."

"Yeah, thanks."

"Thank *you*, sir. I'm sure you'll enjoy your stay at Havre de Poisson."

"Oh, I intend to, indeed."

Chapter
31

After breakfast on Saturday, Lou went down his readiness checklist: Gasoline had been delivered, bait cage was full, Angelo had everything he needed, Alessandra had all the cottages ready, the Abenaki guides were all lined up.

"Well, everything seems in order," he said. With less than a half a day before the first sportsmen would be arriving, Lou decided to take one last walk over to Rocky Point, just to enjoy the peace and quiet.

Kate lingered in the lodge helping Alessandra clean up. "Kate, Lou looks like he's carrying the weight of the world on his shoulders," Alessandra commented to her.

"He's feeling more than a little overwhelmed right now," Kate acknowledged. "He's taken on way too much over at the village, but he's too proud to admit it. He's very concerned about where the money is going over there not to mention there's a poacher who has been taking a lot of deer recently. He also chased a group of surveyors off Abenaki land this past week. And to top it all off, both the village, and Lou have been notified that their land is going to be taken by some development group."

"Oh, my," Alessandra said. "And the second half of the season starts tomorrow."

"Yes, it's a lot, right? Hopefully this solicitor he has engaged will be able to protect the land. I don't believe that Lou understood just how much time his being on the council would require, and he won't delegate anything."

--

Lou was definitely "stuck in the weeds" with everything he felt was his personal responsibility. On the way back to their cottage, Kate decided she'd try to help Lou out by putting a little order into everything he had piled on his plate.

--

On Saturday, shortly after noontime, the first float plane set down and taxied over to the dock. Lou and the Abenaki guides were waiting to greet the arriving guests and help carry their gear up to the cottages. As soon as the plane was secured to the dock, a flurry of activity engulfed everyone.

No sooner had the first float plane left the dock, than two more planes were seen coming up the valley. By late that afternoon, a total of seven planes dropped off twenty-four guests, all in a matter of hours. As soon as they arrived, a few guests took boats out to try their luck fishing before dinner. A couple more guests walked over to the mouth of the brook to fish from shore, but most guests decided to just get settled in before enjoying their first gourmet meal. As usual, on the first night, most guests retired early, as they planned on getting an early start in the morning.

By the time Lou finished making his final rounds, it was close to eight-thirty in the evening. Knowing they'd be up well before daybreak, he and Kate had a night cap and went to bed, enjoying 'a quickie' before falling asleep.

--

Breakfast at Havre di Poisson started at five-thirty a.m. By six-thirty, it was rare to see any boat still tied up at the dock. Once the last boat was off, Lou returned to his cottage and was surprised to see Kate logged onto her computer.

"Are you working on a Sunday, Kate?"

"No, I was just doing some personal things. Why'd you ask?"

"These boats won't be back until late afternoon. I was wondering if you'd like to take a skip over to the village with me?"

"I'm going to pass, Lou. I told Alessandra that I'd help her get the lodge ready for dinner tonight."

"Right. Okay, I won't be too long, I'm only going over to meet with my mentees, once I send them out, I'll be back."

And you'll tackle whatever else that shows up while you're there, Kate thought, but knew better than to say out loud.

As soon as Lou walked out the door, Kate returned to the high-level list of everything she knew of that was on Lou's plate:

<u>Havre de Poisson:</u>

- Operating Havre de Poisson – *averaging fifteen hours a day, seven days a week.*

- Sleep – *maybe six or seven hours a night*

- Uncommitted time – *maybe two hours a day*

- Time to actually enjoy life - *none*

<u>Other Commitments:</u>
- Sitting on the tribal council – *four hours every other week, plus travel and follow-up time.*

- Getting the village back into shape –*unknown, could be significant*

- Mentoring four young Abenaki – *three plus hours every other week, plus travel*

- Serving as the "War Chief"–*totally dependent upon how big the fire is*

- Following up on the legal issues –??

Kate had never run an owner-operated small business before, let alone a seasonal business, like Havre de Poisson. The more she thought about all the moving parts, the more she realized that owning one's own business was no walk in the park. The days were long and dealing with whatever showed up so every client had a memorable experience, was not something one could plan ahead. In the short time she had known Lou, she learned that:

(a) He had only two speeds: On and Off

(b) He didn't have boundaries and often wandered outside his lane

(c) Once committed to something, he was all in and

(d) The art of delegating was not among the tools in his toolkit.

Kate sat back and looked at the list she had made. Then, she pursed her lips. "There's no time left for us," she said and placed her hands on the keyboard, adding another line item to the list. "Time for us – zero."

"The truth is, my dear husband, you do things very well, but you take on too much," she said out loud to no one, but herself. Kate sat back in her chair. "He's got himself so far down in the weeds, he can't even see it." She drew a deep breath. "I have to find a way to help him."

Running that survey team off Abenaki lands, was important, she thought. *But it sucked up whatever remaining down time Lou had left. The surveyors are at least temporarily gone; hopefully, Josh Barnard will come up with a legal angle to protect the land.*

Kate knew that it was critical for Lou to insert himself into village life and provide the missing pieces of leadership that were lacking. But the question on her mind was: Could he continue to juggle it all for the next nine weeks, without burning out?

Chapter
32

On Monday Josh Barnard had time to review the documents that Lou Gault had faxed over. After a quick read, Josh was doubtful there was any legal avenue that he could pursue to alter the course of events soon to unfold, let alone remedy the situation. What was interesting to the young solicitor, was seeing the deeds that represented some of the earliest legal work in which his grandfather had been involved.

It was Felix T. Barnard, himself, who had inspired his grandson, Josh, to pursue a career in law. As a young law student, his grandfather had taken Josh under his wing and frequently counseled him on the importance of researching the law for obscure precedents, especially oddities, when it appeared the legal issue at hand could not be argued for, or against, in a straightforward matter.

While the law firm never destroyed any files, after ten years of being inactive, files were transferred to a storage vault in the basement. Josh Barnard had another appointment waiting. So, he decided he would go down to the basement later and take a look at any records he might find among his grandfather's files around the time these deeds were created.

When word reached corporate counsel of the Canadian National Railway that surveyors working on their behalf had been driven off a worksite by an irate group of Abenaki, the skeletal crew of young lawyers covering the department during its annual vacation shutdown, ordered all further work at the site to cease until they could look further into the matter.

--

Meanwhile in another city, Elwood Pritchard sat at his desk fuming that the expropriation legislation for which he'd been waiting, was now stuck somewhere in a committee. With provincial elections coming up, very little would happen in Parliament now, as most of the legislative assembly members had gone home to campaign for re-election .

--

Back at Havre de Poisson, all boats were out on the water and Lou was on his way to the village. Kate had a little time to herself before the first of many conference calls she planned to make later this day. So, out of curiosity, Kate decided to take a look at the deeds that Lou had faxed over to Solicitor Barnard the day before.

--

A few years ago, Kate had been dragged through the mashed potatoes and gravy of transferring an ancient deed, when she acquired the Irish cottage where she grew up from her parent's estate. More than anything else, she was curious to see how different the deeds in Ireland were, from the deeds written in Canada.

At first glance, the deed had the usual reference points which defined the property boundaries, and was basically, very similar to an Irish property deed. However, there was a paragraph imbedded in the deed that referenced a *treaty* between the British Crown and the Abenaki. The deed specified that the treaty of 1796 was incorporated into this deed and was the legally binding covenant that took precedent over all others in establishing perpetual ownership for the property.

At first, the wording seemed rather unique. *But, perhaps, all lands belonging to the First Nations had that type of clause,* she thought. With her first conference call only moments away, she managed to key in a search criteria to her computer for any treaties between the Abenaki and the British Crown in the late eighteenth century. Then, she logged on as moderator and kicked off the first of many virtual meetings she would have during this day.

--

As soon as the last boat headed out, Lou powered up the mahogany runabout and headed down the lake to Moose Cove where one of the villagers stood waiting for him with a freshly painted ATV.

"Morning, Raven Claw, today is a good day to be in the forest. Many wait for us at the council lodge," his morning chauffeur said.

When they arrived at the council lodge, twenty-three Abenaki had already gathered there waiting for his arrival.

"It is good to see so many of my brothers willing to protect our deer from those that trespass upon our lands," Lou, as Raven Claw, said. "The poacher's village is known to me but we must catch him on our lands. He has killed men who sought to capture him, and he is wise in the ways of the forest, so we must be careful. We will go to the edge of our western boundary, then we will wait and watch for him to kill another of our deer."

"Raven Claw," Kasko spoke, "Do you see how many follow you? The story of how you drove the surveyors from our land has already been told around many lodge fires."

"Capturing the one we seek today, will be risky," Raven Claw said. "He is as cunning as the fox, and he fights like the badger if cornered. When we reach our western boundary, I want each of you to take cover, use the skills that you learned when you played butterfly-hide-and-seek. Once he is on our land and has taken one of our deer, then we will take him. Do not shoot to kill this one. The Mounties want him alive."

The Abenaki worked their way through the forest on

ATVs, leaving them in a clearing about a mile from the edge of their lands. Once everyone was in position, Raven Claw made the sound of the whip-poor-will and they blended into the forest.

--

Around ten o'clock that morning, Arthur Turnbridge emerged from the land that his people had occupied for generations. Muzzle loader in hand, he walked across the dirt road onto the land of the Abenaki. By this time, Turnbridge had killed a significant number of deer and the number of bucks were no longer as plentiful as they had been.

To compensate, Turnbridge had begun setting out salt licks. The lick that he headed toward today was in a ravine, next to a stream. There was a ridge that offered him not only a comfortable place to sit and wait, but a commanding, unobstructed view of the target area below. He headed in that direction, unaware he was being watched.

Every Abenaki who had traveled west with Lou saw him walk across the dirt road, then the small field, and finally enter onto Abenaki land. At one point, Turnbridge passed within a few yards of an Abenaki hidden in tall grass, completely unaware of how close to him he walked.

It wasn't long after Turnbridge had taken a seat overlooking the ravine, when three doe approached the salt lick. Now on high alert, Turnbridge waited for the buck that might be following them. Suddenly, the wind shifted, and the deer caught his scent. Their tails flashed up, and they bounded off. Turnbridge was a patient hunter, but only to a point.

Another half hour passed, and he was about to move to a different salt lick, when he noticed movement to his right. A large buck appeared but was in no hurry to enter the ravine. After taking a few steps, it would stop, absorb whatever was in the air, and listen. The scent of the three doe had drawn it to the ravine, but he was skittish, and remained in the brush.

Being naturally cautious, this buck had seen a number of winters and had survived in the wild. But every muscle in his body was now tense and he was ready to take flight, should he sense danger.

Turnbridge was amazed at the size of the rack, once the buck came into view. He had obviously foraged extremely well during the past winter. Now Turnbridge took aim as the buck entered the ravine, and gently squeezed the trigger. The sound of the muzzle loader reverberated throughout the forest, putting every Abenaki on alert.

By the time Turnbridge had sawed off the antlers, the Abenaki had begun circling the area near the ravine.

If nothing else, Turnbridge was a creature of habit and never lingered at a kill site for long. He also traveled with a loaded weapon. Today was no different. Before he had even approached the buck, he had already reloaded his rifle. Once the antlers were off and incased in plastic, Turnbridge climbed out of the ravine, ready to head home.

When he reached the top of the ravine, he briefly looked back down toward the lick, he caught a glimpse of movement. At first, he thought it was another deer, then he realized that two men were standing next to his kill. A wave of panic swept over him.

Both men had their backs toward Turnbridge as he lifted his rifle and took aim. Then, just as he pulled the trigger, both men stooped down as if it was part of the Great Spirit's plan, or maybe just plain luck. The projectiles sailed over their heads by less than an inch before completely taking out a tree on the far side of the deer that had at least a fifteen-inch diameter girth.

When the tree buckled over, one man rolled to his side, coming up with his bow at the ready. Smoke from the shot gave away the location of the shooter, and the man let his arrow fly which struck a tree next to Turnbridge.

The second man had always been fleet of foot, and immediately scaled the ravine. When he reached the top, he saw Turnbridge barreling down the other side. He quickly notched an arrow and let it fly, then he notched a second arrow and let that one fly.

Turnbridge stumbled when the first arrow entered the back of his right thigh, but he kept going. Knowing enough to zig zag, he avoided the second arrow as it ricocheted off the stock of his muzzle loader and lodged in his leather belt.

Another Abenaki stood up when he saw Turnbridge crashing down a slight incline coming directly toward him and let loose an arrow that struck Turnbridge in the right front shoulder.

Still, Turnbridge continued on, as if nothing had happened. Another arrow was let loose that embedded itself in the back of Turnbridge's left thigh.

Still, Turnbridge continued to crash wildly through the underbrush, jumping over streams, and dodging trees like a man pursued by a swarm of bees. When he zigged left, another Abenaki stood up and fired an arrow that lodged itself in the front of Turnbridge's left thigh, just above the knee, a second arrow entered the back of his left thigh, just above his knee and slightly below the first arrow embedded there.

Finally, the brute began to show signs that he was human; his frantic pace began to slow, as he ran through the forest with arrows sticking out of him at all angles. As Turnbridge approached the clearing that marked the end of Abenaki lands, he had a resurgence of energy, and picked up his pace again, continuing to power forward.

When he broke through the edge of the tree line, he looked like a pincushion running with his head down.

Now, Raven Claw raised his bow, took aim, and embedded an arrow squarely in the back of Turnbridge's right knee. The force behind Raven Claw's arrow knocked Turnbridge off balance and he briefly went down onto both knees. But he quickly recovered and hobbled across the dirt road, disappearing into the safety of the woods that represented the outer boundary of Turnbridge lands.

Two Abenaki entered the clearing and began chasing Turnbridge, until Lou yelled, "Stop!"

When both Abenaki stopped, the man in the lead stooped down to pick up the muzzle loader that Turnbridge had dropped. He held it over his head and let out a warrior's yell. The second man picked up the sack that Turnbridge had dropped and began swinging it over his head as he, too, let out a triumphant yell.

Their quarry had escaped, but the two prizes they had captured made the day victorious. The mystery of who was behind the poaching had not only unraveled; it was all but over.

Chapter

33

When Turnbridge disappeared into the woods, Lou walked to the edge of the dirt road and could see Turnbridge hobbling in the distance, among the ferns, heading for home. Then, he took out his cell phone and called Kate.

Kate was on a conference call on her computer when she saw Lou's name popup on her cell screen. She asked for a break, put herself on mute, and took his call.

"Lou, I'm on a call, what's up?"

"Kate, if you send some Mounties over to where the Turnbridge Clan lives in Five Fingers right now, they'll find a man with a half dozen arrows sticking out of his body. Eyewitnesses will attest to seeing him kill a deer earlier today on Abenaki lands. After he sawed off the antlers, he attempted to kill two Abenaki while trying to get away."

"Anyone hurt?"

"Only the deer hunter."

"How bad?"

"He'll make it."

"Okay, let me make a call."

"We've got his weapon and the antlers," Lou said. "I gotta go; my warriors are beginning to really whoop it up over here.

Love ya!"

Kate quickly dialed Sergeant Major Fletcher Martin. "Fletcher, it's Kate."

"Hey Kate, I understand congratulations are in order for you two!"

"Thanks, Fletcher, but listen, I just got a call from Lou. The Abenaki just put a bunch of arrows into the guy who appears to be the shooter who killed the two game wardens. Lou said if the Mounties raided the Turnbridge clan compound over in Five Fingers ASAP, they'd find him. The perp is wounded."

"Thanks Kate. I'll take it from here."

--

Arthur Turnbridge was barely able to walk by the time he reached his father's home and literally collapsed on the front porch. His brothers dragged him into the house without making comments about the arrows, and his sisters immediately began tending to his wounds. It was as if this was an everyday occurrence.

Turnbridge had lost a considerable amount of blood by the time he had reached home but was fortunate that none of the arrow tips had hit any arteries nor were lodged in any bone.

In less than a half hour, two helicopters were hovering over the cluster of ramshackle buildings where the Turnbridge clan lived. Moments later, six SUVs came roaring into the Turnbridge compound, lights flashing, with men who were carrying an arrest warrant.

The father of Arthur Turnbridge was absolutely *certain* this was a raid on the still he was running further up the hill and started to run. But he stopped when he heard a shotgun go off, and a voice yell: "Stay where you are!"

It wasn't long before the Mounties found the trail of blood that led from the porch into the room where Arthur Turnbridge lay on a bed.

The elder Turnbridge was visibly relieved, once he realized it was his son the Mounties were after, and not him, or his still.

In Canada, there is no requirement to read anyone their rights when they are taken into custody. So, the Mounties simply put cuffs on the younger Turnbridge and escorted him toward an SUV. But when the young man saw his father, he suddenly became violent, and momentarily broke free from the hold that two Mounties had on his arms as he ran toward the older man.

"Pa! help me!"

With total indifference, the elder Turnbridge looked at his son, shook his head, and said, "I told ya' to stay on our land boy! But you wouldn't listen to me. Now you've gone and got yourself into a damn mess. That's what you've gone and done. Maybe this'll learn ya'."

When Arthur Turnbridge realized that his father was not going to come to his aid, he gave up resisting and hung his head. The Mounties helped him hobble to the nearest SUV and settled him into the back seat, closed the door, and drove away.

When Kate received a text that Turnbridge had been taken into custody, she interrupted whoever was speaking on the conference call. "Excuse me, I've just received word that a suspect in the murder of the two game wardens has been taken into custody over in Five Fingers. Hold while I patch Sergeant Major Fletcher Martin into this call; he wants to brief us." Within seconds she spoke again.

"Sergeant Major are you on the line?

"Yes, I am, Kate."

"I've only shared the fact that a suspect has been brought into custody."

"Right. Okay, at this point, we don't know if this suspect was acting alone, so let's keep this quiet until we've had a chance to interrogate him."

"Sergeant Major, where was he captured?"

"A SWAT team brought him into custody over at the Turnbridge compound in Five Fingers."

"What led you there?"

"Earlier, the suspect had shot a deer on Abenaki lands, then tried to kill a couple of Abenaki. The Abenaki tried to take him alive, but he escaped. However, they were able to put a few arrows into him. That's when we received the call."

"Anyone hurt?"

"To my knowledge, only the suspect. Currently, he's receiving medical care."

Fletcher Martin stayed on the line and took a few more questions from the others until he wasn't able to add anything further at the time.

"Sergeant Major, thank you for joining us."

"Kate I'll share what comes from the interrogation with you, once it's available."

When Kate knew for certain that the sergeant major was no longer on the call, she sat back and listened to the banter among the others on the call.

"I'd be interested in knowing how the Abenaki found this guy," one said.

"One of my guys ran into a couple of Abenaki over in Five Fingers a few days ago. They were out looking for him," another said.

"I don't think I'd ever wanna be 'the fox' with a bunch of those 'hounds' chasing after me," a third person said.

Kate allowed the chatter to continue a little longer, until she decided to take back control of the conference call. "All right, let's move on. This deer killer certainly wasn't the one flying that ultralight we know killed one of our constables. Nor do we know if he's connected in any way to the death of Corporal Burkett."

"Kate, I'm about halfway through checking with the airports for ultralights; we should be able to complete that in another day."

"Good. Let's go down the list of actions from our last call."

Just as the call was ending, Fletcher sent Kate a text that they'd be sending a float plane up in the morning to collect the shooter's weapon and the bag with the antlers. Additionally, he would be sending a crime scene team to take pictures of the kill site and specifically the wounds on the deer. They also wanted to know about the escape route the shooter had used.

Well, Lou's just gonna love this, another day will be shot, Kate thought. She sent Lou a quick text, letting him know that he needed to bring back the evidence that Fletcher wanted.

The Abenaki who had grabbed the bag of antlers didn't care that he wasn't able to keep it. His story would be told around the fires even if he no longer had the bag in his own possession. But the man who picked up the muzzle loader refused to give it up. Raven Claw finally secured it from him after he promised he would replace it if the Mounties didn't return it.

Chapter

34

Arthur Turnbridge received emergency medical treatment at a clinic in Kedgwick before being transported down to Fredericton Union Hospital.

The two Mounties who were about to question Turnbridge sat on opposite sides of his hospital bed. Arthur faced his interrogators alone since there is no constitutional right in Canada that a citizen is entitled to have a lawyer present during an interrogation.

"Arthur, I want you to know that if you cooperate with us, and answer our questions, this will all be over in no time at all," one Mountie said.

Turnbridge mistakenly took this to mean that he'd be able to go home, once he left the hospital. So, he readily admitted to countless charges of poaching deer out of season. Upon further questioning, he eventually admitted to killing the two game wardens. That's when the line of questioning changed.

"So, tell me Arthur, you shot a lot of deer, yet you didn't take any camp meat, venison's mighty tasty this time of year. Why didn't you take any of the meat?"

"We don't need none. We raises hogs; 'sides my momma says hogs is sweeter tasting!"

"Well, what about the hides? Hides can bring in a fairly good price, you know."

"Ha, not as much as antlers. I gets me a hunnert dollars for a rack a' antlers, brand *new* dollars, too."

"Arthur, you're pulling my leg! Nobody pays that kind of money for antlers."

"Yessir, a hunnert dollars. Biggest damned fool I ever met, and that's a fact. I got me lots of hunnert dollars, too. All's I gotta do is wrap da antlers in plastic, and go meet him, and he pays me."

"For that kind of money, I'll take last year's rack off of my garage, and sell it to him, too. When are you going to see him again?"

"He don't want the old ones."

"Why is that Arthur?"

"Don't know. All I knows is he wants new ones, with the velvet on them."

The interrogator decided to circle back. "Arthur, there's a buck that comes into my back yard every morning, nice rack, lots of velvet. If I shot that buck, would you be able to sell this guy the antlers for me?

"Yes I would. He don't care how I gets them."

" When will you see him, again?"

"Next week. But it's at a new place."

"A new place? Where's the new place Arthur?"

Arthur looked around, as if to make sure no one else was listening. "He's gonna meet me at the edge of the field, behind the general store."

"Which general store?"

"The one over in Five Fingers."

"What's his car look like?"

"I ain't never seen his car."

"You've never seen his car?"

"Nope, he's gonna *fly* in like he always does."

"He *flies* in?"

"Yeah, he's got himself a tiny little he-lo-copter. All's I gotta do is wait in the woods for Ying."

"Ying. Is that his name?"

"Uh-huh."

"What's his full name?"

"I don't know."

The second interrogator who had been taking notes, suddenly dropped his pen, and stared at Turnbridge. Neither Mountie could believe what they'd just heard. They had never connected Turnbridge to the pilot of the ultralight who had decapitated one Mountie and injured another. Up until now, everyone thought the helicopter was part of a drug ring.

The connection to the helicopter suddenly placed Turnbridge near the scene of Corporal Burkett's murder, and he became a suspect. All Turnbridge could offer about the pilot was that his name was Ying. When the interrogation ended, and the aids came in, Turnbridge thought that he was going home. Instead, he was given a clean set of prison denims, released from the hospital, and taken to a holding cell in Fredericton.

--

Elwood Pritchard had been meeting with various lenders in Quebec City all day, hoping to generate interest in his Carleton Mountain Development project. Montreal banks had shown absolutely zero interest in any involvement in spite of the fact that he had the Crown land lease in hand, and that Canadian National had committed to laying track. Additionally, legislation was pending in Parliament that would give him the authority to acquire additional lands needed at a reasonable price.

One lender in Montreal told him, "Mr. Pritchard not today, not tomorrow, not *ever* will this bank invest another dollar in one of your projects." Another banker told him that the name "Elwood Pritchard" had been blacklisted by the bank's senior loan officer. Pritchard was at his wit's end trying to raise enough capital to back his project.

--

As soon as Kate heard the powerful runabout coming up the lake, she took a walk over to the boathouse. When the mahogany bow glided in, Lou threw Kate a line to secure to a cleat on the dock.

"The Mounties picked up the deer killer shortly after you called me, Lou, they're interrogating him now."

"Good, I'm glad that's over. It's been one helluva day. I didn't get a single thing done over there today, except chase this guy. I'll tell you, I'm looking forward to being able to just sit back and relax tomorrow."

"I'm not so sure about that. I think your tomorrow is being planned out for you."

"By who?"

"Fletcher is sending a crime scene team up tomorrow. He wants them to have a look at the latest kill."

"Well, they can look all they want, but someone else is going to take them over to the kill site. Tomorrow is my day to rest, and that's exactly what I'm going to do."

"How's the gas in the boat?"

"You mean 'the HMS Guzzler', she's over half full, why?"

"Alessandra said that Angelo was hoping to take it out tonight for a twilight cruise. She said they often did that when they lived on Lake Como in Italy."

"Yeah, Angelo said he had almost the exact same boat,

except it was Italian made."

"I think they're hoping that we'll go with them. Are you too tired?"

"No, we'll go."

"Good."

"Give me a few minutes, I need to tell the guides that I'd like them to come over early tomorrow and handle getting everyone launched in the morning."

Chapter

35

The following morning, Kate slipped out of bed as soon as she heard the loons. Lou was on his feet once the rich aroma of freshly ground coffee percolating on the stove reached the master bedroom along with the crisp smell of bacon.

He could tell immediately it was going to be a beautiful day. The sky was clear and the air wasn't anywhere near as heavy as it had been. Kate had all the windows open in the main part of the cottage letting a fresh breeze in off the water. It was so pleasant that she tied the curtains back.

"Good morning, my husband. Sit yourself down and I'll pour you coffee!" Kate surprised Lou with a hot sticky bun she had just taken fresh out of the oven.

"Now, this is the way every day should start," he said appreciatively. With that, Kate's cell phone began to ring.

"Hello? Yes, this is she . . . They're leaving now? Okay, I'll let him know . . . Yes, today's call starts at ten o'clock . . . Right, speak with you then." When she hung up, she looked over at Lou.

"Dare I ask?"

"The float plane just left Fredericton. They should be here in a little over an hour."

"Well, after I give them the muzzleloader and the bag with

the antlers, I'm sending them down to Moose Cove on their own," Lou said. "I'll text Kasko. He can take them to the kill site."

"How would you like your eggs this morning, husband of mine?

"Looking up at me," he said, "which is exactly what *you're* going to be doing right after breakfast, when I carry you back into the bedroom . . . and I have my way with you!"

"Oh, is that right?" Kate tousled Lou's hair. "Well, maybe we'll just have to arm wrestle to see whose head is on the pillow looking up and who's eyes are looking down."

An hour later, when the Mountie's plane landed, Lou was waiting at the end of the dock with the muzzleloader and the bag with the antlers in it.

"Morning, fellas!" he greeted them. "Here's the evidence you came for. Now, you wanna head back down the lake a little over three miles. Land in the first large cove on the right. That'll be Moose Cove. The water will be deep enough for you to taxi between the islands. Tie up at the dock, and a fella will meet you and take you to the kill site. He was with us yesterday and will answer any questions you have."

"You're not coming with us?"

"Not today, fellas. There'll be someone waiting for ya." With that, Lou turned around and walked back to their cottage, stopping in just long enough to tell Kate that he was going over to the outcrop they knew as Rocky Point, to get his head around a few things.

--

While Kate was waiting for her conference call to start, she had time to do a little research on antlers and a connection with the Shang Ho Laboratory in China. Earlier, she had downloaded a feature article from their website and converted it into English. Most of the information in the article talked about IGF-1 a substance which Kate was already familiar.

The article reinforced the fact that their refined IGF-1 product had already proven to be undetectable in human blood because of DNA differences. But it was the last paragraph in the article that caught Kate's attention.

Shang Ho's most urgent need was to expand their supply line in retrieving velvet. At the end of the paragraph there was a link to a page that outlined how one could become a partner in their material supply chain.

Moments before Kate was planning to kick off her conference call for the day, she received a text from Sergeant Major Fletcher Martin asking her to delay the call for at least an hour.

Given the extra time, she decided to pull up a file containing the Abenaki treaties she had queried the day before. Kate had never seen a treaty before. The language and spelling in the document was consistent with an earlier era of English grammar.

There were two treaties in the file. The most recent treaty was pretty straight forward and read more like a sale of land than her idea of a peace treaty. In it, the Abenaki agreed to exchange certain parcels of land along their western border in exchange for Crown lands which surrounded the southern and western base of Carleton Mountain. It appeared to be an exchange of Crown land in order to keep the peace and compensate the Abenaki for lands which settlers had encroached upon.

The earlier treaty of 1796, between the British Crown and the Abenaki, was much more involved, and for the most part, pretty boring to read. However, there was one section in the treaty that did catch her eye.

Section 20 read: *In exchange for peace, from this day forward, all current and future rights, claims, privileges, jurisdictions, and interests in the remaining Abenaki lands by the Crown are dismissed with prejudice. Furthermore, those lands shall forever remain as, and be known as, the sovereign lands of the Abenaki.*

Just as Kate began to ponder about the meaning, a cell

phone on Lou's desk began to ring.

"Hello?"

"Hello. Is Lou Gault available?"

"May I ask who's calling?"

"This is Solicitor Josh Barnard."

"Just a moment, I'll see if I can get him." Kate looked out the window expecting to yell over to Lou about the phone call, but he wasn't at Rocky Point.

"I'm sorry, Solicitor, he's stepped away at the moment. He left his cell phone here on the desk, so I can't connect you. May I help you? I'm his wife."

"Do you know if he'll be around this afternoon?"

"Yes, I expect he will be. Would you like me to have him call you back?"

"Actually, I thought I'd fly up there today and meet with him in person. There's some work that requires his signature. Then, once that happens, we can discuss legal strategies."

"I see. Well, I'll let Lou know that you're coming."

"Thank you. I look forward to meeting you later today."

Chapter
36

Elwood Pritchard spent several days in Old Quebec City attempting to bankroll his project. Time and again, bank after bank, every loan officer he met, listened to his pitch, then turned him down. The only encouragement he received was from one bank which expressed a slight interest in investing in Phase Two.

Discouraged and empty-handed, Pritchard took a late flight out of Quebec City and flew into Moncton, the largest financial center in the province of New Brunswick. The maritime provinces were Pritchard's last hope. Surely a few of New Brunswick's larger banks would see the huge economic boom his project would bring to their province. But if the Maritime provincial banks weren't willing to be investors, the only option he had would be what Buxton Thomas had put on the table.

During the flight to Moncton, Pritchard decided to try a different tactic. Instead of going directly to the banks, he would first pitch his Carleton Mountain Development plan to the chamber of commerce.

Upon hearing Pritchard's plan, the Greater Moncton Chamber of Commerce business development officer said, "Mr. Pritchard, I'm impressed, how can I help you?"

"Well, the project needs a few more investors, so an introduction to the right people would be a start."

"Let's go, I'll get you in front of the people you need to

talk to."

When the president of the Third Bank of Moncton began to visualize the number of loans that businesses participating in Pritchard's project would be seeking, and the number of people who would be looking to finance a second home around Carleton Mountain, he realized the financial opportunities Pritchard's project could bring to his bank. At the end of the presentation, the bank president not only agreed to invest in the project, but he also committed to opening a branch office near the project and buying the rights to be named the official mortgage lender for the entire development.

While his success with the Third Bank of Moncton boosted his spirits, in no way did their investment represent the amount of capital Pritchard needed.

As Pritchard was walking toward the elevator, the bank president's secretary stepped out of her office and called out, "Mr. Pritchard. the president would like another word with you."

Pritchard's first thought was, *I hope he hasn't had a change of heart.*

"You may go right in, Mr. Pritchard, he's expecting you."

"Thank you."

Pritchard opened the door, not knowing what to expect.

"Come in, come in, sit down," the president said. "I've given this project of yours a little more thought."

"And?"

"And I want to do a little *more* for you. Now, I know that my bank can only invest so much, and that you're looking to raise more capital. So, here's what I'm going to do: I'm going to *personally* introduce you to the presidents of the other lending institutions in Moncton who I suspect would be interested in investing in a project of this nature."

Pritchard couldn't believe what he was hearing. By the time he left Moncton, he headed over to Nova Scotia with commitments for roughly thirty-five percent of the upfront capital that he needed for Phase One. He was very pleased.

In Halifax, Pritchard again made his pitch to the chamber of commerce before meeting with any banks.

When the president of The Central Bank and Trust of Halifax saw the sizable commitments from the banks in Moncton, he also wanted in. Pritchard ended up leaving Halifax with additional capital, as well as a commitment that a second bank would open a branch office near the project.

Buoyed by his recent success, Pritchard called his assistant. "Marsha, see if you can arrange a meeting with Buxton Thomas for Thursday." He had an idea how he wanted to play one hand against the other.

Chapter

37

In Fredericton, Josh Barnard removed the canvas fuselage covers on the de Haviland DHC-2 Twin Beaver in which he owned a quarter share and was finishing up his pre-flight inspection routine.

One of his pleasures in life was flying, but since his father had retired, he hadn't had much time to log many hours because of the case work he had inherited from the older man.

Felix T. Barnard had mentioned Havre de Poisson to his grandson more than a few times. The elder Barnard had been impressed with what Grey Elk was doing there, and the two had actually bartered a portion of his fee in exchange for several weeks at the resort which the elder Barnard had completely enjoyed.

A half hour after taking off, Josh's plane entered the western end of the valley that surrounded Lake 980 and he began to look for signs of the resort. Halfway up the lake he saw the wooden dock extending out into the water, with the bright orange windsock.

--

Lou wasn't too pleased when he found out that the lawyer was flying up. "I wish you would have told him not to come up, Kate; why couldn't he have just faxed whatever it was that I needed to sign? This is going to punch a hole in my day. Well, it is what it is, let's see what the hell he has to say."

"Lou, I found something that you should take a look at before he arrives."

"What'd you find, sleuth?"

"I took a look at the deeds you had out yesterday and noticed a reference to an old treaty. Then, I was able to find the actual treaty online. Section 20 is quite interesting. Here, I printed the whole thing out."

After reading the document, Lou looked up. "Grey Elk always said this would be our land forever, maybe *this* is what he was talking about. Did the lawyer mention the treaty when you spoke with him?"

"No, all he said was that he had some things that you needed to sign."

"Well, that sounds like a bird coming up the lake now, I might as well get down to the dock and secure his lines."

--

As Josh Barnard taxied his plane over to the dock, he saw Lou standing there. *If this guy isn't a poster child for the quintessential outdoorsman, nobody is,* he thought.

As soon as Lou had secured the de Haviland to the dock, Josh jumped out of the cockpit. "Lou! Josh Barnard. Good to meet you! I've heard a lot about this place. My grandfather came up here a few times to fish and always said it was the best fishing he ever did."

"That's what we like to hear," Lou said. "I hope you can help me find a way to keep these claim jumpers from taking our land. Come on, let's take a walk over to my cottage."

As they walked along the path Josh asked, "Are you closed? I thought you'd be busy this time of year?"

"We are, the boats are all out. If you wanna see 'busy,' come back at five o'clock, or this weekend. We've just reopened after a four-week shut down in mid-summer. Fishing is slow then, and we're always ready for a breather after going full throttle for the first twelve weeks."

As they approached the front steps to Lou's cottage, Josh commented, "Wow, now *that's* a fantastic view." He nodded toward the lake.

"Yeah, it is special. Come inside and meet my wife." He opened the door and let Josh walk in first. "Kate, Josh Barnard is here," he called out as he entered.

"It's a pleasure to make your acquaintance, Josh," she said while entering the living room.

"I thought I detected a slight Irish brogue when we spoke on the phone," he smiled. "The pleasure is all mine. May we use the table?"

"Make yourself at home."

"Lou, I've had some time to take a look at the situation," he said after he'd taken out a few papers from a case he'd been carrying. "First thing we need to do is get the other two deeds out of your grandfather's name and into *your* name to satisfy the instructions in his will."

"I'm not sure I know what you're talking about."

"My grandfather created three deeds for Grey Elk. There was one for his personal property, which is basically this fishing lodge, and the land around it. There was a second deed for the land he wanted to set aside and lease out the logging rights on, and there was a *third* deed for the land that he set aside as a village for his band. Only the deed for his personal property was probated. The other two deeds are still in his name, so we need to take care of that before we can do anything else."

"What are you telling me?"

"I need to transfer the other two deeds to you."

"Are you saying that I own *everything*?"

"According to Grey Elk's will, yes, everything was to transfer to you upon his passing. I have no idea why the other two deeds were never probated."

Lou took a deep breath, realizing for the first time that he now had even more responsibility for the land than he previously believed. "Okay, then what?"

"Then we've really got our work cut out for us. The courts generally side with the railroad on right-of-way issues, but we may have an opportunity to argue that they need to move the spur *beyond* your property, there is legal precedent for that in the case of Mitchell vs. Canadian National. As far as the expropriation legislation, that's a different matter altogether. Now, we may be able to *delay* the developer from taking title to any of your land, but realistically, once parliament passes that bill, the only way to stop anyone from taking your land, is to introduce a second bill that *excludes* your property from the original bill. That will be costly."

"How costly?"

"Costly, with all capital letters, and then some. I don't have an exact figure, but plan on something well north of two hundred grand, just for openers. Lou, none of us really *own* the land in Canada. The Crown owns the land, we're just allowed to use it. If the Crown determines that it wants the land, they have the legal right to take it. People have spent a lot of money trying to contest that, but in the end, the Crown always prevails."

"What about the reference to the treaty in the deed? Doesn't that protect the Abenaki lands?"

"I did see a reference to a treaty in each of the deeds. But those treaties were made between the First Nations and the Crown and didn't actually change the ownership of the land. They were just agreements on the *use* of the land. Remember, the land belonged to the Crown, especially back then."

Lou passed a copy of the treaty Kate had researched across the table to Josh. "Take a look at Section 20 in this treaty. I'm not a legal scholar, and I don't pretend to be one, but it certainly appears to me that the Crown *gave up everything* in this treaty."

While reading, Josh raised his eyebrows and nodded his head. Then he sat back and ran a hand through his hair. "I've read a lot of treaties . . . but, I'll tell you, I've never seen one worded like *this*. How did you know where to find it?"

Lou pointed to Kate. "I didn't, but Lieutenant O'Grady over here was the one who found it. She knows her way around the Internet. In fact, that's the reason the Mounties recruited her, to be their investigative consultant."

Turning toward Kate, Josh said, "I could use someone like you on my team."

"Sorry, I just changed jobs," she smiled.

Then Josh pointed to three documents spread on the table. "Okay, Lou, just sign here, here, and here. Then, I have what I came up for and just maybe this treaty is the game changer that we need. I'll file a motion to get before a judge which will bring everything to a standstill. Once we have a hearing, I'll attempt to put things on hold for at least a week until I can determine just how much weight this treaty might have, if it has any weight at all."

Lou signed, after which pleasantries were exchanged. Kate offered tea, which was declined, and Josh gathered his papers to leave.

--

As Josh's plane taxied down the lake, Lou looked over at the unspoiled pristine beauty of Carleton Mountain. *I wonder if the landscape will look this way when the next generation steward takes over*, he thought.

--

The flight back to Fredericton was smooth. After landing and securing the float plane, Josh did something he vowed never to do and went back to the office after five o'clock. Upon entering the building, he went directly down to the vault and retrieved the complete file that his grandfather had on Grey Elk.

Somethings just cannot be left to chance, he thought.

Chapter

38

When Elwood Pritchard walked into Buxton Thomas' office in Ottawa, he was feeling very confident. The banks in New Brunswick and Nova Scotia had collectively committed to forty-five percent of the additional Phase One capital he needed for the project.

Buxton was his usual congenial self in welcoming Pritchard to his office. "Woody! It's nice to see you again! Come in, sit down."

"Thank you, Buxton. Well, we're moving forward and things have changed *considerably* from an investment perspective. We're now only looking to you for *thirty* percent of the upfront Phase One capital. Of course, you'll be able to invest further in Phase Two, if you choose, when we reach that point."

"Well, I'm actually very pleased to hear that thirty percent is the level of investment you're looking for from us, as we've determined that was exactly where we wanted to participate. My investors felt that was the upper limit on any risk they were willing to carry, but they *do* want to be investors."

"Wonderful! That's what I was hoping to hear," Pritchard said. "I'll have my people send over the necessary paperwork tomorrow, and we'll put this to bed."

"Yes," Buxton was now ready to play hardball. "However,

there's been another *slight* change . . . the cost of money has gone up."

"Oh. . . and?"

"We'll put up the thirty percent, however in exchange we want *fifty-one* percent ownership in the project."

Pritchard was taken aback; it took him a few moments to recover. "Buxton, a thirty percent investment does *not* warrant a fifty-one percent ownership! The other investors will *never* go along with it. A *thirty* percent ownership would be far more in line with your level of investment."

"Woody, we have several investment opportunities that we're looking at and yours is only one of them. If the terms aren't agreeable to you, there's no hard feelings on this end."

Pritchard knew he was stuck between a rock and a hard place. More importantly, so did Buxton.

"All right Buxton, I'm going to say 'Deal,' but I'll need to pass this by the Board before it's official. By the way, the legislation to acquire the land seems to be stuck in committee, somehow. See if your contacts can move that forward for us."

"My investors will be happy to hear that we'll be a part of this project. Odd that your legislation is stuck in committee, though. I'll have someone look into that. Politicians are a strange lot. We'll get it moving again, even if it takes a little well-placed cash in a few pockets."

"Thank you, Buxton, I appreciate your help."

Even though he had given up too much, Pritchard was relieved that he finally had the capital he needed. However, he was furious at being manipulated by Buxton Thomas. *At least Jesse James had a horse and a gun*, he thought as he walked toward the door.

When Elwood Pritchard left Buxton's office, Buxton Thomas immediately placed a call to his solicitor. "Aaron, how much money will you need to lift the hold on that expropriation legislation?"

"Not even a grand."

"That's all?

"Absolutely."

"Fine. Take care of that for me when parliament comes back in session, will you? Oh, and Elwood Pritchard's people will be contacting you. When they do, just wire transfer them the money, we've come to an agreement."

"He agreed to fifty-one percent *ownership*?"

Buxton Thomas paused to finger his mustache, he was pleased with himself. "He had no choice; no one else was going to give him any money."

Pritchard had never been a wealthy man. Over the years, his failed marriages, and the courts, had taken away whatever personal wealth he had been able to accumulate. Now, these past few months, Pritchard had been under a lot of stress while peddling this development plan.

Finally, feeling flush, and proud of the millions that he had just raised, he decided to live it up a little. When he arrived at the Ottawa airport, he changed his return flight to a later one that offered first class seating. Then he walked into the airline's private lounge which was maintained only for first-class travelers.

Being the *only* board member for the Carleton Mountain Development Group, Pritchard knew he had no choice other than to accept Buxton Thomas' offer. Therefore, after ordering his second double martini, he sent a cryptic text to Buxton: *'Board has accepted your terms, pls wire money.'*

He leaned back to savor his martini while thoughts ran through his head. There were still several unsettled civil judgements hanging over his head from previously failed development projects. Pritchard also owed a considerable amount of money in back taxes to the Canadian government. The courts had ruled that until all claims were settled, any bank account in Pritchard's name with a balance of more than three thousand dollars would be subject to immediate confiscation by the Canadian government.

However, Pritchard was confident that the Carleton Mountain project would be the one to finally enable him to settle all back judgements against him and free him from the constant feeling of insolvency which hung over his head like a dark cloud.

Unfortunately for Pritchard, things began to unravel even while he sat in the airport lounge.

The Carleton Mountain Development Group's organizational structure was pretty much a shell game consisting of various holding companies, each one having multiple bank accounts and only one of which had Pritchard's name on it. The only reason Pritchard wanted his name on a bank account, at all, was so that he could sign the weekly payroll check for his assistant. The account balance never exceeded the dollar limit set by the court and, in truth, usually carried a negligible balance, just enough to pay his assistant, which wasn't much at all.

When the Third Bank of Moncton attempted to wire money to the account that Pritchard had provided to them, they ran into a problem. So, they called Pritchard's office. Being unable to reach anyone else in the company, Pritchard's assistant took it upon herself to enter Pritchard's office, open his desk drawer, and give them the routing number and account number from which her weekly payroll check was drawn against.

When the bank attempted a transfer using the new account number, multiple bells and whistles went off. The bank's inhouse proprietary security software detected that Pritchard's account had been tagged for immediate seizure of funds by the Canadian government.

A few hours later, Pritchard's administrative assistant received another call, this one from the law office used by Buxton Thomas. They, too, requested an account number where they could wire money. Again, Pritchard's assistant gave the paralegal the same information she had provided to The Third Bank of Moncton. Within the hour, all fifty-seven million dollars that Buxton Thomas had directed his solicitor, Aaron, to wire over to Pritchard had been seized and now sat in an account for the Canadian government.

At about the same time the Canadian government seized the money Buxton Thomas had invested in Pritchard's project, the president of The Third Bank of Moncton notified all other banks that his bank was no longer interested in investing in the Carleton Mountain Development Project. Their interest had soured as a result of the background checks they had made. When the smaller banks heard the reason prompting the larger bank to pull out, they all followed suit.

Ironically, it all happened while Elwood Pritchard sat quietly in the airport, toasting to his success with a second double martini.

Chapter

39

In Fredericton, Josh Barnard was pouring over notes his grandfather had placed in the file decades earlier, back when the elder Barnard had successfully argued for the Abenaki to hold sovereign ownership of their lands going back to the treaty of 1796.

The file contained a brief that the ruling was subsequently brought back to court on appeal twice in the first year, and both challenges were denied based on "being frivolous."

Josh also found another claim made by the now defunct narrow gauge Brunswick Rail Company that sought an easement across Grey Elk's lands. When this challenge came to court, the request was denied on the basis that the Crown *had no sovereign right to the land*, therefore, the Canadian courts held no jurisdiction over the lands. Based upon what the elder Barnard had left in the file, the younger Barnard began to assemble an argument that the Abenaki had full and indisputable sovereignty over their lands.

When Josh Barnard finished drafting his argument, he sat back. *Why was I so ready to just dismiss this case as being indefensible? Grandfather, I believe that your penchant for looking at oddities and obscure precedents will continue to protect the lands of the Abenaki.* He bowed his head with reverence.

Then Josh placed a call to the Canadian Railway's inhouse attorneys to give them a heads up that he would be filing an argument to contest their ability to take any lands belonging to the Abenaki for a rail corridor.

"Thank you, solicitor. Actually, it has already been brought to our attention that there was a potential issue, so we've recently placed the project on hold. Will you be representing one of the property owners?" the person on the other end of the line said.

"Yes, I expect to file today."

"Then, we'll see you in court. Thanks for the professional courtesy."

Knowing that parliament would remain in recess for another week, and that no action would be taken on any legislative bills during that time, Josh Barnard decided to wait a couple of days until the judge with whom he really wanted to file, would be back on the bench.

Josh was quite certain that once his arguments were filed with the court, and the judge made his ruling, then Canadian National would immediately abandon all efforts to create a corridor from their main line over to Carleton Mountain. He believed that when the legislative aids of the bill's sponsor learned there was a legitimate reason to question whether the Crown actually had sovereignty over the Abenaki lands, they wouldn't even wait for the ruling; the bill would never leave committee.

His two-day delay gave Josh some breathing room, so he decided to skip out of the office before lunch and fly back up to the Carleton Mountain area, just to have a leisurely look around at the natural beauty of the landscape.

--

Across town, formal charges were being brought against Arthur Turnbridge and immediately sealed by the judge. Although Turnbridge was now wearing prison garb, his transfer to the provincial prison was placed on hold and he remained in a cell at RCMP headquarters in Fredericton.

The reason for the delay in moving Turnbridge was strictly based upon the Mounties investigative process. In the last session, Turnbridge had given them the date and time of day he was to meet Ying in the field behind the general store over in Five Fingers. Once they had that information, the Mounties began planning the air support that would be required to take Ying down.

--

After Ying had decapitated the Mountie, there wasn't any doubt that every airport within a radius of two hundred miles would receive a second visit from the Mounties as they intensified their search efforts for the ultralight. All airports were placed on notice to contact authorities immediately should any ultralight land at their location.

Kate chose not to have the strike force commander share advance details of exactly *how* he planned to capture the ultralight's pilot, but she did share that there was reason to believe Ying would be in custody shortly.

She also sent out a synopsis of the research she had done on IGF-1 which brought Ying's role into focus. Once it became clear to the team that the product from Shang Ho Lab was, indeed, made with IGF-1 extracted from the velvet on deer antlers, and that the lab was aggressively trying to create a supply chain, they understood that Ying was the connection.

If ever there was a suspect the Mounties wanted taken alive, it was Lee Wong Ying. On the morning Ying planned to land in the field behind the general store in Five Fingers and connect with Arthur Turnbridge, the Mounties would be waiting.

Hours before Ying would arrive, the Mounties were in position. Among them was a Mountie similar in size and stature to Turnbridge who had donned Turnbridge's clothing, including the wide brimmed hat that he always wore and who waited patiently at the edge of the woods.

Given the fact that this was the first time Ying and Turnbridge were meeting at this location, the Mountie dressed in Turnbridge's clothes had been instructed that when the ultralight appeared, he was to step out of the tree line and wave to Ying, then retreat back into the woods. Once the ultralight actually set down, the Mountie posing as Turnbridge (or "the bait," as he was being called internally,) would re-emerge from the tree line, approach the ultralight, fake an injury by falling to the ground while holding his ankle and roll around while yelling for help, all in the hopes that Ying would get out of the ultralight and come to his aid.

In addition to "the bait," there were fifteen Mounties hidden in the underbrush, all dressed in camouflage and armed with various weapons. Instructions were to shoot only to wound the pilot or disable the ultralight.

As soon as Ying stepped out of the ultralight, the plan was for three Mounties to rush in and subdue him with tasers while the rest of the Mounties would surround everyone including the ultralight. As a precaution, the Mounties had aircraft on standby in the unlikely event that Ying somehow smelled a rat and took flight.

--

Time passed, and the Mounties had been waiting in the forest long enough that the usual sounds of the forest had begun to return. Off in the distance, a dog who had been barking incessantly, had either given it up, or someone was finally paying attention to it.

At exactly two in the afternoon, the high-pitched whine of an ultralight broke the silence. Within minutes, it came floating over the roof of the general store.

The Mountie playing 'the bait' stepped out from the tree line and waved both arms before stepping back into the woods.

Ying began circling the field's perimeter, looking for anything suspicious. After three passes, he was apparently satisfied, and set the craft down about thirty yards from the tree line very close to where "the bait" had stepped out and waved at him.

When "the bait" came running out again, he held

Turnbridge's bag in one hand and held Turnbridge's hat down low over his face with the other. The strike force commander watching from among the trees thought: *Easy now, don't get too close to the ultralight. All right, stop right there . . . you're getting too close . . . now fall to the ground.*

Just like in practice, "the bait" landed with his back facing Ying, then started rolling around, clutching his ankle, in what appeared to be total agony. One of the Mounties watching from the brush even wondered if "the bait" had actually hurt himself, and if there'd be a change in plans.

Ying watched 'Turnbridge' roll around until it was apparent that he wasn't getting up. So, he finally stepped out of the ultralight. As soon as that happened, three Mounties raced from the tree line with tasers in hand, each from a different direction. Ying saw them coming and realized it was a trap. He ran to the figure he now knew wasn't Turnbridge and with one swift kick delivered a vicious blow to "the bait's" head with his right foot while looking for a bag with antlers. Finding none, he turned and raced back to the ultralight. In a heartbeat, Ying had the throttle in hand and was lifting off.

The three Mounties who had raced toward Ying, fired their tasers hoping they might still be able to restrain him. But the angle was wrong, and their prongs bounced off the plastic shield protecting the cockpit and underbelly, accomplishing nothing.   The remaining Mounties immediately began firing at the ultralight attempting to disable it. By the time the ultralight had cleared the treetops, its two-stroke engine was sputtering and a visible thin line of black smoke was coming from the exhaust.

Immediately, the strike force commander called for support aircraft to execute a suspect pursuit.

Ying was flying close to tree top level as he headed north, hoping it would give him the best cover. But the Euro copter EC 130 that had been standing by, was onsite in less than four minutes, and quickly established eye contact with the now-disabled ultralight. With a top speed of 187 miles per hour, it didn't take long for the Euro copter to overtake the ultralight.

Ying knew he couldn't outrun the pursuit helicopter but hoped that once he cleared the lake ahead of him, he could find a small clearing where only he could land. Then he could melt into the wilderness.

But the ultralight's sputtering engine was struggling. Ying was losing altitude and flying far closer to the lake's surface than he wanted. Then, when the pursuit helicopter made a second pass over Ying, it came in low and the larger helicopter's downwash created just enough turbulence that Ying's ultralight entered a retreating blade stall which forced the ultralight into an uncontrolled nosedive. At that point, Ying's tail rotor was thrown up into the air, missing the underbelly of the pursuit helicopter by mere inches before crashing into the water.

The ultralight hit the water hard about thirty yards from shore and upon impact, broke into multiple pieces. The pursuit copter pilot immediately radioed: "Suspect's craft is down. Repeat: ultralight is down and broken into pieces. We will circle back to see if the pilot survived."

Within moments, the pilot of the pursuit helicopter came back on the air. "We are not seeing a swimmer. It does not appear likely anyone could have survived the crash. The craft is really broken up."

Dispatch came on the line: "Make a couple more passes before returning to base. Make absolutely sure there is no swimmer."

"Roger that. Out."

Chapter

40

As the week passed, Lou's guests at the lodge had all hit their stride and no longer required much TLC. After Lou made sure everyone had the different kinds of bait they wanted, and the boats were all out, he walked back into the lodge for another cup of coffee, knowing that Kate would still be there.

"Kate, I'm heading over to the village around noon; the council is holding a special meeting, and I suspect my mentees will have returned."

"Anything you need me to do while you're gone, Lou?"

"Nah. One of the Abenaki guides didn't go out today; he should be able to handle anything that comes up. I'll be back by four-thirty at the latest."

"Okay. I'm on a call shortly."

--

Kate's afternoon conference call with the major crime unit team was about to end when she received a text telling her to stand by for a debriefing by the strike force commander who had just run a takedown operation over in Five Fingers.

"Stay on the line, everyone, the strike force commander has just joined us." There was a brief silence, then Kate said, "Go ahead, Sergeant."

"Thank you," a man's voice said. "I'll make this brief, then take whatever questions you may have. Earlier today, we attempted to bring the pilot of an ultralight into custody. We were unsuccessful. One member of our strike force sustained a serious injury when the pilot of the ultralight was briefly on the ground. That man has been airlifted to Montreal and will be operated on tomorrow to reconstruct his left orbital eye socket. The doctors say they won't know if he'll regain sight in that eye until the swelling goes down.

"As far as the suspect is concerned, he is believed to have perished when his craft went down in a lake about seven miles south of Kedgwick. The wreckage is floating in the water as we speak. Divers from Search and Rescue are on their way to the scene now and will remain there until a Piasecki H-21 chopper can arrive to lift the wreckage out of the water and transport it over to the crime lab in Kedgwick."

"Sergeant, do you have a positive ID on the body of the pilot?"

"Negative. Initial reports from the pursuit craft say that the pilot was most likely thrown from the cockpit upon impact; his body is somewhere in the lake."

"Sergeant, this is Kate…knowing what you know now, is there anything you would have done differently, if you had to do it all over again?"

"I would most likely have had a couple of snipers disable the ultralight as soon as it landed, ma'am."

"Arnold Cunningham here, Sergeant. Was there any scenarios where you might have been able to extract the pilot without putting any of your men at risk? This suspect seemed to be quite proficient in martial arts."

"Roger that; he is known to be a dangerous man, sir. I would have immobilized him by shooting out his knees. But to tell the truth, I'd have felt more confident if we had been allowed to use a damn tranquilizer gun and treated him like a rogue bear."

Once the strike force commander finished his report, he left the call, and the conversation began to wind down. Just before the call ended, one participant made the comment: "It's pretty unusual for two aircraft to go down on the same day, but I just heard that Search and Rescue is out looking for another plane." There was further conversation, but without more facts, the call finally ended.

Kate finished her meeting notes before clicking over to the Search and Rescue site to see what information might have been posted on the ultralight, or on the second plane that had crashed.

--

Earlier that afternoon, Josh Barnard had been enjoying the magnificent landscape as he circled around Carleton Mountain.

The first time he made the circle, he saw the land stretching to the south and west of Carleton Mountain in a beautiful display of nature. He smiled knowing that once his argument was presented before the judge, the Abenaki claim on this pristine area of New Brunswick would, again, be upheld.

The second time he circled around the mountain, he noticed the winds coming off the lake were creating more than just a little turbulence, so he decided to stay to the east side of Carleton Mountain.

One of the things Josh loved most about flying was the ability to execute what is referred to as a "wing-over-wing" maneuver, also known as a "crop-duster turn." The maneuver definitely wasn't something a novice would try, but then, he wasn't a novice.

First, the airplane would make a steep climb followed by a vertical flat turn which meant the plane then turned on its side, without rolling, and was followed up with a vertical dive. Josh had first attempted this aerobatic maneuver in a Beechcraft CT 156 trainer when he was in the Canadian Air Force. The only reason he didn't receive disciplinary action for the maneuver back then was because Josh's enlistment period was up in a matter of days and his commanding officer was just as much of a cowboy as Josh. He had, in fact, silently applauded his bravado.

Now, after Josh enjoyed his wingover maneuvers a few times, he tired of them and decided to make a few low passes over the water before heading home. As Josh banked the plane, he saw the sun glistening off the surface of the perfect lake and was so mesmerized by its beauty, he decided to practice a few more low runs just a little further to the east.

Unlike a "touch and go" maneuver, the "low pass" was prohibited at airports. Even though, upon occasion, a waiver was granted for some air shows, even then, the plane had to maintain an altitude of at least five hundred feet. Josh loved to push the envelope and often when he was off in the boonies, he tried to skim the surface of the water with the plane's low-hanging pontoons before entering into a steep climb. The thrill never left a pilot who executed it correctly.

Josh did a time check, and figured he had just enough time to make one more "low pass" before he needed to head back, refuel, and leave the plane at Echo Lake for one of the other owners who had reserved the plane for two o'clock.

As thorough as Josh was, he had forgot that the de Haviland's extremely precise digital altimeter had been temporarily replaced with a used barometric altimeter which is only accurate to within five hundred feet – give or take a little.

Whether it was the inaccurate altimeter, or the blinding sunbeam that strayed into his eyes as he came from the east on his last "low pass," Josh totally misjudged how close he was to the surface of the lake. A sudden downdraft caused the nose to dip and the front tips of both pontoons dug into the surface of the water. It caused the plane to do a half summersault before landing upside down in the water, both pontoons pointing skyward.

--

A few minutes before two o'clock, Josh's friend arrived at the dock and was surprised the plane wasn't there. He assumed Josh was still refueling the Twin Beaver; but as time passed, and

Josh hadn't returned with the plane by two-thirty, nor was he answering his cell phone, his friend became concerned and called air traffic control at Fredericton. He wanted to find out what VFR flight itinerary Josh had filed.

By three o'clock, the RCMP Search and Rescue team had dispatched two search planes to look for him, hoping it was search and rescue and not - retrieval.

Chapter

41

Back in the village of Grey Elk, the special tribal council meeting came to order when John White Owl led those attending in a traditional invocation prayer. Then he began with a question. "Kicking Bird, are you ready to tell us what our financial situation is?"

Kicking Bird was in his late seventies. "Yes, but my eyes are not good. I will remain seated as I speak, so that I can read what is written in these books." The carefully kept books allowed Kicking Bird to account for every nickel and dime that had ever come into or gone out of the Abenaki accounts for decades. He then reported, "As of today, our village has over a million dollars in the bank".

Kasko stood up now to address the council. "Kicking Bird, if we have so much money in the bank, why do you always say that we have no money?"

"After the first of every month, after the bills are paid, we have no money left."

"But you have just told us that we have over a million dollars in the bank."

"Yes, and that is because on the first of every month, money is deposited into our checking account. I pay whatever bills we have from that amount. On the second day of the month, whatever is left from the day before, I put into a long-term certificate of deposit. When I do that, we have no more money in our checking account to pay for things until the following month when more money comes into our checking account."

Raven Claw put his head down and smiled. Then he asked, "Why do you do this, Kicking Bird?"

"Grey Elk once told me that whatever money was left after paying all the bills should be put into CD's."

White Owl then asked, "Are there any more questions for Kicking Bird?"

No one spoke.

"Raven Claw, are you satisfied with what Kicking Bird has told us?"

"Yes. However, given that Kicking Bird's eyes are failing, I think the time has come for us to thank him for all that he has done. Let us ask someone with younger eyes to manage the finances of our village."

There were more than several affirmative grunts and heads that nodded in agreement.

A member of the audience stood up and asked, "Kicking Bird, why did you not tell us about the surveyors when you first saw them trespassing on our lands?"

"I did not need to. I told my wife. She told others. Soon everyone in the village knew."

Raven Claw, and all the others laughed. They all knew Kicking Bird's wife who was appropriately named "Tongue-That-Wags." When the laugher ended, Raven Claw asked him a question.

"Kicking Bird, why do you hide in the bushes and watch me?"

Kicking Bird boldly raised his chin and said, "You

mentor my grandson. I listen to make sure that you teach him well." After a pause he said, "So far, I am pleased."

Raven Claw smiled again and nodded. "There is no need for you to hide. Sit among us from now on."

The moderator asked, "Is there anything else that we need to discuss?"

No one spoke.

"Then we will begin our closing ceremony."

--

When Lou left the council lodge, it was noticeable that the air had changed; the wind had picked up, and the western sky was dark. By the time he reached Moose Cove, rain was beginning to come down in large drops. After untying and climbing onto his boat, he blew out the bilge and glided over to the shallows. Then Lou pushed the throttle full forward, hoping to stay ahead of the storm. He reached the boat house just as the full force of the gale storm hit. After tying up the runabout, Lou looked out the window and counted the number of boats at the dock; all twelve had made it back. Satisfied, he ran for their cottage.

As he reached the porch, he saw Kate standing at the door. "Lou, something awful has happened!"

"What?"

"A plane went down east of Carleton Mountain. A search and rescue plane has been sent out to look for signs of wreckage."

"It wasn't Jake, was it?

"No . . . they believe the pilot was Josh Barnard."

"I'm calling Fletcher!" he said, while reaching for his cell phone. His call was answered on the first ring. "Fletcher . . . it's Lou Gault. What do you know about the plane that went down east of Carleton Mountain? Kate and I think we know the pilot."

"Hey, Lou, funny you should call. I just got off the line with Andre Girard who was telling me how many times he used you to lead search and rescue operations. Are you interested in doing some work now?"

"That's why I'm calling, Fletcher. Do they know where the plane went down?"

"They spotted a wreck in the water. The pilot who reported the crash said it's sitting upside down in Lake 991, wherever the hell *that* is."

"I know *exactly* where that is," Lou said. "Is the search plane still in the area?"

"I doubt it. That report came in over an hour ago."

"Listen, have a plane pick me up and drop me off on Lake 991. If he's alive, I'll find him."

"Can't, Lou, the search and rescue planes are all grounded until a storm in that area moves through. But it's fast-moving, they tell me."

"It's already starting to let up here. Have them call me when they take off. I'll be waiting on the dock."

"You sure you don't wanna wait until morning?"

"Damn sure. If it's who we think it is, I've got a lot riding on this pilot,."

Lou threw together what he would basically have taken if he was heading out on an overnight. Thirty-five minutes later, when a float plane taxied up to the dock, Lou was standing there, waiting with a kayak which they quickly strapped to the pontoon struts.

Within fifteen minutes, they set down on the east end of Lake 991 and Lou was paddling over to the wreckage. The first thing he did was check to see if there was a body trapped inside the cockpit of the Twin Beaver. The water in these unspoiled remote lakes was extremely clear, often down to a depth of sixty feet, and the plane was listing just enough that Lou could tell from the surface there wasn't anybody inside.

Lou yelled over to the pilot, "There's no one in the plane. I'm heading ashore. Maybe I'll find some tracks before the sun goes down. Come back sometime tomorrow morning."

"Roger that. I'm heading home."

Lou thought. *Well, the wreck isn't in the middle of the lake, so I'm guessing if someone survived, they'd try for the nearest shore.* He began his search near the outlet and paddled slowly along the northern shoreline looking for signs where someone might have gone ashore.

Mostly sand, the shoreline was edged with underbrush that was impenetrable. If someone had gone ashore, Lou would easily have recognized it. Years ago, he had hiked around Lake 991 a few times, but had never floated a kayak on it before. Now, he was surprised to find the lake had a strong current. *We've just had a heavy downpour and I'm close to the outlet, maybe both things are causing that*, he thought.

As he continued paddling up along the northern shoreline, he came to a section where the underbrush seemed to have been disturbed. He moved as close to shore as possible, only to determine that it was an animal trail. Then, he decided to circle back and try the southern shoreline before paddling any further up the long lake.

It was beginning to get dark by the time Lou had circled back and paddled a good distance up the opposite shoreline. Frustrated at not finding anything, he brought the kayak up onto a sandy stretch and proceeded to make camp for the night.

--

When the Twin Beaver had summersaulted, Josh's harness had broken free from the floor mounts and his head had bounced off the instrument panel. Though he never lost consciousness, still, he was a little disoriented by the time he reached the surface. Knowing that night came early in the wilds and that it would be hours before any search was launched, Josh decided to swim to the nearest shore.

He had been schooled in survival techniques when he was a pilot in the Canadian Air Force. In the pockets of his flight jacket, Josh always carried a compass, a whistle, a mirror, and a waterproof container of stick matches, plus he had snatched the first aid kit from the plane, more for its buoyancy than anything else.

Although it was the third week in August, the nighttime temperatures in New Brunswick had already been dipping down into the low thirties and everything Josh had on was soaking wet. The first thing he did after finding a suitable place to spend the night, was to collect wood, build a fire, frame a shelter, and start drying out his clothes to prevent hypothermia from setting in.

As Josh piled boughs of evergreens onto a makeshift shelter, he thought he heard a plane down around the east end of the lake, but before he could be sure, a storm suddenly came through, blocking out all but the sound of the wind and the rain.

Later, just before dusk, he again thought he heard the sound of a plane, but it too, was off in the distance further down at the far end of the lake. At the moment, Josh's main concern was gathering enough wood, drying out and staying warm. The first aid kit had four mylar space blankets inside. One he used to cover his shelter, another became a ground cloth, and he wrapped the remaining two around his body as best he could. His survival training, and the first aid kit that he had taken from the plane, eliminated the risk of hypothermia, however, he had nothing to quell the growling of an empty stomach.

Meanwhile at the opposite end of the lake, Lou had erected a shelter, had a rabbit roasting over a low fire on a spit that he had caught in a snare, and was sending a text off to Kate that he had put up for the night. Accustomed to sleeping out in the open, Lou quickly fell asleep. He awoke once to the sound of wolves off in the distance, then threw a few more logs onto the fire to finish incinerating the remains of the rabbit he'd had for dinner before rolling over and going back to sleep. The only thing close to a weapon that he had brought along was a six-inch long blade tucked in his belt

Shortly after first light the following morning, Josh walked down to the water's edge. When he didn't see the upside-down plane, his first thought was that it had sunk to the bottom. Then he saw the sun's rays reflecting off something way down at the eastern end of the lake.

Josh figured he had two options: Hike a good mile along the rugged shoreline to the eastern end of the lake where the plane was or stay put and build a smokey signal fire. Building the signal fire was the choice that won out.

--

Meanwhile, Lou had also broken camp early and was back out on the water paddling up the southern side of the lake carefully examining the shoreline for any indication where someone might have come ashore.

He smelled smoke long before he actually saw it rising up from the trees on the far side of the lake. As he headed toward the opposite shore, he yelled: "Hello, the fire!"

There was no response.

When he reached the far shoreline, he cupped his hands and yelled again: "Hello, the fire!"

"Hello!" came a distant response.

"Josh Barnard?"

"Yes!"

"Come to the lake."

Within minutes, Josh walked out onto a sandbar, all smiles and not looking too stressed.

Once Lou was satisfied that Josh didn't require any immediate first aid, he sent a text to Fletcher Martin and Kate that he had located Josh Barnard and that he was safe. He also texted that they'd be waiting along the shoreline at the west end of lake 991. "Why'd you hike all the way back here, Josh?"

"I didn't. The plane flipped over just about there," he pointed to an area close by. "The storm must have pushed it down the lake."

"We were looking for you at the other end, last evening."

"I figured I'd stay put and not get lost."

"Smart move."

Chapter

42

When Elwood Pritchard returned to his office, he had several faxes from the banks in Moncton and Nova Scotia, each one notifying him that they had decided *not* to invest in his project.

Pritchard slammed his fist down on his desk shouting, "Damn, what the hell happened?" Then he called to his assistant. "Marsha, see if you can get the president of The Third Bank of Moncton on the line for me."

While he waited for Marsha to make the phone call, he scanned the summary of calls, events, and changes to his calendar, which he usually expected to have waiting on his desk whenever he'd been away. As he went down the list, he noticed six entries for "account number provided to wire money."

"Marsha, what's this about an account number for wiring money?"

"Just a moment, Mr. Pritchard, I'm on the line with The Third Bank now." She sounded harried. "Okay, Mr. Pritchard, you can go ahead now. I have the bank president on line one."

Pritchard, was still in the dark as to what was going on when picked up the phone line. "Hello?"

"Good morning, Mr. Pritchard, I was anticipating your phone call."

"Yes, yes, good morning to you, too, James. Listen, I'm looking at a fax from your bank that says you are no longer interested in investing in the Carleton Mountain Development project. What happened?"

"Yes, that is correct," James said. "When our monitoring software identified the account that we were given as an account that was subject to immediate seizure of funds by the Canadian government, we decided to cancel the transfer. We do need to safeguard our depositors' money. That is paramount here at Third Bank."

"There shouldn't have been any issue with transferring the money to the account that I gave you. What happened?"

"Well, the account that *you* provided happened to be one digit short. When we called your office, we were provided with a different account number."

"I see. Well, I'll fax you the *correct* account number, so you can wire the money right over."

"I'm afraid we're not going to be able to do business with you, Mr. Pritchard," James said. "Our head loan officer ran a Dun & Bradstreet on you and has recommended that we not make the investment. Sorry, but we should have done that in the beginning. Good day, Mr. Pritchard."

As Pritchard hung up the phone, he muttered to himself, "Good day? How the hell can I have a *good day* when one of my major investors tells me that they have just backed out!"

Pritchard looked at the sheet his assistant had left on his desk and saw that a wire transfer was to have occurred yesterday. He yelled out to his assistant. "Marsha! What bank account did you tell people to wire money to?"

"I couldn't reach anyone in accounting," she said, "and they wanted an answer right away, so I gave them the information on the checkbook that you have in your desk, Mr. Pritchard."

When Elwood Pritchard internalized what he had just heard, something deep inside the very core of his existence snapped. He was totally unable to focus on where he was. His mind was racing through a thousand thoughts.

Marsha was having difficulty distinguishing whether the noise coming from Elwood Pritchard's office was laughter, or sobbing, or perhaps a combination of both. Whichever it was, her curiosity ended when Elwood Pritchard emerged from his office, placed a pistol against the back of her head and pulled the trigger.

Chapter

43

Ying was badly shaken from the crash, but he survived without serious injuries. Each time the pursuit chopper circled back looking for signs of a survivor, he managed to hold his breath and conceal himself under pieces of the wreckage.

Once the Mounties headed back to base, Ying came out from underneath the ultralight wreckage and swam to shore. When he reached the beach, he wasted no time disappearing into the woods, just in case the pursuit helicopter returned for another pass.

Without a compass, Ying was still able to determine where north was by the position of the sun. He knew that Five Fingers was behind him and that he had flown far enough north that the next settlement would most likely be Kedgwick. After pushing his way through the thick underbrush for a while, Ying entered into an area that someone must have been managing as a wood lot, as it wasn't quite as dense.

Eventually he came upon a logging road and made better forward progress. Ying stayed on the dirt road, knowing that it had to lead somewhere. He took shelter whenever he heard a plane fly overhead. Eventually, he realized the planes weren't searching for him, but rather were heading toward an airfield that was probably close by.

Ying stayed on the dirt road until he came to a gate which was perhaps thirty feet inward from a paved road. His clothing hadn't made it through the crash as well as he had, so rather than attract attention, he decided to remain in the woods and continued to walk north, parallel to the paved road.

The further Ying traveled, the more apparent it was that he was near the approach corridor for a runway. Planes were now flying overhead close to tree top level.   An airport meant transportation, a change of clothes, food, and water.

When Ying reached the runway approach path that had been cut out of the forest, he held back as a Twin Otter suddenly glided overhead toward the runway. Once the plane passed overhead, he ran across the paved road and headed toward the nearest hangar.

It was late in the afternoon, the lone mechanic in the hangar was standing on an elevated platform, replacing a few rivets in the cowling of a Beechcraft with a pneumatic hammer. Between the noise of the air compressor and the small prop plane that was taxing past the open hangar door, the mechanic never heard Ying sneak up behind him.

Once Ying changed into the mechanic's coveralls and finished off the leftover pizza that had been sitting on the break room table, he walked back out into the hangar. There were only two planes parked there and neither one was flyable. One plane had the engine out, and the other's propeller sat on a balancing device that had been set up on a work bench. Ying stepped into the shadows and began eyeing the planes directly across the tarmac in the tie down area.

--

When Elwood Pritchard's assistant hadn't come home from work by six, her husband became concerned. Marsha was a creature of habit and rarely deviated from her normal routine. He tried calling her cell, but it went directly to voicemail. She'd been having trouble with her car starting, so when he hadn't heard from her by six-thirty, he decided to drive over to see if she was stranded in the parking lot.

Marsha's husband was initially relieved when he saw her car in its familiar spot, but once he saw that she wasn't in the car, he went inside to see what was up. Except for Pritchard's office, everything else inside the building was in darkness. He could see Pritchard at the far end of the building, bent over, looking at something that he had strewn across his desk. It wasn't until he reached the doorway to Pritchard's office that he turned and saw his wife, slumped over her desk, her head sitting in a dark pool of blood.

When the Mounties responded to Marsha's husband's 911 call, Elwood Pritchard was still in his office making notes and talking to himself as if nothing unusual had occurred.

--

The following day, when Pritchard was brought before the court for arraignment, the legal aid lawyer assigned to him requested a postponement until it could be established that Pritchard was mentally stable enough to stand trial.

Whatever it was that had snapped inside Elwood Pritchard's mind the previous afternoon, it didn't appear to be temporary.

--

On Thursday mornings, Jake always flew out of Kedgwick Airport several hours earlier than normal so that he would be back in time to refuel the Otter and drive over to the One-Eyed Jack Pub in time to play darts. Jake had been on the same team or the past four year and rarely missed a meeting. His team was in third place and if everyone showed up this night, they might have a chance to move up into second place. The first time ever.

--

At the precise moment Ying was about to run across the tarmac to steal an old Piper Cub, he saw the Twin Otter which had passed over his head a short while ago, taxiing over to the tie down area near the fuel depot.

As soon as the pilot exited the craft, Ying raced across the tarmac. The pilot had his back to Ying but saw the reflection of someone running toward him in the plane's window. He turned just in time to avoid a vicious kick that would have definitely broken a few ribs. "Whoa! what's going on here?" Jake shouted.

Ying moved into a martial arts stance.

Jake quickly moved away from the body of the plane to give himself a little freedom of movement in all directions and mentally shifted into fight mode. His attacker came at him three or four times before he recognized the moves of a Silat fighter, one of the more vicious forms of martial arts. Jake was a proficient pugilist and had taught Mixed Martial Arts when he was in Canada's elite JTF2 commando division, so now he countered with a form known as Krav Maga, a style he had trained recruits in for street fighting.

"Look, you wanna dance?" he said. "Let's do this another time, okay?"

Ying responded by coming in with another swift movement, which Jake narrowly avoided. He had no idea why he was under attack but had no doubt that he was up against an extremely fast and unpredictable opponent. It had been quite a few years since he had gone up against anyone this talented . . . or this quick.

Ying came at him again and seemed to be a powerhouse of tireless energy who just kept coming at Jake again and again.

After several attempts, Ying connected with a sweeping left foot that caught Jake in the hip. He swallowed the pain. The next time Ying attempted that move, Jake was ready and countered with a move that struck Ying's right knee, causing him to stumble backward, only to charge forward with a leaping attack. Jake easily stepped aside and hammered Ying with a powerful blow to the shoulder as he passed by.

Then Ying retreated a few steps and stared at Jake. He hadn't anticipated this pilot would prove to be such a formidable challenge. His shoulder felt numb from Jake's last blow, but he was beginning to enjoy this unexpected battle between warriors which would ultimately end in his opponent's death . . . or so Ying thought.

Jake rarely went on the attack at the outset of a martial arts contest. His approach was very much akin to a gunslinger in the old wild west, coercing his opponent into drawing first. He was far more inclined to react to his opponent's moves in a match, believing that it gave him a better opportunity to use his opponent's strength against him. He liked to watch his opponent's eyes and facial movements for anything that might telegraph a next move.

Now he studied Ying. His opponent was smooth and showed very little emotion for Jake to pick up on before he struck with lightning speed. Jake soon realized that he was up against someone who had competed professionally.

In the next hanger, three mechanics had been working on an engine until they heard what sounded like a fight coming from next door. They moved over to an open doorway to see what was going on. Having been a fixture at the airport for over four years, all three of them recognized Jake at once but they didn't recognize the man who was fighting him.

Suddenly, Ying surprised Jake with a roundhouse kick. Jake stepped back just in time to avoid a crushing blow to his face. As Ying's leg came down, Jake hammered his attacker's Achilles tendon with the side of his shoe.

Ying's Achilles was damaged and he hobbled somewhat but showed no signs of slowing down his attack.

Jake blocked a couple of dangerous kicks to his midriff, either of which would have damaged his kidneys.

Then, Ying rushed at Jake and landed a few well-timed chops on Jake's upper arms but failed to connect with a chop which would have broken Jake's collar bone.

Suddenly, Jake went on the attack with a groin kick. Ying was able to back step which left Jake vulnerable for a moment.

Within minutes, the mechanics realized this wasn't just a couple of guys fooling around, it was for real. One of them dialed 911. "Hey, ya' better send a couple of cars over to Kedgwick Airport fast! There's a couple of Kung Fu guys over here in the hangar area, going at it. It looks like they're trying to beat each other's brains out."

Ying continued on the attack. Jake blocked most of Ying's moves and delivered counter blows, but he was beginning to tire. Although he was in good shape, Jake was nowhere near the shape required for a match of this caliper or with an adversary like Ying.

Ying could sense that Jake was tiring. All Ying wanted was the plane, and this one man stood between him and his escape. But Ying was tiring also, yet he pressed onward.

As Ying advanced, Jake bolted out of his guard stance and attempted a straight knee strike which Ying was able to avoid.

--

When the 911 call came in, the desk sergeant thought it was odd that the caller had described the fight as a couple of "Kung Fu fighters going at it." The corporal who was about to relieve the sergeant said, "Wasn't that guy in the ultralight some kind of a Kung Fu fighter? You think there was more than one of them?"

"I'll dispatch a couple of cars," the other Mountie said.

--

Ying decided he needed to end this fight sooner than later and picked up a rope that was attached to a wheel chock. He began swinging it over his head. Jake wasn't quite sure how to counter an attack with something akin to a medieval ball and chain flail, beyond retreating and trying to find a weapon of his own. But he was tiring fast. The intense battle had also begun to wear Ying down, too.

As long as Jake stayed beyond the reach of the flail, he knew he was relatively safe. The only thing he needed to watch was anything behind him. Ying began to regret having picked up the chock as it was causing his opponent to back up, taking him further and further away from his goal: the Otter, the plane he wanted to commandeer.

Without warning Ying let go of the rope, deciding to use the chock as a distraction. The wedge sailed toward Jake and in the same fluid movement, Ying charged with lightning speed. Ying's intention was to end the fight with a fatal blow to the head. Jake was momentarily distracted but still able to dodge the missile and deliver a powerful chop to the back of Ying's neck. Ying fell, rolled left, and jumped up.

"You die *now*, fly boy!" he yelled. Ying swayed back and forth like a cobra assessing his adversary before he sprung at Jake, knocking him to the ground. Ying began delivering punishing chops to Jake's neck and shoulders.

But Jake was able to grab Ying and catapulted him overhead before jumping to his feet.

Ying smiled at him.

As Jake prepared for Ying's next attack, two Mountie patrol cars pulled up. Both officers jumped out of their vehicles with tasers ready, yelling: "Back off! Stand down!"

Ying immediately felt trapped and turned to face these new challengers. In that instant, Jake laid him out with a vicious Krav Maga move to the head. Ying collapsed.

The two Mounties immediately recognized him. "Jake! What the hell is this?"

"Guys, just put the damn cuffs on this crazy bastard before he recovers, will ya? I'm friggin' wiped!"

--

Ying was booked at the Kedgwick RCMP facility and immediately transported down to the holding area at the Fredericton RCMP headquarters.

When Arthur Turnbridge saw Ying walk by his cell, he yelled, "Ying! They ain't let me out yet so's I can't git you more antlers!"

Once the Mounties realized who they had in custody, Ying was placed in leg irons as well as hand cuffs. They weren't taking any chances.

Chapter

44

When the Search and Rescue Twin Otter set down on lake 991, Lou and Josh were waiting at the shoreline.

After a quick stop at Havre de Poisson to drop Lou off, the pilot flew Josh down to Fredericton where he waited for over three hours at the Fredericton Union Hospital before he was examined. Once released, Josh headed directly to his office, grabbed his arguments and walked over to the courthouse to present them to the one judge he'd been waiting for.

--

Around midafternoon, Lou was standing dockside when his clients' boats began returning, "How'd the fishing go?

The fellow seated in the stern pulled their stringer out of the water to show him.

"Now those are some beauties," Lou said. 'Which part of the lake did you fish?"

"We just trolled back and forth down by the outlet at the end of the lake."

"It's usually good down there, there's a shelf that the big ones seem to hide under."

"Figured it was something like that. Every time we made a pass, we had a hit."

"Yup, they'll wait there and come right up for the fingerlings as soon as they come off that shelf."

"Today clinched it for us, Lou," the sportsman in the bow said. "Between the fishing and the food, you've got us coming back again next year."

"That's what we like to hear," Lou said. "Give those fish to one of the guides and they'll dress 'em up for ya' and put them in the freezer with your name on it."

--

That afternoon Buxton Thomas sent a fax off to Elwood Pritchard that his solicitor had spoken to a legislator and the bill they had talked about would be out of committee as soon as parliament resumed. Buxton was somewhat surprised that he didn't receive any acknowledgement back from Pritchard by end of day.

Just before Buxton Thomas' solicitor left his office for the day, he texted Buxton: *"The name 'Elwood Pritchard' just came over wire service regarding a shooting in NB. Pritchard in custody."*

Buxton texted back: *"Hold off wiring $$$ 2 Carleton Mt project until U find out more."*

Aaron texted back: *"Money may have already been wired."*

Buxton texted back: *"Get it back asap . . . need 2 go . . . dinner guests tonight."*

--

Later that evening, two skilled interrogators sat down at a table with Ying in Fredericton. One Mountie sat across the table from Ying, the other sat to his left.

"Mr. Ying, this can go very easy for you, if you cooperate with us. May I have your full name?"

Ying stared straight ahead and said nothing.

"Mr. Ying. May I have your full name, please?"

Ying remained silent.

"Mr. Ying, your fingerprints have come back as a match with the name 'Lee Wong Ying.' Is that your full name?"

Again, Ying did not answer.

"Mr. Ying, we know that you have been paying Arthur Turnbridge to procure deer antlers. Why is that Mr. Ying?"

Silence.

"Mr. Ying, you have been charged with one count of murdering a police officer, another for murdering a civilian, and two counts of assault on a police officer and an assault on a mail carrier. You are also being charged as an accessory to the murder of two game wardens, and a police officer, and with being an accessory to multiple charges of taking deer out of season. These are serious charges. If you cooperate with us, it will go easier for you."

Ying spat across the table at the interrogator.

"Mr. Ying, who are you procuring these antlers for?"

Silence.

"Mr. Ying, are you working on behalf of Shang Ho Laboratories?"

There was a flash of recognition in Ying's eyes, but he still remained silent.

"Mr. Ying, how did you first become acquainted with Arthur Turnbridge?"

Silence.

The interrogator sitting across the table continued asking questions while Ying just sat there, motionless.

Eventually, the lead interrogator, on the left of Ying, had enough of the stonewalling. "Let's return Mr. Ying to his cell."

In the blink of an eye, as the guard entered the interrogation room, Ying pulled his knees up to his chin, lowered his shoulders, and using a contortionist's move, passed his cuffed hands under his feet. Suddenly Ying's hands were in front of him.

Then, in one fluid movement, Ying stood up, used the table like it was a pommel horse, lifted his legs and rotated his body, wrapping his leg irons around the neck of the lead interrogator.

Ying's back landed on the tabletop with a thud. He began twisting and jerking his legs with such violence that he began crushing the lead interrogator's windpipe. It took two officers to subdue him. The interrogator Ying had assaulted slouched over the table, gasping for air and coughing up blood.

Ying was immediately fitted with a belly chain to which both his leg irons and his handcuffs were secured before he was returned to his cell. Even in chains, he was a dangerous prisoner.

Chapter

45

As usual, Lou spent most of his Saturday morning jawing with several of his guests before they departed for home. He listened to their stories and about how much they wished they were living the life he was living. In any given week, nearly half the guests at Havre de Poisson were visitors who had previously stayed at the lodge.

By eleven that morning, every guest ending their stay had departed and were on their way home.

Now that Kate was partnering with Alessandra on Saturdays, they were able to turn the cottages over for the next week's incoming guests in half the time that it had previously taken.

By noon, Angelo had lunch ready. Lou, Kate, Alessandra, and the Abenaki guides all sat down with Angelo to enjoy a peaceful meal together before the next wave of incoming guests arrived.

Around two o'clock, the first float plane landed, shortly thereafter, six more planes arrived with new guests and week two of the second season was off and running.

Lou counted only one no show. However, later that

afternoon, Jarl Ohlson sent a text saying that he would be arriving on Monday.

Angelo always liked the first meal he served to be memorable and this week was no exception. When Angelo came out of the kitchen to the chants of "Angelo, Angelo, Angelo" on this Saturday night, every guest rose from their seat and applauded his culinary talents. This week's guests seemed exceptional.

--

Sunday was the most hectic morning of the week. Guests were anxious to down an early breakfast and get out on the water. Once the boats all left the dock, Lou headed over to his cottage.

"Woman-of-the-House, do we have any freshly brewed coffee?"

"We will in a moment," Kate answered. "Are all the boats out?"

"Yeah, the last boat just left. But I don't think the two over in Cottage Eight are serious fisherman. I guess we'll see."

"I'm sure they'll have plenty of stories to share by week's end."

"I suppose so," then pausing a moment he said, "Kate, I need to start listening to you a little more closely."

"Really? What brought this on?"

"I gotta tell ya, between everything that I have to do here and what I've raised my hand for over at the village, I don't have a damn life anymore, it's just too much. I need to outsource a few of these village projects."

"I think that's a good idea," she smiled. "By the way, Jake called. He's flying in on Thursday night and will be staying over the weekend. I'll have the spare room ready for him."

"Well, that's a surprise. Angelo will be happy. I'm sure they'll watch *Skyfall* again like it was their first time, then argue about the dialogue like they always do."

--

Later in the day, Lou was at the dock helping folks tie up as they came back in. When the two from Cottage Eight returned, he noticed that the stringer wasn't hanging over the side of their boat.

"How'd it go, fellas, did you have any luck today?"

"Nah, no fish today," one of them said.

Lou never wanted to hear that an angler came back in without having caught a single fish. "Well, tomorrow before you go out, let's talk about where you might want to try your luck and how you'll want me to rig up your lines."

"No worries. We had a good time. We just got in a few more games of cribbage than we thought we would."

--

On Monday morning, everyone was out on the lake before seven. Around two-thirty that afternoon, Lou heard a plane coming up the valley. *This must be the late arrival.*

Because Lou had promised Angelo that he'd give him a hand leveling the stove before dinner, he asked one of the Abenaki guides to greet the incoming guest, help him with his luggage and get him set up in his cottage.

When the plane arrived at the dock, the lone passenger got out and waited for the pilot to pass his luggage out. The Abenaki guide approached him. "Welcome to Havre de Poisson."

"This is it?" the man looked around with almost a scowl on his face. "I expected something a lot less rustic at these prices."

Within minutes, the pilot finished unloading his

passenger's luggage and was already moving away from the dock.

"Which of these cottages am I staying at?" the man asked.

"Number seven."

With that, Jarl Ohlson stepped over his luggage and started walking down the dock.

"Whoa, sir," the guide said. "We work together here. I'll *help* you carry your luggage, but I'm only making one trip. You'll need to pick up these last two."

"Hmmm, no trolly? I would have expected that you'd at least have a luggage trolly . . . at these prices."

"Sir, like I said, we work together here. I'll take these two, but you'll need to take the other two."

Ohlson picked up the two pieces of luggage remaining on the dock and followed the guide as he proceeded over to cottage number seven.

"The large building is where meals are served," the guide told him. "Breakfast begins at five-thirty, lunch is whenever you get back, and dinner is at six. Over to the right are the showers. Behind your cottage to the left is the closest outhouse to where you'll be staying. There's another one behind cottage five, if that one's taken."

"Outhouses?" he said incredulously. "You're shitting me! *Outhouses?*"

Smiling, the guide responded. "I wouldn't *shit* you, sir. That's what the outhouses are for."

--

That evening, Jarl Ohlson was the last to arrive at the lodge for dinner. Even though there were more than a few open seats available at several of the tables, he chose to sit at a table by himself.

Before the meal was over, Lou walked over to him. "Mr. Ohlson, nice to meet you. I'm Lou Gault, your host. If there is anything that you need while you're here, or that I can do for you, just let me know."

Ohlson answered in somewhat of a surly voice. "How late do they serve breakfast?"

"The kitchen opens at five-thirty and most everyone is out on the water by six-thirty. I suspect that if you wanted to sleep in a little late tomorrow, there will still be someone in the kitchen at seven."

"That's pretty early for me," Ohlson said.

"We try to accommodate everybody, but the kitchen staff is up around four-thirty in the morning to prepare breakfast. They shut down pretty soon after seven, so I'd advise you to mosey over before that happens, unless you want to wait for lunch. But fishing is best early in the morning, anyway."

"I didn't anticipate this place would be as . . . *rustic* as it is. No running water in the cottages and with outhouses and all."

"How'd you find out about us?"

"You might say it was a referral."

"Did you check out our website?"

"I looked at it briefly. Just to get the phone number."

"We make it pretty clear on our website that we're a rustic sportsmen's resort. That's not anything we try to hide in the small print."

"Yes, well at these prices, I expected flush toilets at least, not outhouses."

Lou decided to call this guy's bluff. "Tell ya' what, Mr. Ohlson, I don't want any of my guests to be unhappy and not have a great experience. So, if this isn't what you expected, and you'd like to leave, I'll arrange for you to fly out tomorrow.

I'll only charge you for the one day."

"No, I'm here and I'll deal with it," he said. "How do I get a boat?"

"All you have to do is walk down to the dock and we'll fit you up with a boat along with any fishing gear that you'll need, including the bait. If no one is there, just grab hold of the rope and clang the bell on the side of the boat house. Someone will come right over to help you out."

"Thanks, I'll remember that."

--

The following morning, both men in Cottage Eight showed up for breakfast a little later than the crowd, but they were down to the dock by quarter to seven.

"Okay, are we thinking of trolling, or still fishing today?" Lou asked.

"I think we'll still fish today, Lou."

"Okay, the rainbows are down at about forty-five feet; lake trout are at about sixty. Put three split shots on about three feet from the end of the line, hook the bait behind the dorsal fin, measure your line as you let it out, and you'll be right where the fish are."

"That's it?"

"Well, you do have to pay attention to the rod tip, but yeah, that's about all there is to still fishing."

--

Just minutes before seven, Ohlson, the lone man from Cottage Seven, sauntered down to the lodge, ordered a full breakfast and took his time eating. Once he finished, unlike most of the guests, he left his dishes on the table instead of bringing them over to the kitchen counter.

Then, Ohlson walked back to his cottage, came out carrying a large duffle bag and proceeded down to the dock where Lou was waiting.

"Ah, Mr. Ohlson, good morning. Are we ready to do some fishing today?"

"I suppose so. Is that my boat over there?" He pointed to the last available one.

"Yes, it is, I'll pull it around for you." With that, Lou walked down the dock, untied the boat and brought it around to the side of the dock next to the boat house. "What do you feel like fishing for today, lakers or rainbows?"

"Doesn't matter to me."

"All right, then I'll rig you up for rainbows. That's a fun fish, and they're starting to hit again pretty good."

Lou rigged up a line for Ohlson and filled up a bait bucket. "Here ya' go. Do you think you'll be trolling or still fishing?"

"Ah . . . still fishing, I guess."

"Okay, I'll rig your lines with some weights, hook the bait under the dorsal fin and let the line play out forty-five feet. You'll be right where the fish are. Don't go much lower than that…you wanna stay above the fish, they'll come up to your hook, but they won't go down to it. I'd recommend you try the west end of the lake. There's an outcrop on the left going down right in front of a couple of trees that extend over the lake at a forty-five angle. You can't miss them. Drop the anchor about sixty feet offshore and you should have some luck. Oh, and keep the bait bucket in the water. That way they'll stay alive and active a lot longer."

"I'll keep that in mind."

With that, Ohlson placed his duffle bag into the boat, fired up the engine and headed *east*, not west. Lou watched Ohlson as he motored away from the dock. *That's just about the biggest damn asshole I've seen in a while. No wonder he's up here all by himself.*

Later that afternoon, when the two men in Cottage Eight came back, Lou asked, "So, how'd it go today?"

"Well, I beat him four out of six games of cribbage."

"The heck you did," the other man protested. "We never finished the last game."

"I can't believe you two are out there playing cribbage, instead of fishing."

"Hey, the air is clean. It's warm in the sun; we're soaking up the rays and there's no stress. We caught a couple of fish, went ashore, and fried them up for lunch. What's not to like about that?

"You'll get no argument from me," Lou said.

A little after five, Ohlson returned to the dock.

"How'd it go?" Lou called out.

"I'm looking forward to tomorrow."

As Ohlson was ready to step out of the boat, Lou reached for the duffle bag. "Let me give you a hand with your bag."

"Don't touch that bag!" Ohlson replied sharply. Then, realizing how it sounded, he corrected himself. "I mean . . . thanks, but I'm good."

Lou thought it was odd that both knees on Ohlson's pants were covered with dirt, almost as if he had been kneeling on the ground.

--

The next few days were a mirror image of the movie *"Ground Hog Day."* Every cottage was up and out early, including the two in cottage eight, long before Jarl Ohlson even arrived at the lodge for breakfast.

Each day, Lou would ask him what he wanted to fish for, then would rig a pole up for him and Ohlson would head off in an easterly direction. Every afternoon, just about five,

Ohlson would return with dirt on his knees, and no fish.

Maybe he's strictly a catch and release guy, Lou thought.

--

On Thursday afternoon, when everyone except Ohlson had returned, Kate walked over to the dock to help Lou move a few boats around so Jake would have room to tie up.

"Kate, I can't figure out why the guys in cottage eight dug deep into their pockets to come up here. Neither one of them are serious fishermen, but at least they seem to be having a good time."

Just then they heard the sound of a Twin Otter approaching. Lou turned around and looked down the valley. "Strange that Jake's flying in on a Thursday. Wonder what's up."

As soon as the plane was secured to the dock, Lou opened the door, "Hey, cuz, surprised to see you here today."

"Yeah, well I decided to use a couple of vacation days and make it a short week after what I went through *last* week."

Lou stared at Jake for a moment. "Okay, I'll bite."

"You didn't hear?"

"Hear what?"

"I played 'Waltzing Matilda' with the ultralight pilot that everyone thought was dead for about twenty minutes last week when I was over at the airport."

"That was *you?*"

"Yeah."

"Kate told me about that, but nobody said it was *you.*"

"My ribs can attest to the fact that he was alive and kicking, and I do mean *kicking.* He wanted my Twin Otter. The bastard killed one of the best mechanics we had over in hanger three before he came after me. But I'll tell you, he could *fight,*

I'll give him that."

"You okay?"

"Left shoulder's still sore."

"You taking anything for it?

"Yeah, the doc's got me on a strict regimen of Crown Royal".

"That's one helluva doc, you've got."

"He's the best."

"Come on, let's go over to the cottage, I wanna hear more about this, then I'll tell you about *my* week."

Later, Jake described the fight that he'd with Ying in such vivid detail that he was virtually reliving the match.

At one point, Lou interrupted him. "Hey, hold that thought, I'll be right back. I need to help this last boat that's coming in."

When Lou returned to the cottage, he said, "I can't figure out the guy in cottage seven. Every day he goes out later than everyone else and never comes back with any fish. Besides that, the knees of his pants are covered in dirt. What do you think about that?"

"Do you think he's fishing from shore?"

"Nah, I haven't sent him out rigged for shore fishing."

"Ya' wanna follow him tomorrow and see what's going on?"

"Yeah, maybe we will."

"By the way, Kate said she was going over to the lodge."

"Yeah, she gives Alessandra a hand in the evenings. Finish your story about the fight, then we'll head over there."

Chapter

46

Friday was no different than any other Friday at Havre de Poisson. The serious fishermen were up early and away from the dock well before sunup; it was the last full day of fishing. Jake had gotten up early to help Lou see the boats off. Once everyone was out, they walked back to Lou's cottage to have breakfast with Kate and found her sitting at the kitchen table reading the daily newspaper that Jake had brought with him.

"Jake your picture is in the paper!" she said, looking up with a smile.

"Yeah, whoop dee do," he said without enthusiasm. "It's below the fold on page six. Last week, I was on page one. Fame is such a fleeting thing, isn't it?" Kate smiled, then heard a phone ringing.

"Lou that's your cell phone ringing. You left it over on the desk."

He pushed away from the table and walked over to grab it. "Hello?"

"Lou, Josh Barnard here.

"Good morning, Josh, good to hear your voice . . . safe and

sound."

"I've got some news."

"And?"

"The judge has just ruled that based on the treaty of 1796, the Crown has absolutely *no jurisdiction* over any land belonging to the Abenaki. You've won!"

He called out, "Kate, we've won!" Then turned back to his conversation. "Josh, you can't believe the weight that's just been lifted off my shoulders. Thank you *so much* for calling right away."

"Thank your wife. It's because she dug up that old treaty. Until then, you really didn't have a snowball's chance in hell."

"The village will be very happy to hear this. This is wonderful news." He was smiling now.

"Oh, one more thing. Remember the Crown lands that were scheduled to be leased to the Carleton Mountain Development Group? Well, that's now been rescinded by the oversight board. Once they realized that the project wasn't going to be able to go forward, a board member brought the matter back up for discussion and changed her vote to 'no.' So, no lease, no railroad, and no eminent domain. Quite a hat trick, eh?"

"Yeah. Let me know when you wanna come up Josh. You're welcome anytime."

"Will do. Gotta run, now, I'm on my way over to the hangar, The insurance adjuster is over there and they're leaning toward saying my crash was due to a faulty altimeter and not pilot error. So, they may pony up some cash on this."

When Lou hung up, Jake said, "Lou, I've got a feeling this is gonna be one of those lawyer bills that I wouldn't ever wanna see."

"He and I actually talked about that when we were over

by lake 991. He felt that my coming to find him was worth more than enough to cover his fee. I told him if he won the case, I'd give him a couple complimentary weeks up here, just like Grey Elk had done with his grandfather."

After breakfast, Jake said, "Lou, how 'bout we take a ride in that runabout of yours and go see what this guy with the dirty pants is up to."

"Let's do it."

As they walked down to the boathouse Jake asked, "Did you see which way he headed out this morning?"

"He went east, just like he has every day."

Untying the stern and bow lines, Jake stepped into the runabout as Lou blew the bilge and fired up the inboard. In no particular hurry to go down the lake, Lou stopped a few minutes to talk to a couple of fishermen in boats that were dragging stringers of fish.

"How's it going, fellas?"

"Had a lot of action on top until about a half hour ago, Lou," one called over. "Fish must be deeper now."

"Add a couple more split shot to the line and see what happens. Have you seen the boat from Cottage Seven?"

"Saw him earlier, he was heading down toward the east end."

"Thanks," Lou tipped his head. "Enjoy your day."

As they rounded Eagle Head Point, Jake stood up. "I think I see one of your boats over to the right." He pointed. "Up on that small beach."

"I see it."

"Think that's him?"

"Yeah, there's a big 'ole number seven painted on the stern. He must have gone ashore to answer the call of nature.

We'll wait out here until he gets back in the boat."

After twenty minutes had passed, Lou shifted into forward gear, giving the engine a quick thrust which glided them up onto the sandy shore. "Come on, let's go see if this fella is all right."

As they walked along, they could tell that it was a relatively new path underfoot.

"Looks like there's been a lot of people coming ashore here, Lou, the grass is all trampled down."

"I'm noticing that, too. Almost looks like someone's been walking in a grid pattern, maybe looking for something."

After walking inland for another ten minutes, Lou held up his hand, signaling that someone was up ahead. Lou and Jake stepped off the path and melted into the underbrush. As they eased their way forward, they spotted Jarl Ohlson, head down, walking slowly, wearing a headset that was attached to a metal detector that he was sweeping back and forth in front of him.

Lou motioned Jake over to him and whispered: "This is the guy in Cottage Seven. Now I know who he is, and he didn't come here to fish."

"What's he doing?"

"He's looking for that old Viking grave."

"Is there anything to that old legend?"

"Apparently, *he* thinks so."

Lou reached into his pocket, took out a quarter, and when Jarl Ohlson's head was facing away from him, tossed the coin a few feet in front of the metal detector.

When Ohlson moved back in their direction, toward the quarter lying on the ground, the needle on his meter went off the scale. Ohlson dropped the detector, went down on his knees, and started digging with a collapsible shovel. Unaware that anyone was behind him, Ohlson kept digging until Lou picked him up by the collar and the back of his pants, swung him back and forth twice, then launched him into a bramble bush. Unfortunately for Ohlson, it was also surrounded by a huge patch of poison ivy.

"Hey! What the hell are you doing?" Ohlson sputtered.

"I was just about to ask *you* that?"

"I got tired of fishing, so I decided to take a walk."

"With a metal detector?"

Ohlson didn't respond.

"I know who you are . . . you're that professor from McGill. Get up. You're heading out today."

"I am not! I paid for the whole week."

"Yeah, for *fishing*. Tough. I told you I didn't want any digging on my land. Now, get up, or I'll *drag* your ass back to the boat."

Ohlson didn't move fast enough for Lou, so Lou grabbed him by the back of his shirt collar and started dragging him along the path.

"Wait! What about my metal detector?"

"Leave it."

Ohlson tried to break free, but Lou had too firm of a grip. "That belongs to the university," Ohlson called out.

"Tough."

"I need to return that!"

"Too bad."

"Let *go* of me!" Ohlson tried breaking away from Lou's grip.

"Jake your cell phone should work from here. Call Smyth Charter. Have them send a plane over."

"Bob Conroy might be cheaper."

"Makes no difference to me. I'm using this guy's credit card anyway."

"You can't *do* this; I know my rights!"

"So, do I."

Ohlson tried to right himself and stand up, but Lou was moving at a pace that made it impossible for Ohlson to get his legs under him.

"Let *go* of me!"

"Lou," Jake said. "Smyth's got a plane leaving Kedgwick now that was deadheading back to Grand Falls. They could be here by the time we get back to the dock."

"Book it."

"Let *go* of me!"

When they reached the boats, Jake grabbed the bowline to Ohlson's fishing boat and pushed it off the beach. Finally able to stand up, Ohlson was angry. "You ripped my collar! And my pants are all grass stained!"

"You're lucky I didn't pull you by the hair. Now, get in the back of the boat and no funny business." He pushed Ohlson's shoulder toward the runabout.

Jake tied the bow linc on Ohlson's boat to the stern of their craft and climbed in next to Ohlson. Lou lifted the bow of the runabout up, pushed it into the shallows, jumped in, blew the bilge, and started up the engine. Within seconds, they were hauling butt back to the dock.

Just as they were pulling into the dock area of the resort, Jake pointed to a plane coming up the valley. "Here comes Smyth."

"Good." Lou tied up at the dock just in front of Jake's Twin Otter. With most of the boats still out, there was plenty of room for Smyth's plane to come right in.

Lou reached down into his boat and grabbed Ohlson by his collar. "Get out, you're leaving."

"I am not."

"Watch."

"I'll *sue* you! I'll *own* this friggin' place!"

"Try that, and I'll hunt you down, and kick the ever-living shit out of you."

"Are you threatening me?"

"No. That's a *friggin' promise*."

"Let go of me!"

"Jake, open the door to that plane will ya?"

When Jake opened the door, he recognized the pilot. "Mike! You flying for Smyth now?"

"Yeah, what's going on Jake?"

"We got some trash that needs hauling out."

"Got it."

"Ya' know, Mike, we really could have used you at darts last week."

"I know. They gave me a long haul that day, but I'll be there this week."

"Good."

For some reason Jarl Ohlson wasn't connecting the dots that he was actually leaving.

"Your ride is here, get in."

"I said, I'm not leaving."

"Get in the plane."

"I'm not leaving without my luggage!"

"I'll FedEx it to you. Get *in*." Lou's tone was now a

menacing growl.

"No!"

With that, Lou turned Ohlson around and grabbed the professor by his shirt collar and belt and bodily launched him into the plane. "He's all yours, Mike." Lou said, and slammed the door shut.

Giving Lou a thumbs up, the pilot backed away from the dock. Ohlson scrambled into the passenger section and held both hands up against the window, giving Lou the finger.

"Lou."

"Yeah Jake?"

"I got a funny feeling you won't be getting a Christmas card from him this year."

Chapter
47

Solicitor Aaron Blake dreaded having to phone Buxton Thomas. He decided to wait until mid-afternoon to make the call with the news that he was reluctant to deliver. But finally, he made the call.

"Hello, Buxton. Aaron here."

"Yes, Aaron, I was expecting your call. I trust that you've reversed the wire transfer?"

"Actually, I wasn't able to; the transfer went through."

"Aaron, don't joke like that! We're talking about fifty-seven *million dollars.*"

"I know that Buxton."

"So, what the hell's the problem?"

"It was wired to the wrong account."

"So, fix it!"

"I can't; it's unrecoverable."

"What the hell do you mean, 'it's unrecoverable?'"

"The government has seized the funds."

"What the hell do you mean, 'the government seized the funds . . . *what* funds?"

"Apparently, Pritchard owed millions in back taxes, and he had a number of unsettled civil judgements against him. As soon as the money hit his account, it was gone."

"And you didn't *know* this was going to happen?"

"No . . . somehow we missed that."

"What do you mean, 'somehow you *missed* that? I don't pay you to miss *anything*!"

Aaron Blake paused before saying, "We didn't expect it to happen."

"Didn't you do any due diligence on Pritchard?"

"Yes, of course, we did."

"And you didn't *find out* about this?"

"Look, Buxton, I'm embarrassed, all right? But nothing like this has ever happened before."

"Fifty-seven million dollars *gone*, and you're telling me that your *embarrassed*?"

"I'm professionally embarrassed, Buxton."

"Oh, you're professionally embarrassed, now that makes one *helluva* difference."

"Buxton, I . . . I just don't know what to say."

"Aaron, you and I go back a long way. I *trusted* that you would fully vet this guy."

"I know."

"So, how do you plan to make me whole again on this, Aaron?"

"I . . . I don't know. I don't have that kind of money. The firm doesn't have that kind of money."

"Aaron, I want you to think about it, and call me back."

"I have thought about it . . . I've thought about it all day."

"Do some *more* thinking about it, and come up with a solution, Aaron. I'm dead serious . . . do you *understand?*"

After Buxton Thomas hung up the phone, a man sitting across the desk from him commented. "You raked him over the coals pretty good."

Thomas sat back in his chair, pulling on his pencil thin mustache. "Maybe, but nowhere *near* fifty-seven million dollars' worth."

"How long are you going to let him sweat?"

"No more than a couple of days."

"You know you've got him dead to rights on malpractice and gross negligence."

"I know. How much do you think I can recover?"

"One, maybe three mill; that's the usual malpractice coverage a firm of his size would carry. Of course, you can always go after his *personal* assets."

"I'm sure he has those well-protected."

"There are always ways to get around that."

"Tell me, how'd you find out so fast that the government had seized the money?"

"I have a pretty good network."

"I'd say you do."

"So, what made you call me?"

"I had a hunch that you might be interested in changing solicitors."

"And you flew all the way over to Ottawa on a hunch?"

"No, I was already here. I came over to cannibalize a few parts off an old Twin Beaver."

Buxton Thomas stopped pulling on his pencil thin mustache. "Well, you played your hunch right. Go ahead and get this thing rolling, Josh."

"My pleasure."

--

As usual on Saturday morning, the absolute diehard fishermen were up early and out on the lake for one last time. Lou spent the morning with his guests, listening to their stories, and especially, for anything that needed to be changed.

One change Lou had already made for the second season was to send everyone home with a Styrofoam cooler packed full of fish they had caught, all cleaned and packed in ice. The guests loved it, and every one of the guides ended up with some additional gratuities, as a result.

The following weekend, when Jake flew in with the mail, he dropped off a copy of the Brunswick Times newspaper. As Kate was going through the paper she suddenly stopped at one news item, then asked Lou, "Wasn't 'Elwood Pritchard' the name of the fellow who was promoting this Carleton Mountain development project?"

"I think it was, why?"

"It says here that he was arrested for the murder of one of his employees."

"I met him once; he made a presentation to the tribal council. He wanted to put a road across our land. The council voted against it. I don't think he wasn't very happy about that."

--

Once the Mounties realized that Arthur Turnbridge knew Ying, Turnbridge underwent more questioning. The additional information Turnbridge quickly shared helped fill in the missing pieces of the puzzle for Kate and her team, and she scheduled a final conference call.

"Good morning everyone. I've let the Crown attorney's office know that we've wrapped up our investigation; they're anxious to start preparing their cases against Arthur Turnbridge and Lee Wong Ying. So, I'm moving things to the next stage.

"To summarize, we're all in agreement, based upon the evidence, that Arthur Turnbridge acted alone in the killings of both game wardens and the killing of Corporal Burkett, and that Lee Wong Ying is implicated insofar as he aided and abetted Turnbridge through an illicit poaching arrangement. Does anyone have an issue with these findings or have anything to add to these findings?"

No one spoke up.

"Okay then, I'll take that as agreement. The evidence also points to Lee Wong Ying acting alone in the killing of a constable and a civilian, and in the assault on two constables and a mail carrier. Does anyone have an issue with these findings, or have anything else to add to these findings?"

Again, no one spoke up.

"Lastly, the evidence points to Turnbridge as the lone shooter in the actual poaching of deer antlers. Does anyone have an issue with this finding, or have anything to add to this finding?"

"Harland here, Kate, didn't Ying aid and abet Turnbridge on this one?"

"I believe that's covered in the illicit poaching arrangement point made in the first finding, Harland. This simply states that Turnbridge is the only one who pulled a trigger on the deer."

"Okay, thanks," Harland said.

Does anyone else have anything?"

No one else spoke up.

"Okay. Next steps. Claude, Harland, go ahead and release the Mounties that were on temporary assignment to your region."

"They'll be happy to hear that."

"Arnold, you can let the conservation director know that we no longer see the need for their officers to travel in pairs."

"Will do, and I'll see about getting the body mics back that we had out on loan."

"Good. Is there anything else that we put in place which has to be addressed?"

"I think you covered it all, Kate."

"Okay then, headquarters and I will be working with the Crown attorney's office to provide them with whatever they need to pull their case together. I could use help on that phase if anyone is interested."

"Arnold here, Kate. I'll lend a hand."

"Great, Arnold, thanks. I'll look forward to your help. Everyone, I appreciate the effort that each of you have put in on this case. Also, I hate to cut this short, but I'm late for a call with the Crown attorney's office. Stay safe out there."

Chapter

48

Every September, the clientele at Havre de Poisson shifted from all anglers to a mixture of anglers and hunters. During the last two weeks of the month, four black bears were taken and two moose were brought in. As a service, chef Angelo butchered, wrapped, and froze whatever was brought back to camp by the hunters.

By October, the montage of vivid fall colors, which nature painted on the forest canopy, had fallen to the ground and were an integral part of the forest floor now.

Temperatures were growing colder at night and the bucks were in full rut. The wood stoves in all cottages were lit and warming the sportsmen during the night. Thermoses of hot coffee were keeping them warm when out on the lake and bow season for deer had also kicked off.

--

After four weeks of back-and-forth discussions with Kate's team, the Crown attorney's office was satisfied with both cases they had prepared against Arthur Turnbridge and Lee Wong Ying.

Arthur Turnbridge was charged with three counts of

murder in the first degree, poaching in excess of fifty deer, multiple counts of wasting of a game animal, hunting on private land without permission, and hunting without a valid license.

Turnbridge's court-appointed legal aid lawyer unsuccessfully argued that Turnbridge was a victim of his environment; he entered a plea of no contest with the hope that leniency would be shown. But when the jury saw the gruesome crime scene photos of all three victims, any possible chance the jury might recommend leniency went out the window. Even the judge was aghast at the carnage.

Turnbridge's lawyer never put him on the witness stand since he knew any possible chance he had for leniency would be destroyed by the prosecutors during cross examination. Turnbridge was ultimately convicted on all charges, and sentenced to three concurrent life sentences, all without any chance of parole.

As a result of testimony given at Turnbridge's trial, The Canadian Centre for Child Protection was instructed to review conditions at the Turnbridge compound and potentially move all the youngsters living there, under the age of fourteen, into foster homes.

Lee Wong Ying continued to prove that he was a dangerous and violent prisoner. Twice, he inflicted bodily injury on officers while he was awaiting trial. Ultimately, the commanding officer of the New Brunswick Mounted Police sought and received approval from the chief medical officer to sedate Ying while he was in custody.

Like Turnbridge, Ying was provided with a court-appointed legal aid lawyer, however, Ying refused to speak with his lawyer. So, on behalf of his client, Ying's lawyer entered a plea of guilty on all counts and merely monitored the proceedings, making sure that Ying had a fair trial.

Ying sat quietly next to his lawyer and never moved once throughout his trial until he was told to stand when the verdict was to be read. Upon hearing the verdict of guilty on all charges, he turned to his lawyer and with a vicious headbutt knocked him unconscious before running toward the judge as best he could while still in shackles. The court bailiff subdued Ying with a taser that he had been advised to carry during the court proceedings. Ying was sentenced to two life sentences to be served in solitary confinement, without chance of parole.

The Crown's case against Elwood Pritchard was also prepared, however, until his release from a psychiatric ward in the provincial asylum, no arraignment date was set.

--

A couple of weeks after Ying's trial, Arnold Cunningham called Kate. "Kate, do you get the Brunswick Gazette?"

"I have it online, why, Arnold?"

"Take a look at page one of the sports section."

"Hold on, let me get there."

"Read the article on the left column."

"I see it: 'Four Hockey Players Suspended.'"

"Yeah, read it."

Kate took a minute to read the article to herself:

Indefinite suspensions have been handed to four National Hockey League players after routine drug tests showed the hormone IGF-1 to be found in their blood systems. A spokesperson who spoke on condition of anonymity due to not being sanctioned to speak, said that all four players had been using an experimental drug manufactured by Shang Ho Laboratory during their injury rehab periods to foster a faster recovery."

As soon as Kate finished reading the article, she cleared her throat. "Well, I guess their claim that it couldn't be detected was bogus."

"Yeah. There's a similar article in the Ottawa Daily Sentinel which goes on to say that Shang Ho Labs is being sued. After acknowledging their earlier testing was flawed, they finally admitted that there was no differential DNA factor which could have prevented IGF-1 manufactured from deer antlers from ever showing up in the human blood stream."

"It doesn't appear that they followed the gold standard in scientific research."

"Peer review?"

"Exactly."

"Justice has been served."

--

The following morning, Lou was up early and watched the twilight turn to gray dawn while sitting over on Rocky Point. It was his favorite kind of meditation. When he returned to their cottage, Kate was up and working in the kitchen.

"Morning Kate. Guess who booked the other four-bed cottage for the first week of deer hunting?"

"I have no idea."

"Fletcher Martin. He wants a shot at that ten pointer he saw hanging around by the old gate last year."

"Is he coming up alone?"

"Nah, Duffy will join him. Those two have been inseparable since we were in Afghanistan."

"It'll be grand to see them, again."

"I told him I'd go out with them once or twice. How about you," Lou asked Kate. "Are you thinking you'll hunt?"

"No, I didn't get a license."

"Kate, you're married to an Abenaki and you'd be hunting on Abenaki soil, you don't need a license."

"In that case, I *might* hunt, but first I need to focus on our trip to Ireland and the ceremony."

"It'll only be for one or two mornings."

"Maybe, I will."

"What's the matter?"

"Not sure. I haven't been feeling great lately, first thing in the morning."

"Well, the invitation is there if you want it," Lou said. "Oh, Jake sent me a text. Remember that professor who we threw out of here?"

"Yes, and don't forget you still need to FedEx his luggage to him."

"Jake said there's an article in the Montreal newspaper that he was arrested for stealing artifacts from McGill. He's no longer a faculty member."

"How about that . . . speaking of the paper . . . were you looking at the news online earlier this morning?"

"I was, why?"

"You left the page you printed out next to the monitor."

"Oh, yeah, I want that."

"I noticed you circled an ad under 'Positions Wanted' placed by a facilities manager."

"Yeah, I've decided to look for a professional to come in and manage the upkeep of the village."

"So, what brought that on?"

"I want my life back. I'm also hiring an accountant for the village. I'll stay on the council and I'll mentor those four young men, but that's it."

"So, no more 'Lone Ranger?'"

"Even 'the masked man' had Tonto to help him."

"Can't say I'll be disappointed to have you around more," she said and tousled his hair. "What are you up to today?"

"I thought I'd call a couple of landscapers over in Five Fingers. I need to make arrangements for fall cleanup and plowing the roads this winter over in the village."

A noise caught Kate's ear coming from the dock area. "Did I just hear a couple of boats come in?"

"Yeah, I asked a few people from the village to come over and help me get a head start on closing things up for the winter. "How 'bout you, what's your day look like?"

"I need to get going on this trip to Ireland."

--

Meanwhile, across the pond, three women were plotting their revenge against Kate O'Grady-Gault.

"Soon, she'll wish she'd never meddled in our affairs," one said.

"She'll wish she'd never been born," said another.

The three women laughed as they gathered around the photos of Kate and Lou.

"Yes, she'll be very sorry, indeed."

Want More Lou Gault Thriller Stories?

Here's a Sneak Peek into Book 3

Howl

of the

Banshee

coming in 2023

Howl
of the
Banshee

A Lou Gault Thriller (Book Three)

By

Dave McKeon

Banshee

The banshee is a mythical creature that dwells in the spirit world. The name comes from the old Irish *bean sídh* which translates to mean "woman of the fairy mounds." Banshees are clairvoyant, and capable of crossing over from the spirit world in a shadowy form.

In Irish folklore, the "howl of the banshee" is an omen of death or great peril in one's family.

The sound is often described as, either a series of mournful wails or a shrill scream.

Chapter 1

It didn't matter to her that it was near midnight, when she finally decided to call her twin sister. Nor did she care that there were still visible traces of dried blood in the crevasses surrounding her fingernails.

She felt no remorse for her actions, she never had. She had no conscience, the only values she had, if you could call them that, aligned with her immediate gratification and her self-fulfillment.

"Beatrice, why are you calling so late?"

"It's done."

"What's done?"

"He's dead."

"You killed him?"

"Yes."

"How?"

"Is that important?"

"No, I...I…I just thought..."

"What?"

"Nothing, it…it doesn't matter."

"You said you wanted revenge, didn't you?"

"Yes."

"Well, revenge costs money, Sweetheart, and he wasn't willing to part with any."

"Father refused us, again?"

"The damn fool actually said, "over my dead body" to me.

"Oh God, Beatrice what if they find out it was *us*?"

"They won't."

"Are you sure?"

"The inquest into the death of Aaron Yardley, former Earl of Surrey, will be permanently closed by late tomorrow."

"That's ridiculous. . . that's too soon."

"Believe it."

"Why?"

"I've made arrangements to squelch it."

"How?"

"Our young coroner has an insatiable desire to bed older women."

"Oh, God! Beatrice you can't..."

"I'm not leaving anything to chance, no loose ends."

Anne More closed her eyes as she took in a deep breath. "So, when will you file?"

"Tomorrow."

"That soon?"

"Yes."

"Won't that raise questions?"

"Perhaps."

"Will the Crown approve it?"

"They could deny the transfer, but it's unlikely. Once the

prime minister's office creates the writ, and places it before our beloved royal sovereign, he seems to sign anything involving a first born."

Anne paused for a moment, "Then what?"

"Then we go after the bitch."

"Beatrice, we'll have money again! Let's just go live out our lives."

"No! She's going to suffer . . . like we've suffered." Beatrice, waited for a response, before saying, "Are you in, or out?"

"I'm . . . I'm in."

"Good. Evelyn, said that she was in, too."

"You spoke with her?"

"Yes."

"When?"

"Just now. She's on her way to my flat now; I'm leaving father's study shortly."

"Do I need to be there?"

"Yes."

"I won't be able to stay long."

"You need to be there."

"I go into work early tomorrow."

"I don't care. You need to be there."

"I'll come . . . but I can't stay long."

"No . . . you're staying until we finish talking this through."

Anne closed her eyes as a heavy sigh escaped from her lips. Beatrice had always been the dominant twin.

"Anne, I hope you're not going to disappoint me. Was that sigh I just heard a 'yes?'"

Anne closed her eyes. *No . . . and stop trying to manipulate me.* But Anne was thinking she always gave in to her sister's demands. Finally, she said, "Yes."

"Good. And use the back stairway this time."

"Why?"

"Because I *said* to. . . isn't that enough? For once, will you cut me some slack and just do as I ask?"

Chapter 2

It was close to midmorning, when the sound of an approaching float plane interrupted the natural serenity of the valley nestled deep within the wilds of central New Brunswick. For the rest of the morning, Twin Otters, and de Haviland Beavers would line up offshore, awaiting their turn to taxi into the dock at the resort known as *Harve de Poisson*.

Once the incoming passengers disembarked, the sportsmen who had arrived the previous week would board the planes and head home. Most would fly west to Grand Falls; others, north to Kedgwick Airport where they'd make their connecting flights back to civilization.

Lou Gault had inherited the remote sportsman's retreat a decade earlier, when his grandfather, Grey Elk, had died. The resort was situated on the south shore of an obscure lake created during the end of the Pleistocene Ice Age when the glaciers retreated. There were a few old logging roads in the area, however, the only practical access to the resort was by float plane. Except for a nearby Abenaki village, the nearest thing that even came close to being called a small settlement, was over thirty miles away, the way the crow flies.

As the last float plane taxied in, Lou and his remaining guests stood up, grabbed their gear, and walked down the well-trodden path to the dock.

"I've got you fellas in the same cottage for this same week next year."

"Thanks, Lou. We like that one."

"Refresh my memory, how many years have you been coming up here?"

"This was our sixth year, Lou."

"I knew it was something like that. We had a group up last week that's been coming for nineteen years.

"How large a party?"

"Eight. A few years ago, they brought down a deer that made the Boone and Crockett record book."

"Is that the same group that caught the lunker trout mounted inside the lodge?"

"Nah, that was a different group. I was actually surprised when they brought that fish in; they're all catch and release guys. But they figured that one would set a new record, and it did."

"Helluva girth on that fish."

"Yeah, well, it had been gorging on smelt all summer."

It was common, for trophy hunting sportsmen to return to Havre de Poisson year after year. For some, the call was so strong, it was akin to a sacred pilgrimage.

The lake itself was obscure. It was listed on maps as merely Number 980. Yet it held the record for the largest lake trout taken by rod and reel in Canada. It also held the record for rainbow trout hauled up from the depths – twice – and topped New Brunswick's provincial record. The potential of hooking a record-breaking fish had always been the allure for most sportsmen who came to the resort.

"We enjoyed the Abenaki guide we had this year, Lou."

"I'm glad to hear that."

"Lou, I gotta tell ya, every time we leave here, we say to

each other that we need to come up and do a little *Spring* fishing."

"Then, do it."

"We're gonna hint around to the wives; maybe that'll be our Christmas present."

"First part of May is prime fishing, fellas, the days are warm, the smelt are running and you can use light tackle since there are no black flies."

"Can't ask for more than that."

"If you decide to come up, get your reservations in before the middle of January. You won't have your choice of cottage, but you should still have your choice of week."

"You book up that quick?"

"Over half of next season is already booked."

"Lou . . . you should add a few more cottages."

"I'm at just the right size now."

"You think?"

"Definitely. Any more than twelve and running this place would feel like work."

"Hell, ya can't let that happen!"

As soon as the plane reached the dock, the men picked up their pace. Once these last two guests boarded the plane, Havre de Poisson's twenty-three-week season would officially come to an end.

As soon as the two sportsmen boarded the plane, Lou passed their luggage up to the pilot. Turning to his friend, one of the departing guests leaned over and said, "There's an enviable independence about him, isn't there?"

"Yeah, he's found his niche in life and doesn't have a care in the world."

To even the most casual observer, Lou Gault projected a

calm self-confident demeanor that masked the warrior's spirit hidden deep within him. His tall, wiry physique belayed the tremendous strength in his limbs. Even though he was no longer a member of Canada's elite *Joint Task Force Two* commando unit, he still wore his hair close on the sides. Today he lived a quiet life far from the daily carnage that had surrounded him when he had fought in the Afghan war.

As the plane taxied away from the dock, Lou eyes scanned the natural beauty of the valley looking for anything unusual. Other than a flock of geese winging their way south, it was a typical fall sky: deep blue, with just a hint of wispy white clouds in the higher altitudes. The heavier snow clouds were weeks away, but still, there was a chill in the air, and thin layers of ice were visible along the shoreline in the mornings.

Lou, had grown up with the knowledge that it was nature itself, not some computer-generated weather report, which told the story of how close winter was. For weeks, the treetops had resembled an artist's palette, filled with fiery reds, brilliant yellows, deep purples, and various shades of orange. The once colorful treetop canopy now carpeted the forest floor, adding to the rich, earthly smells of fall. Clumps of balsams were more pronounced, their dark green color contrasting with the naked grey branches of the hardwoods.

Then Lou zeroed in on the far shoreline. *Well, the loons are still here,* he thought, *always the last to go! They're the real bellwether for when fall will give way to winter.*

As Lou turned to walk over to his cottage, the furthest thought from his mind was that the quiet, peaceful life he was living was about to come to an abrupt end.

If you've enjoyed this except of

Howl

of the

Banshee

This third book in the Lou Gault Thriller series

will be out in 2023.

Watch for it on Amazon.com

Acknowledgements

Seldom have I been as grateful to take hold of an opportunity as I was during early 2020 when we were all sequestering due to Covid-19. It was March, when in-between fine-tuning my culinary skills, I decided to depart from writing short stories and enter the rhelm of the novelist.

I am beyond thankful for the early encouragement that I received from my wife. She devoured every word of my initial chapters, before her advancing Alzheimer's robbed me of her insights and helpful critiques.

Special kudos to my early readers, especially: Barry Covin, Barbara Cheney, Tom Mullin, and Carl Johnson.

I can't adequately express my appreciation to Paula Howard, my editor and publisher, for all the work she has done to help me bring this book to the public. Paula, it's been an enjoyable journey.

Books by Dave McKeon

Relentless Pursuit
War Chief

Coming Soon

Howl of the Banshee
Sabotoge

About the Author

Dave McKeon is an award-winning author of short stories and creator of the Lou Gault Thriller series.

His stories reflect a diverse background of life experiences, and an unquenchable love affair with the outdoors.

A native New Englander, he has hunted, fished, hiked, camped, skied, and traveled in the eastern United States and throughout New Brunswick, and Quebec his entire life.

A Vietnam-era veteran, Dave has formerly held both a Top-Secret Clearance and the Department of Energy's "Q" Clearance. His stories are influenced by experiences working with the NSA, the EPA and the Department of the Navy.

To learn more about Dave McKeon,

visit www.avillagewriter.com

284